Breaking The Moon

Dream Catchers Series - Book 2

A Novel by Sandy Lo

Hugs, kisses, & Stars,

Sandy Lo

www.sandylo.com

This book is a work of fiction. Names, characters, places, and incidents are the product of the author's imagination or are used fictitiously. Any resemblance to actual events, locales, or personas, living or dead, is coincidental.

Cover art by Sandy Lo.
For more information, visit www.sandylo.com.

Printed in the United States of America
Second Edition: April 2017

ISBN: 9781521005781

In Loving Memory of
Sierra Eileen Williams

Acknowledgments

Kathlyn Lo Grasso - My beloved sister-in-law, I am so grateful for your input and attention to detail with this book. You really came through for me as an editor, a friend and a sister. Thank you! Sebastian Lo Grasso – Thank you for always protecting your baby sister and for all of your generosity and love. Cindy Monaco – Thanks for being my biggest fan and spreading the word. Suzie Lo Grasso – Thanks for all the laughs, support and love. Little Sebie & Samantha – Aunt Sandy loves you!

To my amazing family: The Lainos, The Williams, The Sadliks, The Boncoraglios & The DelRosarios – I love you and thank you. To my wonderful friends: Danielle Manzello, Diana Callahan, Teresa Abbate, Natalie Hoskins, Tami Lemble, Geetha Bailey, Flora Terrelle, Sandra Cerrone, Vanessa Mourner & Mike Morgan.

To my Starbucks crew in Hauppauge – Especially Edda Titus for encouraging the growth of my writing career. Thanks to all who have supported me in any way throughout the past year. You all will be sadly missed when I leave this summer.

And thanks again to those who allowed me to base characters off them in this book: Danny DeQuatro, Darren Colvil, Sebie Lo Grasso, Meghan Williams-Trusa, James Manzello & Colette Seodat.

To my network of creative forces helping to spread the word: Shawn "Harlem Witness" DeBerry, Mandi Leigh, Tamala Baldwin & Aaron Carter. Thank you!!! My amazing readers—You brighten up my world! A special thanks goes out to Julie Alesi and Mary Jimenez for their unwavering support.

Finally, to my angels up in Heaven, especially Mom... I miss you and love you. Thank you for always providing a happy memory on a bad day.

December 20th

The sound of a baby crying rang through my head like church bells tolling. She was *my* baby; making the most beautiful sound I have ever heard; though haunting at the same time. The sound was shrill and consistent, as if the baby needed to be picked up. Somehow I knew the baby was a she.

Daddy's little girl.

I couldn't find her no matter where I looked. Times Square. Battery Park. Columbus Circle. Every direction I turned was a mistake.

I was wandering New York City looking for someone I wasn't sure even existed. Every turn I made seemed to bring me further away from the crying. The city was desolate; no honking horns, no tourists. The lights of the buildings and streetlights were far too dim to be accurate.

I turned onto a dead end street and the last person I wanted to see was standing there; with her long, flowing chestnut hair and dramatic make-up. She looked plastic. Had she always looked that way? Why was I ever attracted to someone like Bippy Reynolds?

"She's gone, Charlie."

Bippy used my birth name—the name I tried so hard to escape; my father's name.

"Where's my baby?"

I was frantic now as I stared at my ex-girlfriend. The same ex-girlfriend who killed the life we made before it could even be born.

"What did you do to her?" I snarled with pure hatred.

"I did nothing," Bippy smirked. "Haley killed her."

She laughed maliciously at her statement before vanishing into thin air. The baby's cries stopped as soon as Bippy disappeared.

Her words made no sense to me. Haley would never hurt someone intentionally—especially not an innocent child. My girlfriend wouldn't deceive me the way Bippy had.

Now, I could hear the sobbing of an adult.

Haley's sobbing.

I turned around and she was sitting on the floor in hysterics. Her blonde hair was matted down and when she looked up at me, her blue eyes were bloodshot. Her fair skin was splotchy from crying and my heart broke seeing her so upset.

"I'm so sorry, Jordan. I can't be with you anymore."

I woke up startled. My breathing was shallow and I turned to look at Haley lying next to me, thankful she was in my bed. It was just a dream—no, a nightmare. I wondered if there was any meaning behind it, but like I had told Haley when she kept having bad dreams about public nudity, it was just her anxiety.

Of course, her anxiety was obvious and on the surface. She was afraid to stand up for herself and follow her heart.

I suppose I have anxiety, too, though I bury mine pretty deep; covering it with bitterness and brushing everything off with a swipe of my hand.

I will always feel a hole in my heart, knowing I could have been a father by now. Somehow I thought having that child Bippy aborted five years ago would right all the wrongs my father did to me. I would turn things around by being the complete opposite of a dad that Chuck Ashton was to me. It was stupid, and I realize that, but my father and Bippy conspiring against me to secretly destroy my child will always cause me pain.

I placed my head down on the pillow and watched my girlfriend sleeping. She healed my heart in so many ways and I'm so grateful for her. I thought I was incapable of love. Haley makes me feel alive inside, as much as I pretend to be on the outside.

-J

Chapter 1

I checked my watch before looking back down at my last final for the term. I relatively enjoyed all of my courses at the New England School of Photography, except my practical business & marketing class. Creativity and technique were much more enticing to me than practicality and money. However, my business course was over now. I circled B for the last question and immediately stood up with my test.

Laney glanced up at me and smiled, holding her finger up to tell me she'd be done in a minute. She and I became friends after working on a group project together two semesters ago.

Unlike the rich overcrowded party institution I used to go to, this school was so much better suited for me. Class sizes were intimate, yet the building was spacious enough that I didn't feel trapped inside. As far back as I can remember I have always had mild to severe claustrophobia tacked onto a minute case of social anxiety.

Needless to say, I had trouble making friends. I was in a large, overpriced university for two years and managed to make just one friend: Tasha Torres. She still remains to be my best friend, even after I transferred. In fact, we now share an apartment together in Boston.

At my new school, I was able to make a handful of friends that included Laney and her twin brother Luke. The students are all free-spirited and dedicated to their art rather than drugs, alcohol and getting laid. Well, of course, that last thing isn't entirely true.

Laney and Luke both are alike in their athleticism along with their blonde hair and blue eyes. Other than that, they are fairly different.

Laney had her fair share of bed buddies since I've known her, but she is young and entitled. Luke worries about her. He isn't nearly as carefree as his sister is with dating. He hasn't dated a single person since I met him. He is a bit on the quiet side with a sweet smile, and I'm sure if he flashed it at some girl, she'd be won over.

When you're in love, you want everyone else to be in love as well. Not everyone is lucky enough to meet the man of her dreams at twenty years old, like I had. I know I am smug about my amazing boyfriend. I just can't help it.

Despite our ability to constantly bicker, after a year and a half of dating him, I am still smitten with Jordan Walsh.

After handing in my exam and slipping into my winter coat, I waited outside of the classroom for Laney. As any other typical college student with a few minutes of nothing to do but wait, I pulled out my iPhone and checked Facebook.

I updated my status about officially starting winter break before noticing an update to Tortured's fan page.

New single "Haley's Letter[1]" is now available on iTunes! Full album coming out in March! Show some love!

I blushed at the mere mention of *my* song. To this day, I still can't believe someone—let alone this amazing musician AKA my boyfriend—wrote such a beautiful song about me. And now, people can buy it? Just like they would a Michael Jackson or Beatles song? Insane!

As I contemplated "liking" Tortured's status, wondering if

---

[1] "Haley's Letter" is available on iTunes under the artist name Tortured. The song was written for "Dream Catchers" by Sandy Lo and James Manzello. Produced by Frans Mernick. For more info: www.sandylo.com.

that would be too vain of me, Laney walked out of the classroom.

"How'd you do?"

I shrugged, "Passable. You?"

"I did okay," she shrugged as well, as we began to walk toward the exit.

Laney's light blonde hair was sitting on top of her head in a messy bun. She wore her black framed glasses, pajama pants and a Red Sox sweatshirt. It was obvious she rolled out of bed before taking the exam. I didn't have the luxury of looking that casual.

Jordan and I are driving up to Vermont in less than an hour. We are spending Christmas at Foster's Ski Lodge—although my name is Haley Foster, my family doesn't own it. However, my family invested enough money in the lodge that old Wilson Bartlett—my grandfather's best friend—named it after him.

The ski lodge is about forty-five minutes south of my hometown of Bakersfield. As far back as I can remember we spent Thanksgiving and Christmas there with the Eriksson family. Sadly, I didn't truly appreciate the place or my parents' friends until more recently. Sure, Mr. and Mrs. Eriksson were always sweet to me, but they were plotting with my parents to hook me up with their son, Christian.

Oh how I despise Christian Eriksson! Who would have ever thought he'd wind up engaged to my best friend? He popped the question to Tasha about three weeks ago and to my surprise, she said yes!

Tasha isn't exactly the tied-down so young marrying kind of girl. I figured she'd want to live wildly, untamed for a few more years, before settling down. Her response to that was simple.

"I will never be tamed."

Tasha was one of a kind and I worried her relationship

with Christian would somehow change that. I am very pleased to see that isn't the case, for the most part. Though, Christian still seems to keep me on his radar a bit too much for my taste—and Jordan's taste. Christian isn't too pleased I am dating his cousin. Jordan is the black sheep in his family and Christian had thought we would just be a fling.

"Holy crap!" Laney shouted as we walked outside, the cold air instantly biting at my cheeks.

"What?" I asked, pulling the zipper up higher on my coat.

She was shivering as she held her phone, looking at the screen.

"Your song is on sale!"

I blushed once more, though with the cold, I'm sure Laney couldn't notice.

"I know," I smiled.

"I'm going to buy it as soon as I get back to my apartment!" Laney grinned. "I've been dying to hear it again since Tortured performed it on MTV2."

"You're such a fan, Lane," I rolled my eyes jokingly.

Lately, it is difficult meeting someone who *isn't* a fan of Tortured. When I had met the guys of Tortured two summers ago, they were this cool little indie-New York City band with a strong following.

Now...

They're not so little and indie. With over 700, 000 sales on the band's three-song EP released last year, they are surpassing their record label's expectations ten-fold!

"Ugh, don't play it cool," Laney rolled her eyes and folded her arms over her chest as we began to walk. "You are the biggest dork when it comes to Tortured...and Jordan," she grinned at me.

I smiled, "I am supportive of my boyfriend."

"You are obsessed with Tortured's music, just admit it."

"Okay, I am. So?"

"It's just funny," Laney shrugged.

I sighed, "Jordan thinks so, too. I think I creep him out sometimes."

Jordan was completely freaked out when he came over mine and Tasha's apartment a couple of days ago when he first saw the Tortured poster I have up in my room.

He is insisting I take it down when he sleeps over. He claims he can't make love to me while looking at a huge picture of his band mates on my wall. I think he's just being modest. Jordan puts up an arrogant front, but I see the humility behind it.

He is so grateful for his fans and his band, and me. Sometimes I can't help to wonder what kind of temptations there have been on the road while I'm sitting in school, however. How many girls were waiting around after every show? Girls who have fallen in love with Jordan Walsh like I have?

Then I remember: he never wrote them a song. He never wrote anyone a song, but me. I can only trust in his feelings for me. I can also trust in who he is and who he never wants to be—his father.

That alone comforts me that I will never be stuck with someone like Chuck Ashton—an uptight, deceitful ass. His son couldn't be more opposite, and I am proud he overcame his upbringing to be the person he is today. I just hope he feels the same about me. Then again, my parents aren't so bad. They have a few traits I wouldn't mind acquiring—like their unwavering love for one another.

"Have fun at the lodge," Laney said, sliding her gloves on.

"And you try to remain patient with your dad's girlfriend," I warned, wagging a finger in her face.

Laney pouted, "But she's so ditzy."

"She could be worse," I shrugged.

"You're lucky your parents are still together," she sighed. "I feel like I'm totally betraying my mom by spending Christmas with Dad and his new concubine, as she calls her. Luke just goes with the flow; like Mom's feelings don't matter."

"Luke loves your mother just as much as you do. He's just not vicious like you," I teased. "I'm sure your mom understands."

"Humph."

"Give me a hug and stop sulking."

Laney hugged me before heading toward the café she was a permanent fixture at. I had to smile thinking about Laney. She was a child at times—stubborn and helpless. That used to be my role, but I hated the helpless part. I will always be stubborn in some respect.

Being friends with Laney reminds me how proud I am of myself for taking control of my life. She didn't seem to want to change those traits about herself. She enjoyed being a daddy's girl and gave each and every one of his girlfriends a hard time. She also loved to play her parents against one another. I assumed it is some need for attention she missed out on as a child.

"Haley!"

I turned to my left and Luke was walking toward me, his breath showing as he practically jogged.

"Hey Luke," I smiled.

"Do you need a ride? I could drive you."

I smiled, "Thank you, but I'm good."

"I'm glad I got to see you before the holidays," he said, reaching into his black messenger bag.

"Me too. You just missed Laney—"

I was cut off by Luke handing me a wrapped present.

"Merry Christmas," he smiled.

"Luke..." I practically stuttered. "I didn't get you anything."

"That's okay. It's not much. I saw it and thought you'd like it," he shrugged. "Open it."

I pulled my gloves off and unwrapped the present quickly. Luke took the torn wrapping paper from me and tossed it in a nearby recycling can as I pulled open the box. Inside was a photo album. "A Picture Says a Thousand Words" was printed on the front. I grinned.

"I love it!" I said, hugging him. "Thank you."

The roar of the familiar engine told me Jordan was coming down the street. I turned to the left, and sure enough his 1983 Mustang GT Hatchback was pulling up to the curb. He purchased the car with his first paycheck from Struck Records.

Unlike his best friend, Danny, who bought the latest, most expensive sports car with the money, Jordan wanted a fixer-upper. He's had the car for a year, and still the dusty red and black paint is chipping, the engine sounds like it's choking, and the passenger side window doesn't open. With me being claustrophobic, it was almost unbearable.

I only had my driver's permit, though, and didn't know where I would be able to park my car at school anyhow. Luke always had to park about six blocks away!

Besides, I am more than a bit afraid to be behind the wheel. When Jordan is in town, though he moaned and grumbled about having to get up early, he volunteered to chauffeur me to and from school any time he could.

I could hear the music from the radio at a decent level as Jordan reached over to open the door for me from the inside.

I turned back to Luke.

“Thanks again,” I hugged him once more. “I’ll call you when I get back to Boston. Merry Christmas.”

I turned toward the car and Jordan offered Luke a wave before I slid into the passenger seat. His green eyes looked tired as he leaned in to kiss my lips softly. God, how I missed him! Being in Tortured, who are already on the rise, has left Jordan little time to come "home", though I know he really didn't consider Boston home.

Jordan is and always will be a New Yorker at heart. I have grown quite fond of the city myself, but I'm sure that mostly had to do with the pleasant memories of falling in love with Jordan there: seeing Tortured perform live at the Canal Room, kissing him for the first time on top of the Empire State Building, sleeping in his arms almost every night.

New York was also where I found myself—the real me, not the Vermont rich girl who did everything she was told and who was afraid to live.

"How'd your exam go?" Jordan asked as I buckled my seatbelt.

"It wasn't as hard as I thought it would be, but still hard," I explained as he drove down Commonwealth Avenue.

"So you passed?"

"I am fairly confident I passed."

“Your Christmas gift will be well-deserved then.”

Jordan smiled; a closed mouth smile. He was being tight-lipped about the whole gift thing, but acting conspicuous at the same time.

"You only have one term left of college. How does it feel?"

"Scary," I sighed.

He rolled his eyes, "And there it is—some things never change."

He of course was referring to my perpetual state of worry

from when we first met. Thankfully, he was exaggerating; my worries have subsided tremendously over the years, but at the same time, I'm still me.

I stuck my tongue out at him and noticed the tattered edges on his grey long sleeve shirt.

"You're right, some things never do change," I played with the worn material.

Jordan winked at me and flashed his trademark smirk. I shook my head to myself and glanced out the window.

You can give this boy all the name brand, high-quality clothes in the world, but somehow, he will only take the tags off what he needs and wear it down to nothing.

Despite Jordan coming from money, he did his best not to rely on it for unnecessary things. He hated how his father threw his wealth around, and even now earning his own money, Jordan banked almost all of it.

I admire him for it, and sometimes wondered if he looked at my luxuries as superficial. Granted, I only really spent money on trips to visit him or on new clothes. I have become quite the shop-a-holic thanks to my fashion designer friend, Meghan. She recently sent me a dress for New Year's Eve—which she refused to charge me for.

Meghan constantly says she owes her career to me. She just turned eighteen—and yes, she already has a career! All I did to help her was brag about one of her dresses to socialite, Bippy Reynolds, and before we knew it, Bippy asked Meghan to design a clothing line for her.

Oh, Bippy Reynolds.

A large part of me despised her. Not because she treated me like an outcast whenever my parents forced me to hang out with her or that she looked her nose down upon just about everyone she comes across. That didn't truly bother me or surprise me about a spoiled rich brat like Bippy. No, my dislike of her was all about Jordan.

They dated in high school, and I later found out Bippy got pregnant. Without Jordan's consent, she, along with the help of his father, went to a clinic and aborted the child.

Jordan had fought hard against this decision, prior to the abortion. They purposely went behind his back, and he never forgave either of them for it. Not that I blame him.

Fortunately, I hadn't come across Bippy since I ran into her in New York almost a year and a half ago. That would change soon, though. I promised Meghan I would attend the debut of Bippy's fashion line. I am doing it entirely for Meghan's sake.

"Why are you so quiet?" Jordan snapped me out of my angry thoughts of Bippy.

"I'm thinking about Fashion Week."

"Haley, you don't have to go," he sighed.

"I'm doing it for Meghan."

"She would understand."

"I know, but it would be like me not being there for your album release party."

"I would understand, too," he took my hand, and rubbed my knuckles.

I smiled at him.

"I wouldn't miss your big day or Meghan's."

"I'm sorry I'm not going with you, but—"

"I don't want you there," I interrupted him.

He laughed, "Thanks."

"You know what I mean," I sighed. "No one wants to see Bippy—not even Meghan, but unfortunately, this is her big break."

Jordan nodded. Though he hasn't said in so many words, he feels working for Bippy makes Meghan a sellout.

"What did Luke give you?"

I was wondering when Jordan was going to ask about that. He won't admit it, but he has a bit of a jealous streak when it comes to Luke. He claims Luke has a crush on me, and maybe he does, but he is a nice guy that I like having as a friend.

"A really nice photo album," I smiled.

"Did you get him anything?"

"No—I didn't know we were exchanging. I didn't even get Laney anything—she always complains about money, so I didn't want to make her feel bad."

We pulled into the parking lot of the nursing home a few minutes later. Jordan's mother, Maggie, hasn't been doing well lately. We have been taking her out on day trips whenever Jordan is able to, and things were going well for a while.

However, this past Thanksgiving, the staff wouldn't let us take Maggie out. She had some kind of seizure that morning and has been having them regularly ever since. Her behavior has become erratic at times, but her face still lights up when she sees Jordan.

Unlike anyone else in his family, Maggie doesn't call him Charlie. She was against following in the Ashton family tradition by naming him Charles J. Ashton. She was the one who began calling him Jordan in the first place.

The roar of the engine dulled before completely turning off. Jordan turned toward me and pulled me into a fierce kiss, surprising me.

"What was that for?" I blushed, seeing an elderly woman staring at us through the windshield.

"I just want you to know how much I appreciate you coming with me to see my mom all the time and visiting her when I can't," he smiled.

I returned his smile and kissed him softly.

“I love you and your mom.”

“We love you, too.”

We got out of the car and Jordan reached for my hand as we walked into the facility.

"Is Tasha working today?"

"She headed up to Vermont early to look at catering halls with Christian," I explained.

Tasha volunteered at the nursing home for the past three years. Jordan always felt comforted by her looking after Maggie. He hated the idea of his forty-five-year-old mother in a nursing home which was a borderline mental facility. She just never recovered from the nervous breakdown she had eight years ago after Jordan's father left her.

Just another reason Jordan resented his father.

"I still can't believe Tasha is marrying my cousin," he laughed. "Does she know what she's doing?"

He wasn’t laughing out of humor; it was out of pure incredulity.

I shrugged, "She says she does."

Jordan and Christian aren't exactly supportive of each other. They got along for mine and Tasha's sake, but there is some kind of family rivalry that will always be there.

Walking into the facility, I thought back to how much time I had spent here over the past year or so. The most prominent memory was after I had returned from New York the summer I met Jordan. I had no idea Maggie was his mother. He had kept many things hidden from me, not because he was some snake out to trick me, but because he suffered so much pain.

To this day, I am the only person he has completely opened up to about his past. I truly hurt for him. It seems blatantly obvious that we were destined to be a part of each other’s lives.

Every major element around me was connected to Jordan somehow. From our fathers' dislike for one another to barely noticing each other as kids at Bippy's parents' Christmas parties. Then there is the fact that my best friend volunteered at his mother's nursing home and his cousin always had a huge crush on me—yet we were never fully aware of each other nor had we connected until we were both in a different element.

Jordan had heard two different stories about me basically. From Tasha's point-of-view, I was this awkward, overprotected, but goodhearted introvert. And from Christian's, I was this "hot" take charge rich girl who couldn't keep my hands off him!

Christian was delusional when it came to my "relationship" with him. Jordan always had his doubts, but when he saw me two summers ago, looking out of my comfort zone, he leaned toward Christian's opinion of me rather than Tasha's.

I am happy to say I showed my true colors to Jordan—and myself—and was even able to overcome some of my social awkwardness.

"Hey Mom," Jordan cooed, as if he were speaking to a child.

Maggie was sitting in a chair by the window. The vacant look in her eyes made my heart sink. She was not having a good day. I had hoped seeing his mother vibrant today would be the best Christmas present for Jordan.

"Hi Mags," I said, in the same tone Jordan used.

Nothing.

Jordan let go of my hand and walked over to his mother. He knelt down in front of her.

"Mom?"

She just stared out the window as if he weren't there.

"It's your baby. Haley and I are heading up to the lodge and wanted to wish you a Merry Christmas. Maybe if you're up to it, we can take you out when we get back."

Jordan stared at his mother, pleading with her to acknowledge him. I said a silent prayer. After another minute, Jordan began talking as if Maggie *was* listening to him.

"So, the big album release is in a few months. The band's going to be really busy, but I'll call to check in on you. Danny says hi..."

Jordan rambled on some more. I didn't interrupt him. He had so much inner strength. Some guys wouldn't be able to handle visiting their mother here, but Jordan, no matter how hard it was, wanted his mom to know how much he loved her and that she would never be forgotten; even if she forgets him from time to time.

He had told me the last thing she said to him before the breakdown.

"I mean nothing, Jordan," she had sobbed. "I am invisible."

I couldn't imagine hearing my mother say that, and all because of things and words my father had said and done to her.

After about ten minutes, Jordan turned toward me and took a deep breath.

"Are you ready?"

I nodded, and he walked over to me. I rubbed his back and pulled him into a hug.

"She was listening," I whispered. "She loves you so much."

Jordan pulled away from me, and he looked as though he would cry. I knew he wouldn't; not here, but I'm sure he wanted to.

I took his hand in mine and we began to walk out.

"Do you want a peanut butter and Cheerio sandwich, my Jordy boy?"

We turned around, and Jordan's face broke out into a huge smile. Jordan only allowed his mother to call him "Jordy". Sebastian likes to torment him with the nickname—I'm sure not realizing how much it hurt his friend to use it. Peanut butter and Cheerio sandwiches were like Jordan's "safe place" with his mother.

He walked briskly toward Maggie and hugged her.

"I love you, Mom."

"I love you. Where's my sweet daughter-in-law?" Maggie asked, completely aware of who she was now.

I laughed and stepped over.

"Right here, Mags."

I hugged her and she smiled.

On our way back to the car, Jordan was grinning.

"Alright, now I'm ready to deal with anything this holiday week throws at us," he said.

I laughed, "Play nice with Christian."

"I'm talking about my dad," he sighed.

I scrunched my nose, "I can't believe your brother convinced you to spend New Year's with them."

I knew Jordan would do just about anything for his half-brother, Andrew, but spending time with their father was usually something he refused.

"Drew doesn't want to have to choose between me and Dad and I know what effect choices like that have on a kid," he shrugged. "I told him I'd give it a shot."

"I'm very proud of you," I smiled at him.

He laughed, "Well, don't polish my medal yet. I still have to get through the party."

Then it hit me, I'd have to get through it all as well. With Chuck Ashton not liking my father, he didn't seem that fond of me, either. And his wife, well, she was like Bippy eight years from now.

Lord, give Jordan and me both the strength.

December 22nd

People always ask me what the inspiration behind Tortured's songs is. Usually, I tell them I write about how close-minded society is. That's part of it, but most of my songs are about my father and his lifestyle.

Don't tell me what to say
Or how to act
I really shouldn't take lessons
From a world class hack
I am taking control
Me, the only one I can trust
And I'm on the edge
About to combust
I'll turn your world to hell
Like a time bomb ticking
I'm ready to blow
And it's me you slap

For taking all your crap
I am never right
Just not good enough
While you're the devil
Right here on Earth

You'll be sorry
When it's me missing
Then you'll know what it's like
To be the one ass kissing
You made me invisible
While I was trying to be a man
Still, a tortured boy
That you never did understand

Those are the lyrics to Tortured's first single "Detonate". Our debut album will be full of songs like these, and then there's "Haley's Letter"...which doesn't fit in, but is probably becoming our most popular song when we perform it live. I thought our male audience would seriously hate it and think we sold out, but they seem to like it.

I still feel so much anger toward my father, and I know songwriting is a good sounding board, but sometimes I think Haley worries I **am** a time bomb waiting to go off. Sometimes I feel like I am, too.

I try and let go of my past, but it's so difficult, especially when my father still acts like an asshole, and I'm still visiting my mother in a nursing home after 8 years and she's only in her forties. She's a constant reminder of why I hate him. I can't forgive him for the pain he caused her.

-J

Chapter 2

The iridescent, newly fallen snow blanketed the pastures below the streetlights. Jordan pulled into the carport of the Killington, Vermont ski lodge and I sighed with relief. The snow was coming down fairly heavy, which didn't make the over three hour drive a smooth one.

The mustang sounded angry the entire trip and I feared we'd break down or slip and slide along the highway.

"See, I told you my baby would make it," Jordan patted the dashboard, almost scowling at me afterward.

"Jor, you have to get this thing fixed soon."

"I will," he nodded, "when we get back from New York."

I rolled my eyes, "If it'll even make it there."

"Lay off, please?" he sighed.

"I'm laid off," I held my hands up with an innocent smile.

He shook his head, trying to fight his own smile as he got out of the car. I pulled my hood up and followed him out of the car. Shivering, I quickly slipped my hands into the gloves Mom sent me in a care package a month ago.

"Shit, it's cold," Jordan shoved his hands into his pockets as I caught up to him and stuck an old hat of mine on his head. "Haley!"

He hated to have his hair messed with.

"You're going to freeze," I protested, and laughed at his pouting face underneath the snow cap with a red pom-pom on top.

"Right, you just like to piss me off," he groaned and stomped his way through the snow.

The pom-pom bounced on top of his head as he did so, and I couldn't keep from giggling as I trailed behind him, almost falling every few feet or so.

"Stop making fun of me," he huffed, half-jokingly.

He was usually the one to tease people, especially me, and he didn't like when anyone dished it back to him.

I tripped as I went to reply and fell face first into a pile of snow. I rolled over laughing as I wiped snow from my mouth. I could hear Jordan's laughter getting louder as he approached. His face appeared above me, and I just laughed harder at him in the hat.

"I came back to help you and you laugh at me?" he asked, pulling the hat from his head.

Now, his hair was standing on end and I just continued my hysteria.

"I'm going to leave you here…" he muttered, as I reached out for him to help me up.

"You are such a bad sport," I grumbled as he took my hands and pulled me up. "Why is it you can make fun of me all the time, but I can't do it to you?"

He shrugged, "You used to think I was cool, remember?"

I had made the mistake of calling him "cool" once when describing my ability to be not so cool.

"I will always think you're cool. Just like you'll always think I'm awkward," I said with a laugh.

"You're cool in different ways. I much rather have you for a girlfriend than some perfect girl."

I didn't know how to feel about that. I knew what he meant, but still, it was a backhanded compliment.

"Uh, thanks?"

"I mean," he sighed. "You're perfect to me; you're perfect for me."

I smiled and kissed him, wrapping my arms around him. Sometimes I felt like I could crush him with love when he said things like that. Other times, I felt like I could just crush him. I guess that's what love is all about.

"Haley Marie!"

We broke apart to see my mother standing in the doorway of the cabin; her winter white sweater looking itchy even from several feet away.

"Are you two crazy? Get in here!" Mom yelled.

Jordan took my hand and pulled me along to the cabin, knowing I would probably fall down at least once more before I got to the door.

"Hi Mom," I smiled as she welcomed me into a hug.

"You're lucky your lips didn't freeze together," she chuckled into my ear.

"Eh, that wouldn't have been so bad."

"Oh Haley," she waved me off before hugging Jordan.

"How are you, Mrs. Foster?" he asked, ever so politely.

"Elena," she insisted before answering him. "I'm well."

We took our jackets off just as three rowdy men walked out from the game room; each holding eggnog in clear glass reindeer mugs.

"Ah, you're here—took you long enough," Dad said, as blunt as always.

"Daddy, the weather is terrible," I said, walking toward him, not wanting him to blame the delay on Jordan.

My father certainly didn't hate Jordan, not like I had originally thought he would. However, he enjoyed giving my boyfriend the business. I'm sure it was something to do with Jordan being the first and only man to capture my attention.

When I began dating him, I finally became my own person, and I'm sure my father resented that, as much as he came to respect it.

"How is my little girl?" Dad asked, wrapping me into a hug.

"I'm great," I said, meaningfully.

"Jordan, good to see you," he nodded at him stiffly.

Jordan didn't miss a beat, though. He strode over and shook my father's hand with a casual smile.

"You too, sir."

He then turned to his uncle and cousin.

"Uncle John," he shook Mr. Eriksson's hand.

"Charlie," he nodded at him, obviously not caring if Jordan hated to be called that.

I saw Jordan clench his teeth before he moved onto Christian, who was wearing a God awful beige turtleneck sweater and khaki pants. He was irritatingly monochromatic.

Jordan patted Christian's back, harder than necessary.

"What's up, Chris?"

Christian straightened up and forced a smile.

"Oh, you know, Charlie, planning a wedding. I won my third case..." Christian bragged, when really he assisted another lawyer in winning, but he never likes to mention that. "Life is falling into place."

He was smug, as if to say Jordan's life was in pieces. Christian acted like the year was 1940 and not 2011. Was Jordan supposed to be married and figured out at twenty-three?

Before Jordan could speak, I hugged Christian. My chest bumped against his, and I regretted moving in so quickly in order to diffuse the situation. Normally, I gave Christian an awkward butt-out type of hug with minimal physical contact. This was too close for me.

"Congratulations," I said. "Stop it," I gritted through my teeth while leaving his arms.

The cabin was stacked against Jordan enough as it was. I didn't need Christian trying to make him feel like he wasn't good enough. Though, I know Jordan doesn't care what Christian thinks of him. I know he did care if my parents liked him. He didn't want them to give me a hard time about being with him.

Christian pulled away from me with a smile and he winked. Chills ran up my spine whenever Christian winked at me. Not the good kind of chills, either.

"Haley!"

I felt everyone in the room cringe at Tasha's loud yell. I was used to it by now. I turned and was met with a face full of Tasha's almond curls as she hugged me like she hadn't seen me in months before rambling on.

"I have to show you something," she grinned before pulling me upstairs without another word.

Mrs. Eriksson was waiting in one of the bedrooms as Tasha pulled me inside, and closed the door behind her.

"What's going on?" I wondered, as I hugged Mrs. Eriksson.

"Haley, you look wonderful," she said, holding my arms out to the side just like my mother always did when she inspected me.

"I do?" I looked down at my simple button down shirt.

"You're glowing," she nodded.

"It's probably because *her* song is playing on the radio now," Tasha rolled her eyes teasingly.

"You heard 'Haley's Letter' on the radio?" My eyes widened.

"Christian and I did on our way up here—he almost changed the station, not realizing it was Tortured."

I snickered to myself knowing he probably knew exactly

who the band was on the radio.

"Wow, that's so bizarre," I laughed.

"Wait, my nephew wrote a song about you?" Mrs. Eriksson asked.

I nodded as I blushed.

"Aww," she smiled. "I must say—I like the effect you have on him, Haley. My brother didn't know what to do with Charlie any longer. I've assured Chuck, with you around—he'll stay in line."

I bit my tongue wanting to say something to her about the big brother she idolized and his warped view on his son. It was pointless to explain things to these people sometimes.

"So, what do you have to show me?" I turned my attention to Tasha.

"This," she said, pulling out a sheet of paper from her zebra print purse.

On the sheet of paper was a scanned sketch of a wedding dress. It was form-fitting instead of a huge, poufy skirt. The top was a sweetheart cut, with tiny sheer off the shoulder sleeves. Flowered embroidery snaked up the sides of the dress.

"It's completely you," I smiled, looking at Tasha, who was obviously overjoyed with the design.

"Isn't it?"

I nodded, "Who's the designer?"

"Meghan," she grinned.

"My Meghan? Meghan Williams?" I confirmed.

"I asked her yesterday—she got so excited that she finished the sketch this morning," Tasha laughed.

"I'm sure she is thrilled to have this opportunity," I said, gratefully.

Meghan is such a nice girl, and she was a big part of me becoming the fashion-confident person I am today. I was an insecure mess when it came to clothing before I met her. I want nothing more for her than to become the successful designer she dreamed of being her entire life.

"Thank you for asking her."

"She's a fashion prodigy," Tasha shrugged. "Her designs are amazing."

"Tell Haley the other good news," Mrs. Eriksson urged.

Tasha sighed, "Trisha, I still don't know if I want to go with Fairmount Grove for the hall."

Fairmount Grove was the most elaborate catering hall in Burlington. The Erikssons held all of their special occasions there and though they were gorgeously done, they always felt like a presidential ball rather than a party.

"Tasha, dear, it is tradition."

"...And I'm not a traditionalist," my best friend argued.

I saw Trisha Eriksson's eyes turn to pointy slits on her long pale face.

"It's what Christian wants. Don't you want to make him happy?"

"Christian will be happy if I'm happy. He left the choice up to me."

"Don't you think that's just a little selfish of you?"

I knew Tasha was two seconds away from losing her temper.

"Look, you still have time..." I interjected.

"Not much," Mrs. Eriksson argued. "Fairmount needs an answer next week."

"I'm through talking about this right now," Tasha sighed. "Haley, let's go see if Elsa needs help in the kitchen."

Oh, how I missed Elsa and her cooking. She was our maid back in Bakersfield and was practically my nanny growing up as well.

We headed downstairs and I didn't see Jordan anywhere. He was probably bored to tears by the law small talk being made near the fireplace between Dad, Mr. Eriksson and Christian.

Christian paused to look over at Tasha. He winked at her as we passed, and she blew him a kiss. I almost gagged. It wasn't that Christian wasn't good-looking, or that I didn't come to think of him as a friend at times; it was simply the fact that when he was interested in dating me, he completely grossed me out. He was lecherous in his attempts to get me interested in him; always putting his hands on me or trying to kiss me.

Sometimes, I still felt that awkwardness around him, like he still had hope for us even though we were both in relationships. On top of that, he was close-minded, judgmental and kind of a jerk.

Once we were inside the kitchen, I heard Mom reprimanding Elsa.

"Tofu, Elsa?" Mom scoffed. "Honestly, who the heck is going to eat that?"

Elsa's eyes traveled toward mine. I had requested a more animal-friendly diet lately. I was always into eating healthy and organic, but thanks to Meghan and her pro-vegan speeches, I decided to cut down on my meat intake.

"I will," I interjected. "...And so will Tasha."

"Sure," Tasha shrugged.

Jordan walked into the kitchen from the back door.

"And Jordan loves tofu," I smiled at him.

He furrowed his eyebrows at me as he shut the door.

"Oh yeah, adore the stuff," he nodded sarcastically.

Jordan mostly ate steak, hot dogs and hamburgers, and basically anything that was bad for him.

"Fine," Mom rolled her eyes. "You and your hippy ways, Haley."

I just laughed. Hippy? Me? From Elena Foster, I take that as a compliment.

I hugged Elsa hello before walking over to Jordan.

"Thanks for agreeing to eat the tofu," I smiled and gave him a peck.

His lips had a slight taste of cigarettes and cinnamon.

"Were you smoking?" I whispered.

"What?" he asked with a laugh. "No..."

Jordan had quit smoking when we first started dating. I didn't ask him to, but he knew how much I despised it.

I pouted, looking into his eyes. He wasn't being honest. His hand was fidgeting against my thigh. Jordan always appeared at ease, but his hands...they reacted to nerves and stress. It wasn't even noticeable to most people. To me, I could tell and he knew I knew.

He sighed, "I'm sorry."

"How long has this been going on?" I asked, trying to hide my disappointment in him.

He had only been back in Boston a couple of days and I hadn't noticed any smoke signals—so to speak—yet.

"A couple of weeks," he shrugged. "Stress of everything—the album, seeing my dad next week..."

I nodded, "I understand."

"I'm going to stop soon."

"Don't do it for me," I shook my head. "Do it for yourself and your career. You're going back on tour soon enough."

"I know. I'll go brush my teeth," he winked before walking out of the kitchen.

I loved when he winked at me. It still made my knees shake. Not like when Christian winked. That was just creepy.

Mom left the kitchen a moment later and I looked at Elsa apologetically.

"I'm sorry."

"Oh please, your mother has chewed me out far worse than that."

"Why do you put up with it, Elsa?" Tasha asked, picking at a vegetable platter.

"I've worked for the Fosters for over fifteen years," she shrugged. "Despite your mother's tantrums," she explained looking at me. "She and your father have been good to me. I never have to worry about money or vacation time—as long as it wasn't during a crazy time of year."

Like holidays, I thought. God bless Elsa for spending most of her holidays with us.

"They put my daughter through medical school," Elsa continued to list things off more for Tasha's sake than mine.

Though, I honestly didn't know they were paying for Elsa's daughter to become a doctor. That was a surprise that made me smile. I had so many torn feelings toward my parents. They were impossible and pompous at times, but they had big hearts to go along with their closed minds.

Christian walked into the kitchen and smacked Tasha's butt loudly.

"Ass," she slapped him in the chest, harder than he smacked her.

"Isn't he?" I smirked.

"Ha-ha," Christian stuck his tongue out and squinted his eyes at me.

"So, you heard my song on the radio, huh?" I asked, wanting to annoy him.

"Your song?" he played dumb. "Oh, that little love song Charlie went soft for in order to get in your pants?"

I scowled at him.

"Get over it, Chris," I sighed.

"Get over what?"

"The fact that I am his girlfriend and I never was yours."

"Haley," Tasha said, surprised.

I usually wasn't so brazen with my words, but lately, when I was in such an antagonistic environment, with people constantly testing my boyfriend and my judgment, I couldn't help it.

I could tell Christian was wounded by not just my choice in words, but my tone. His hands were in his pockets and he wasn't looking anywhere but down.

"I'm sorry."

"Forget it," Christian sighed.

Tasha stared at him for a moment as if she were burning a hole through his head.

"Unbelievable," she muttered before hurrying out of the room.

"Wha—what's up with her?" Christian asked, staring at the swinging door to the kitchen.

"I'm going to talk to her," I said.

I had an idea I knew what was bothering her.

I walked back into the living room. Jordan was charming my mother and his aunt with some story of his. He looked over at me, slightly concerned. I just ran up the stairs, and walked into mine and Tasha's room.

"Get out, Haley."

"Tash, come on…you know, you *know* how I feel about Jordan."

She nodded, "…And I also *know* how Christian feels about you."

"He loves you. He's marrying *you.*"

"Yeah, because you would never marry him," she said, and it was then I realized she was crying.

"Wow..." I said, sitting down next to her. "You're not supposed to be the insecure one. That's me, remember?"

I was trying to make a joke, but Tasha didn't laugh.

"When I'm with Christian," she sniffled. "I never feel good enough."

"Are you crazy?"

"His parents look at me like I'm trash. So do your parents," she sighed.

Mom and Dad were never exactly happy I found a best friend in Tasha Torres.

"Who cares? Christian loves you."

"What if he's settling for me?"

I was frustrated now. Why couldn't Christian just get over his rejection? I didn't understand.

"Tasha, Christian will always be bitter," I explained. "You know how competitive he is. Everything comes down to winning or losing with him. In his eyes, he lost to Jordan."

Tasha looked up at me with her big sad brown eyes.

"Christian considers you a win, though," I said, rubbing her back.

She forced a smile at me, but I could tell she would need to hear that from Christian.

We sat there in silence for a moment.

"If you don't want to marry him Tash, don't. You don't have to settle," I said, putting my hand on top of hers.

I wanted her to know it was okay to back out. Honestly, I wish she would. Christian didn't deserve her. She deserved someone who knew how to have fun and who knew how to love someone more than himself.

I was going to hug Tasha, but she spoke up.

"Can I just be alone for a while?"

I nodded before leaving the room. I felt guilty. It was my

fault Tasha was miserable. I tried to make sense how we got into this conversation. Tasha was usually the drama-free girl and now she was in tears.

I slowly made my way downstairs. Jordan walked away from Mr. Eriksson to talk to me. I could tell he was curious to know what was going on.

"Is everything okay?"

"You have one of those cigarettes for me?"

His eyes widened.

"Kidding."

Normally, even jokingly, I wouldn't ask for a cigarette.

"It's that bad?"

I just took his hand and led him upstairs. We went into his and Christian's room. Why our parents insisted on being old fashioned with sharing rooms was beyond us. I shut the door behind us.

"I don't know if Tasha and Christian are going to make it."

"Well, I knew she'd smarten up sooner or later," he smiled.

"Jordan, they're having problems because of me."

"What?" he laughed.

"Tasha thinks Christian is still in love with me and that he's settling for her."

Jordan groaned.

"Is he trying to ruin the rest of his life? He has to let you go."

"I'm going to talk to him—" I spun around and headed toward the door.

"Whoa, wait..." Jordan grabbed my arm. "You've done nothing but try to keep the peace since we arrived."

He was right. It's only been an hour and I've tried to prevent fights between Tasha and Mrs. Eriksson, Mom and Elsa, and Christian and Tasha.

"Just relax for a few minutes."

"I can't relax," I shook my head. "Tasha's crying her eyes out. Christian is sulking somewhere. My parents are probably thinking we're up here doing it—" I rambled on worriedly.

Then the words stopped tumbling out of my mouth. Jordan was kissing me. Not just one of his casual pecks, but the kind of kiss that always made me drunk. I wrapped my arms around his neck and pulled him closer.

His kisses trailed down my neck and I moaned.

"You really know how to shut a girl up."

I felt him smile against my skin.

"Next year," he said in between kisses. "We go somewhere else," he kissed right behind my ear. "Just you and me."

His left hand traveled under my shirt and I kissed him again.

"What about our families?" I asked, shivering when his cold fingers traced a line along my waist and up my torso.

"Screw them," his voice was soft, almost growling.

I closed my eyes as his fingers reached my breast.

"I only care about you, Hale."

I love when he called me that. I don't know why, but Jordan's voice sounded incredible anytime he shortened my name.

I opened my eyes.

"That's not true—and we both know it."

He shrugged, "I mean—we don't need to deal with all this bullshit."

"While I've been preventing fights, what have you been up to?" I wondered.

"Aunt Trish was telling me how grateful she was that I turned my life around."

I laughed, "Turned your life around?"

"Apparently, my father hinted to the family that I was on drugs."

"What?" I asked.

"Because I was distant and in a band...I guess that means I'm on drug binges all the time, you know..."

I laughed.

"Don't you laugh," he shook his head at me as his hair fell into his eyes.

He moved his fingers down my stomach again, once more making me shiver.

"It's funny."

"You worried I was into drugs when we first met."

He pinched my sides.

"Ouch," I whined. "I'm sorry—I was naïve and worried you were too good to be true."

He smiled at that before kissing me again. His hands once again found the lace of my bra and I moved my lips down to his neck. He let out a low moan, and I caught a piece of his skin between my teeth.

"Ow," he looked at me surprised.

"Don't pinch me," I said, getting him back from before. I flicked my tongue against the spot I bit before sucking on it softly. Jordan's eyes closed, and his hands slid around my back to the clasp on my bra.

"We can't," I whispered.

"If they already think we are..." Jordan argued.

"They'll call us for dinner any minute."

I reluctantly pulled his arms from around me. He pouted. His eyes telling me how much he wanted me.

We were rarely in the same place at the same time for extended amounts of days. If I was at school in Boston, he was in New York or on the road. If he was in Boston, I had to be in

Bakersfield for some important family thing. I missed having more than a few days in a row with him.

"Tonight," I promised.

"How's that going to work?"

Originally, the plan was that Tasha and I would switch rooms once the parents were asleep. Now, with Tasha and Christian at odds, the plan was a bust.

"We'll figure something out," I promised, kissing him. "Thank you for calming me down."

"It was my pleasure," he smirked.

December 23rd

I took a sharp intake of breath as I jolted awake. Haley mumbled something in her sleep next to me. I slipped on my boxers and got out of bed.

I walked to the window of the cabin and looked out on the haze of white, trying to remember my dream, but all I could piece together were random images. My mother sobbing. My father yelling. Haley letting my hand go. A full moon breaking into pieces. And Christian smirking.

Wanting a cigarette badly, I put my clothes on and as quietly as possible I walked out of the room. I grabbed my coat from the closet near the entrance to the cabin. I bundled myself up and walked outside.

The temperature was sharp and cold, but the snow had stopped. I pulled out the cigarette and ignited my lighter. The fire was a vibrant orange against its surrounding shades of murky white.

I suddenly wanted to write a song about cigarettes or

addictions maybe—since everyone seemed to think I fit the bill to be some sort of addict.

Once the cigarette was lit, I brought it to my lips and inhaled. I hated that I needed this stupid habit. I hated that I kept having these stupid nightmares that woke me up at least once a week.

The vibe I got from each nightmare always pointed to me losing Haley. Realistically, the thought was ridiculous. Wasn't it? Why would I lose her?

I could never bring myself to cheat on her. I never would think she'd cheat on me. I'm sure other things could get in the way—like our families, but that was nonsense. If we didn't let them get to us after a year and a half, why would we start now?

Unless it was out of our hands.

Death was something I never feared. I had only been to one funeral, and that was my grandfather's when I was seven. He was old and happy when he passed away.

The only other pain that I felt related to death was my unborn child. I'm sure most guys didn't feel as attached to the idea of a baby as a teenager, but in the three weeks that I knew of

Bippy's pregnancy I accepted that fate, and was excited about it.

And then there was my mother. She was alive, but sometimes it was like part of her was dead; empty and that hurt the most.

Haley would turn twenty-two in February. She ate healthy. She took care of herself. Fear of losing her to death was crazy.

Then why was she always leaving me in my dreams? She was always sobbing and in pain. And I could feel her pain so strongly and yet I couldn't take it away.

While I was standing outside smoking, the cabin door opened and I jumped. Thankfully, it was only Tasha peeking her head out of the cabin.

"Does Haley know you're smoking again?" she asked.

I nodded, "It's temporary."

She laughed, "Mind if I join you?"

"Nope."

Tasha closed the door and came back out a minute later wearing her coat.

"Hell, it's cold," she shivered, grabbing the cigarette out of my hand and taking a drag.

"Since when do you smoke?"

"I don't. Smoking is idiotic."

I raised an eyebrow and laughed.

"Leave me alone," she nudged me. "I've been arguing with Christian all night."

"Are you guys okay?"

She sighed, "Yeah. I wish he'd stop caring about Haley so much."

I just looked at her. Her eyebrows smoothed and her frown turned even.

"I mean—that sounds terrible. She's my best friend and I love her..."

"You just wish he didn't?" I asked.

"You too, huh?"

I kicked some snow under my boots.

"His feelings don't matter to me," I thought how that sounded. "For your sake, I want him to let go."

"Why do you pretend you don't care about Christian?" Tasha asked me.

I laughed, "I never said that. I don't wish harm on him,

but he's always been an asshole to me, Tash."

He's either insulted me or avoided me like the plague. It didn't bother me, though. The feeling was mutual.

"You know, Haley felt guilty tonight for his feelings."

Tasha bit her bottom lip.

"That's kinda my fault."

"No, it's definitely Christian's fault for not letting this go," I rolled my eyes.

Tasha sighed deeply and I realized I didn't make her feel better.

"He loves you. I know he does, but he will always care about Haley. And he'll always feel rejected by her."

"Haley says he sees it as a loss to you."

I nodded.

"Are you kidding me? Christian was in competition with me over everything—Haley was the only thing I won over him. It just pisses him off. It doesn't mean he loves you any less."

Tasha smiled and handed me back the cigarette.

"Haley is a lucky girl."

"Thanks."

I put the cigarette out and covered the evidence with a clump of snow. Tasha and I headed back into the cabin, which felt like a furnace compared to outside.

"I guess we should switch rooms now," Tasha whispered.

"Yeah," I nodded, reluctant to share a room with my asshole cousin who harbored feelings for my girlfriend.

Tasha deserved better than him. She always seemed to settle for these headstrong guys who argued with her over everything.

We walked into Haley's room. Tasha stomped over to her bed as if she were ready to collapse before she said good night to me. I sat down on Haley's bed and she opened her eyes.

"What's wrong?" she asked, worriedly.

"Nothing," I said, brushing her tangled blonde hair off her face. "I'm going to my bed."

She pouted her lip at me and I leaned down to kiss her.

"I'll miss you."

"Oh God, Haley..." Tasha groaned and I laughed.

Haley was a sap when she wanted to be, but then again, I turn into a romantic around her, even though I never considered myself one. She had such a good heart, and she felt everyone else's emotions so deeply, as if they were her own. My happiness was her happiness; the same as my pain. She was like that with anyone she cared about or could empathize with.

That was why it was difficult for her to hate anyone, even if they deserved it. That prevented her from completely despising Christian or resenting her parents more or clawing Cami's eyes out when they first met.

Haley felt bad that she never returned Christian's feelings. She understood her parents' need to protect her and wanting the best for her. And she knew it must have been hard for Cami to accept I could move on from her so easily after we broke up. I admired her for it. I couldn't be that generous to people—especially the ones who hurt me.

"I'll miss you, too," I said, tapping her butt before getting up and walking out of the room.

I couldn't sleep after that; I figured now was a good time to write this.

-J

Chapter 3

By the time Christmas Eve arrived, Tasha was back to her rambunctious-self, and Christian was back to doting on her—and rubbing in their engagement to Jordan and me every chance he got.

Christian thought marriage to be an accomplishment more than anything it seemed. Finding a wife was right up there with winning a case. His competitive nature considered Tasha a win—against whom, I'm not sure. Maybe against Jordan since we were nowhere near getting married—though with the onset of me graduating college, I am wondering if it was our next step.

I suppose I am a little old-fashioned in the sense of me wanting to get married after college. My parents married right after law school, and though, I've gone against their other traditions, that one seems fine to me. Jordan is the only person I want to be with—I have no doubts.

Before dinner, my stomach was cramping oddly. I figured I was just hungry. I excused myself from the gossip Mom and Mrs. Eriksson were discussing, not really listening anyhow, and headed into the kitchen.

I opened the swinging door quietly and to the far left were Christian and Jordan talking. The kitchen was incredibly huge; it would be a chef's dream.

"I can't believe Haley is still with you," Christian laughed. "I figured she was just sewing her oats that summer and—"

"That she'd run to you?" Jordan laughed harder. "Chris, Haley was never yours and she never will be. Leave her alone and focus on Tasha. Don't hurt her," he said.

"Are you threatening me?"

"Just stop being a dick for once in your life," Jordan sighed.

He turned to walk away and that's when he noticed me. Christian looked over at me and smiled before walking past me and out of the kitchen.

"Why do you even bother speaking to him?"

"I was just trying to talk to him about Tasha and of course, he has to insult me. You don't know how much I want to punch him sometimes."

"Well, thank you for restraining yourself," I said, wrapping my arms around his neck.

He kissed me and we stayed in the kitchen for a few minutes; the thought of food was lost again until it was time for Elsa to serve dinner. Strangely enough, after a few bites I was stuffed.

After dinner was over, the cabin turned into a scene from a cheesy sitcom. My parents were both wearing festive turtlenecks—sitting by the fire drinking eggnog and hot chocolate along with the Erikssons and Tasha.

Mrs. Eriksson asked Jordan to play guitar while they sang carols off key. It was absolute torture. Tasha was practically hiding her face into Christian's arm to keep from giggling, even though he was merrily singing along like the giant dweeb he is.

In the middle of "Deck The Halls", I felt extremely nauseous and had to run to the bathroom. I vomited, but still felt sick afterward. I hardly ate anything at dinner. In fact, I hardly had an appetite today, so it couldn't have been something I ate. There had been all kinds of flu symptoms flying around. Danny and Darren both had fevers the last week that Jordan was on the road with them. Maybe he was a carrier and passed their illness onto me.

"Feeling any better?" Mom asked when I reentered the living room.

"A little."

"It was that damn tofu, I bet," she insisted.

I'm sure it was her turtleneck snowman sweater that really nauseated me.

"Mom, the tofu was fine," I rolled my eyes.

"Why don't you go up to bed?" Dad suggested.

I did feel exhausted suddenly. I nodded and made my way upstairs.

"I'm just going to say goodnight," I heard Jordan say as I shut the door to my room.

I'm sure my father wasn't pleased about him coming upstairs.

I drowsily tried to get undressed. I pulled my dress over my head, but it got stuck on it—maybe because my head felt like it weighed a hundred pounds.

"Try locking thc door, baby," Jordan laughcd coming into the room and turning the lock behind him.

"I can't...get...this...stupid dress...off," I said, finally yanking it off my head.

"There you go," he smiled at me as if I were a child.

"Don't make fun of me."

I climbed onto the bed and crawled over to the pillow.

"You're going to sleep in your underwear?"

"I'm hot—Tasha won't care," I said, throwing the blanket back and pulling the sheet over me.

Jordan felt my forehead as I sat down on the bed.

"You don't feel warm."

"That's good—maybe it's just a stomach virus then and not the flu," I said hopeful.

"I wanted to give you your present," he frowned.

"I'm sorry."

"Well, I'll just tell you what it is," he shrugged, and lifted his shirt to reveal his tattooed chest.

I narrowed my drowsy blue eyes. I loved Jordan's chest—yes, but was *that* my present?

"You? You're giving me you? I already have that," I rolled over, pretending to go to sleep and he laughed.

"No—this," he said pointing to his dream catcher tattoo.

"Huh?"

"You said you wanted a similar tattoo. So, that's my gift to you."

I stared at him blankly. I know I said I wanted a tattoo, but I was terrified of actually getting one. It was so permanent and painful. Needles were no friend of mine—I was a big baby about them.

"I said *if* I ever got a tattoo, I'd get a dream catcher, but—"

"Haley, overcome your fear," he teased me.

"Is that really my present?" I scowled.

"Yup—oh, and this..." he said, getting off the bed and leaving the room. He came back with something behind his back.

"Sorry I didn't get a chance to wrap it," he presented me with the latest Nikon camera.

My eyes must have brightened and the biggest smile took over my face.

"I can't believe you got me this," I said, pulling him down to me for a kiss. "I love it and you."

"Love you, too," he pecked my lips. "Now, get some sleep while I go entertain your family with more lame carols," he rolled his eyes.

"Sorry," I giggled.

Sometime in the middle of the night—well, it was probably

only nine at night—I was pretty out of it, I stumbled out of bed to go to the bathroom, but remembered I had no clothes on. I threw a robe on and walked to the door. Just as I was about to open it, I heard hushed voices in the hallway.

It was Christian and his mother.

"Please Christian, think about what you're doing," Trisha Eriksson pleaded.

"Mom, this wedding is happening whether you accept Tasha or not."

"You don't look at her like you do Haley."

Christian sighed, "Mom…"

"She's just going through a rebellious stage, honey," Trisha argued. "Just like you're going through yours with Tasha. Haley will come around. She's going to get tired of playing second fiddle to Charlie's music and all those girls…especially once she realizes he will never want to settle down," she said with disgust in her voice.

"I wouldn't be surprised if he's sleeping around on her," Christian said, as if he were concerned about me.

I was infuriated to hear them discussing Jordan and me this way. Some rich people think they can get whatever they want. No matter how much the Erikssons want me to marry Christian—it will never happen.

I worried about Tasha, though. She wasn't someone to stand in the background while her man puts the focus on another girl. I didn't want to be that other girl.

I gagged and put my hand over my mouth. I pulled open the door to my room and ran right past Christian and Mrs. Eriksson to the bathroom. When I heard someone knock, I groaned and assured them I was fine. Part of me imagined puking on both Christian and his mother.

December 24th

Why do people expect me to propose to Haley as soon as she graduates college? Aunt Trish and Tasha both seem to bring up the topic to me every chance they get. The only time Christian talks to me civilly is to brag about his pending nuptials as if he freed the slaves or ended war.

The society that Haley and I were raised in thinks you should be settled down and married before the age of 25—I was going to be 24 this upcoming year. Maybe to someone like Christian, marriage was a major accomplishment; to me, it was a setup for failure.

Call me a cynic, but marriage was a legally binding piece of paper that suffocated a relationship. If my parents aren't proof of that, I don't know who is.

I tried to remember when there was a resemblance of love between Mom and Dad. Mom was devoted—warm and accommodating while he was cold and bossy. He left the parenting to her.

She wasn't allowed to have a social life outside of him, and she wasn't allowed to control any of the money. But King Chuck came and went as he pleased—sometimes disappearing for days, and somehow, Mom would get screamed at when he came home.

The only real evidence of love I heard about was on their wedding day. Mom said he cried—I couldn't imagine that. I wondered if those were happy tears. Mom also said he couldn't wait to share the rest of his life with her. Yet now they live two-hundred and twenty miles away from each other and never speak. I will not let marriage turn me into a resentful bastard who ignores his wife and kid.

-J

Chapter 4

...And this is my letter... Haley, I'll miss you when you're gone...

The car radio played the song, and I smiled with my eyes closed. The station changed and I opened my eyes to scowl at Jordan.

"Hey!"

"You know I hate listening to Tortured on the radio," he laughed.

He was so strange when it came to hearing himself on the radio or seeing himself on TV. He didn't want to be seen as a luminary. He wanted to be a normal guy who plays guitar and writes songs. What he doesn't get is there is a light that shines off of him and draws the world to him. Loving him is involuntary for me; like a magnetic force I don't even want to block.

"How are you feeling?" he asked.

"Other than car sick, fine," I turned slightly to try and figure out how far away from New York we were.

"We're almost there," he said, and just then the car stalled. "Shit," he groaned and started it up again.

"Uh, what's up with that?"

"It's fine—we'll get there."

"I hate this car," I grumbled.

"Shh, she'll hear you."

"Loser," I rolled my eyes.

"You've been hanging out with Seb too much," Jordan laughed.

Sebastian calls everyone a loser. If you like a song he hates, you are a loser. If you get yourself coffee and not him, you are a loser. And if you know too many questions on Jeopardy about Shakespeare, you are really a loser.

I know Jordan and his friends don't seem like intellectuals on the surface. I'm sure to the judgmental people of my hometown—Tortured is just a rebellious band of punks. I'm sure they'd be surprised we have Jeopardy marathons at Darren's, and that he is a college graduate. Though Jordan, Sebastian and Danny dropped out of college, they are intelligent and motivated. Sebastian, in particularly, craves knowledge and is always testing the rest of us.

About twenty minutes later, we were in the parking garage and gathering our things to bring into the hotel. We always stayed at the same hotel near Times Square—not the one with the scary concierge, but the second one we stayed in that first summer; the one we shared our second kiss in, which counted more than our first for us. The first kiss was just awkward.

We settled into our hotel room and I excused myself to the bathroom. I felt a few cramps in my lower stomach and groaned. I thought about the date. It was the 30th and I figured I was having a bad bout of PMS. Being that I had to spend the next couple of days dealing with the Ashtons, this wasn't a good thing.

"Haley," Jordan called.

"What?" I asked.

"I want to show you something."

"Jordan, I am not watching any type of History Channel war stuff," I warned.

He loves watching war movies and documentaries, and

would always call me into the room to see gory scenes. I hate the idea of war, though I understand why we do it. I hate fighting in general, which is why I always try to keep the peace.

I opened the bathroom door and I laughed loudly. Sitting on the bed was Jordan...with his guitar...in just his boxers and my hot pink bra. He was emulating the photo I took of myself for him.

"Hold that pose," I said, still laughing as I ran to get my camera.

I snapped the shot and Jordan began strumming a song on the guitar.

"I'm going to take a shower," he announced, standing up.

He handed me my bra and I shook my head at him.

"I'm going to lay down for a bit," I yawned.

"Don't get too comfortable. We're meeting the band in a couple of hours for dinner."

That night, we went to Carney's, the Irish pub we always hang out at in New York. Jordan and his friends are creatures of habit. Aside from Jeopardy marathons, his visits with the band consist of the same things: rehearsals, some kind of athletic activity with Danny, most nights spent at Carney's and ordering Thai takeout for lunch after rehearsal.

That night, Sebastian and Darren were both flirting with two blondes at the bar while I sipped a Shirley Temple and watched Jordan and Danny play pool.

I was never a big drinker, and Shirley Temples are so delicious that most of the time I opt for them rather than some fruity cocktail. The guys tease me all the time about it.

"So, where's Cami tonight?" I asked as Danny took a shot at the nine ball.

He shrugged, "Don't know, don't care."

Jordan laughed, "You guys are fighting again?"

"She's pissing me off. I think I'm done, bro."

I must have frowned because Danny and Jordan both stared at me.

"Come on, Haley, she's a bitch," Danny sighed.

"But you love her."

"Not enough to deal with her attitude anymore."

"What about the band?" Jordan asked.

"This won't affect us. Cami will get over it—she'll be bitter, but when isn't she?" Danny laughed.

For some reason, I was infuriated. I know Cami isn't the warmest person on the planet, but she is my friend—kind of. She got me my first gig as a photographer. And my second. And my third.

Sure, she and Danny fought, but he isn't exactly an angel. His temper flared up fairly often; in public no less. I wouldn't be able to put up with Jordan cursing at me in front of people—let alone at all.

I was annoyed with Jordan, also, for only caring about the band and not Cami. She is his ex-girlfriend. I know he didn't have feelings for her in that way, but he must feel something toward her as a friend; as someone who has helped better his career.

"Unbelievable," I threw my hands up.

"What's up with you?"

"Do either of you care about Cami's feelings?"

"Haley, I care. She's just unbearable at times."

"And so are you!" I yelled.

"Excuse me?" Danny asked, placing the pool stick down on the table.

"D, just calm down," Jordan put his hand on his friend's chest.

"Tell your girl to leave me alone, Jordan."

“Jordan doesn’t tell me what to do.”

“Haley, shut up already,” Jordan growled at me.

Danny smirked and I just hurried toward the front of the bar.

“Haley, what’s wrong?” I heard Sebastian ask, but I just walked outside.

The cold air hit me hard. I was wearing a short-sleeved sweater dress, and my arms instantly goose-pimpled. I looked up at the December sky and there was no moon. That was disappointing.

I hated new moons; it was like the sphere was my nightlight to guide me along, and when it was gone—I was lost.

I heard Jordan walk up behind me. I kept my back to him; pretending to see something of interest in the sky.

“Hale,” Jordan sighed. “I’m sorry—I didn’t mean to yell at you.”

I didn’t look at him. I continued to stare at the blank sky, hoping for some change, though I knew the moon was not going to magically appear.

“It’s just—you know how Danny gets when he has a few beers in him. I didn’t want you to get him going even more.”

I felt his arms wrap around me and still I didn’t react.

“Will we end up like them?” I whispered.

“Like who?”

“Cami and Danny? Tasha and Christian?”

“What do you mean?”

“Fighting over nonsense. Trying to make something work that just doesn’t.”

“We fight over nonsense now,” he laughed into my ear, before kissing it.

I wrapped my arms over his.

“We don’t have to try to make something work,” he

whispered. "We just work."

I squeezed his hands underneath mine.

"I'm scared," I admitted.

"Of what?"

"That we'll lose each other."

I didn't even know I had such fears until that moment. Maybe it was the realization that Jordan is my only boyfriend—and nowadays first loves didn't usually last.

Maybe it was the fact that all of my friends were in and out of troubled relationships. Before Christian, Tasha dated Ricky—that was an emotional roller coaster. Laney's relationships only lasted a month at a time. And then there was Meghan. She was with Mike for two years and they decided to take a break since they were so young when they got together. They wanted to experience other things. I couldn't imagine wanting to experience someone other than Jordan, but he might feel differently one day.

Ultimately, I'm sure my fear had something to do with college graduation this spring—and nothing to actually do with my relationship. There will be so many changes. I will start my career and Jordan will basically be touring nonstop. We will have to decide on our future, and to be honest, we never really discussed it. The possibility that our lives might head in two opposite directions terrifies me.

Even more so than the moon, Jordan is my nightlight. When everything else in the world goes to hell, he is always there to help me forget and move on.

Jordan was quiet far too long. I looked back at him.

"We won't lose each other," he said. "Tasha and Christian will be fine. They're already onto planning the honeymoon."

I wasn't sure if I was happy about Tasha and Christian, though. I don't want my best friend to get her heart broken, but I just can't imagine Christian making her happy.

"And Danny and Cami..." Jordan continued. "We all knew there was a huge chance they probably wouldn't last. He's just angry; it's best not to argue with him. He'll wake up tomorrow ready to apologize to Cami. Don't worry," he said.

"I'm sorry I got so bent out of shape back there," I said, realizing I had overreacted to Danny simply ranting to his best friend about his relationship.

Jordan shrugged, "This is why guys don't talk to girls when they complain about their girlfriends."

"Oh, does that mean you talk to him about me like that?" I wondered.

He shook his head and laughed.

"Miss Sensitive today," he rolled his eyes. "Not once have I ever said I was going to break up with you after a fight."

I smiled, "Can we go inside now? I'm cold."

"Who told you to come out here without a jacket?" he said, grabbing my hand and pulling me back inside the pub.

"Were you going to pass out again, Haley?" Darren asked, laughing.

"Ha-ha, very funny," I squinted my eyes at him.

Darren loved to tease me about my claustrophobia and social awkwardness—though even he can't really pick on me about that anymore. I have overcome many fears and phobias in the past eighteen months.

Sebastian had his arm around the blonde he had been flirting with.

"Jordy, you better be treating my girl right," he winked at me.

I laughed. Seb loves to mess with Jordan by flirting with me—that is his nature anyhow. Danny walked toward us from the back room.

"I'm gonna split," he said.

His blue eyes looked weary. Gone was the cocky, self-righteous guy who didn't care about his girlfriend. Danny isn't an easy nut to crack. He is one of the sweetest guys I know, yet his temper can get him into trouble easier than his smile can win over any girl—which is pretty damn easy to begin with.

"I'm sorry I snapped at you," I said.

Danny pulled me into a hug.

"It's forgotten. Wish me luck with Cami," he sighed.

"Good luck," I smiled at him.

Danny bumped his fist against Jordan's before leaving.

Late that night, I woke up alone. I slid out of bed and looked out of the hotel window, hoping the moon somehow appeared while I was asleep. Although I knew the science of the moon phases, that never took the magic out of it for me—like wishing on stars, I prayed to the moon.

I walked into the bathroom, desperately having to urinate. I had a few drops of blood on my underwear. Relief washed over me. Though I chalked my cramps up to my period coming, the nausea along with it did set the pregnancy alarm off since my period is late and I am on birth control. Usually the pill did its job of keeping my menstrual cycle on track.

I dream of the day Jordan and I are married—both successful in our careers—and with a child on the way; the child Jordan missed out on, the one I can give him. I took comfort in that dream, but with a semester to go of college and with Jordan at the start of his career—not to mention we are unmarried—this is not the right time. My parents would lose it, and though, I don't think they'd react the way Jordan's father did when Bippy turned up pregnant—they would have their own opinions on how we proceeded.

After finishing up in the bathroom, I walked out and

Jordan was flipping through channels on the bed, wearing just sweatpants.

"Did you go out to smoke?" I asked, with a hand on my hip.

"Sorry," he said.

I took out body splash from my purse and began spraying him with it.

"Haley!" he yelled. "I'm going to smell like girl!"

I laughed, "It's better than smelling like smoke."

"I'm dousing you in men's cologne while you sleep," he said, pulling me on top of him.

"Jerk," I said, bouncing hard on his stomach.

"Ow," he winced, while laughing. "Come on, let's get some sleep…big party tomorrow," he rolled his eyes before turning the TV off.

I flopped down next to him.

"It's just one night," I reminded him.

I fear Chuck's party just as much as Jordan is, but I am trying to be uplifting. I despise these ritzy parties with stuffy schmucks who bring out my social anxiety more than anyone in the world.

Around five-thirty the next night, I walked out of the bathroom in a strapless red dress as Jordan was fixing his tie in the mirror. There haven't been many times that I've seen him in a three-piece suit. I know he hates wearing them. It was a little much for New Year's Eve, but Chuck always has overly formal parties. Jordan could have played the part of the rebellious son tonight—he did that well, but he wanted to coast through the party—we both did.

Jordan hates when his father starts with him in front of me or with his brother around. He tries to tolerate Chuck once in a while, for Andrew's sake.

"Wow, is that my boyfriend?"

To be perfectly honest, I like him dressed down better anyhow. Jordan looks good in anything, but in a suit—you can tell he isn't comfortable. I'm sure I come off that way in the heels I decided to wear.

He looked me over with a grin; which usually meant he wished we'd just stay in and fool around. I wouldn't have objected. He scanned down my legs to my feet.

"Heels?" he asked.

"You don't like them?" I wondered, turning my feet to the side.

"I do, but can you walk in those?"

"Tasha gave them to me—she said flats aren't sexy enough for this dress."

He laughed, "You'd make anything look sexy."

"Does that mean I did well?"

He just walked toward me and pecked my lips. He hates that I can be so insecure.

"You look amazing."

"But not slutty? This is a formal—"

"You're perfect. Don't care what *they* think."

By "they", he meant the rich friends of his father.

"I care what *you* think. Do I look like a respectable young lady?" I asked, pouting innocently.

He scratched the back of his head.

"Respectable—sure, but hot as hell."

I just laughed at him.

"Let's go, I'm starving," I pulled his hand and dragged him toward the door.

The New Year's Eve party was held at the grand ballroom of a hotel chain Chuck recently invested in. Jordan and I were hoping the spacious area would mean less time to actually speak to him. Chuck would be distracted with business associates and high profile friends—we would be a speck on his radar. In Jordan's eyes, being ignored by his father was better than being scrutinized by him.

When we walked inside, I could understand why Andrew would want us there. He was probably the youngest person there at twelve and a half. It was like he had been keeping a lookout for Jordan because as soon as we crossed the threshold, he was coming toward us.

"Hey J!"

"Looking sharp, Drew," Jordan gave him a hug.

"You too," he smiled before looking at me. "Wow…"

I blushed and Jordan smacked the back of his head. Andrew developed a bit of a crush on me. He is such a little flirt and he often embarrasses me with his comments. Jordan is amused watching his brother make me uncomfortable.

"You look very handsome," I said, kissing Andrew's cheek.

I thought he was going to pass out.

"Easy there, Romeo," Jordan smacked his chest. "Isn't there someone a little younger for you to gawk at?"

"Do you see anyone younger?" Andrew rolled his eyes. "I hate these parties."

"You and me both," Jordan sighed, looking at me.

"Same here," I said, looking around, spotting several people my parents were friendly with.

The usual New York City wealth was in attendance. I spotted the Reynolds, and I could tell Jordan did, too. It was as if he swallowed a lump in his throat. Mr. Reynolds used to be extremely good friends with Chuck until Jordan and Bippy broke up. Her father didn't think Jordan was good enough for her.

Jordan's resentment toward his own father had given him

a bad reputation over the years. Chuck was fairly vocal about his disappointment with his son. He took no interest in Jordan's accomplishments, only the fact that he was nothing like himself.

To do nothing to help change his image, Jordan would often throw in a sarcastic jab at his father at parties like these to put him in his place. Chuck's friends and colleagues just take that as proof of what an ungrateful and unmannered son he has.

Thankfully, Bippy probably had some club hot spot she was appearing at, so we wouldn't have to deal with her. The Ashtons' stuffy New Year's Eve ball was not on the hit list for her if she wanted to be on page six tomorrow.

Looking away from the Reynolds, I could see the queen of the party charging toward us. Jordan's stepmother, Coryn, has a determined walk that I could see across the room. She always walks with purpose as if she didn't want to be left out of whatever is happening.

Coryn was only eighteen when her affair with Chuck began. Now, at thirty-two, she had several plastic surgeries to change her already youthful face. Sometimes I felt like she could be Jordan's older sister rather than stepmother, but they weren't close enough for him to feel even a shred of relation to her.

"In coming," I whispered to him.

"Wonderful," Jordan groaned.

"Well, look who decided to show this year," Coryn approached us with her hands on her hips.

She didn't come from money, but she sure as hell plays the part well. Her unnatural blonde hair was pulled back too tight. The diamonds in her ears, around her neck and on her finger sparkled noticeably and she wore a designer gown as if she were on the red carpet. Actually, she doesn't play the part *that* well—she was overdone. Chuck's old money friends are a bit more subtle.

"Coryn, how are you?"

Jordan spoke to her with a sharp tone; a certain scathing in his words that was obvious. She knew he couldn't stand her. How *could* he like her? She was sleeping with his father for years—who was married at the time. She weaseled her way into his family and their money, though Jordan truly doesn't consider it *his* money. He doesn't care if he gets a dime of it, and his father doesn't seem to get that. He still thrusts it at him every chance he gets.

"Wonderful. And you?" Coryn asked, looking at me from head to toe.

She stared at me every time I saw her, which wasn't often.

"Great. You remember Haley, right?"

"Yes—how are you, dear?" she asked as if she were thirty years older than me rather than ten.

I held back my laughter.

"Oh, I'm just fine, Mrs. Ashton. Did you do something different with your hair?" I asked, but motioned to her cheek area, which had obviously been surgically enhanced.

Now, I could feel Jordan hold back a laugh as Coryn scowled. He loved when I threw in a surprising zinger to someone who deserved it. I was never one to put others in their place—especially people like Coryn who talked down to me. Jordan brought out many other sides of me. It was also easier for me to disrespect people who showed the people I cared about no respect.

"Did my son tell you the news?"

The way Coryn said "my son" made it sound like he wasn't Jordan's brother at all.

"No," he said, glancing at Drew.

"Don't be modest, Andrew. I've just been telling everyone," Coryn waved her hand in the air. "He was accepted into

Wedgewood Academy."

"What is that?" Jordan asked.

Andrew looked uninterested in the conversation.

"It's only the best prep school in Connecticut," Coryn bragged.

"Connecticut?"

Could this really be happening? Chuck and Coryn practically ignore Andrew as it is, and now they are shipping him off to boarding school? I knew Jordan was about to lose it.

"Where is Chuck?" he snarled.

"Charlie, calm down—Andrew wants this."

He looked at his brother.

"Do you?"

Andrew nodded stiffly, not looking him in the eye.

"Bullshit!"

"Jordan," I said, hoping he would calm down.

"You're just going to get rid of him?"

"Drew, let's dance," I said, not wanting the kid to witness what was about to happen.

Andrew looked at me and then at Jordan with this look that I didn't quite understand. It was as if he didn't want Jordan to fight for him. I knew that Jordan would always fight for his brother, though; whether he wanted him to or not.

We walked out to the dance floor and Drew looked back at his mother and brother briefly before resting his hands on my waist. I placed my hands on his shoulders. He was kind of short for his age, which made him eye level with my breasts. He smiled stupidly as he stared at them.

"You're making me uncomfortable," I sighed.

"Sorry," he laughed, looking up at my face. "What do you expect from an almost thirteen-year-old boy?"

"Some manners?" I teased.

Drew shrugged, "Jordan says girls like it when guys are jerks sometimes."

I rolled my eyes, "No, they don't."

"You liked him and he was a jerk to you," Drew reminded me.

I sighed, "Well, I was a jerk to him, too. That's not what made me fall in love with him, though."

He nodded and glanced through the crowd.

"I don't want Jordan to fight with Dad. I chose to go to prep school."

"Why?" I wondered.

He shrugged, "It's better than being at home. I'm alone most of the time anyway or just in the way."

My heart broke for this kid.

"I wanted to go to school in Boston to be near Jordan…and you," he smiled at me. "But Dad won't let me."

"Why not?"

"He says it's too far, but I think he's just jealous that I want to be with Jordan."

Andrew didn't say much else while we danced; not as much as he usually spoke. He just didn't want Jordan and his father fighting. He was always afraid Chuck was going to forbid him from seeing Jordan one day. I told him Jordan would never stay away. Underneath all of his wit and inappropriate remarks, Drew was a sweet kid. He was a lot like Jordan, and I felt like Andrew was family to me—just as I did Jordan.

"May I cut in?"

Jordan was standing there with a tiresome look on. I offered him a smile before breaking away from Andrew.

I walked off the dance floor and crossed my arms uncomfortably. I hated these huge parties with so many people I didn't know. A waiter passing by with a tray of stuffed mushrooms offered me one. I took two. I was fairly hungry and I hoped dinner would be served soon. I wondered if I was comforting myself with food to deal with Chuck Ashton and the rest of the snobs.

"Haley Foster, my God have you grown up!"

After I had shoved the second mushroom in my mouth, I turned to see Mr. and Mrs. Reynolds staring at me.

I tried to chew and swallow the appetizer, but it didn't go down so easily.

"Hewwo," I said, before swallowing once more. "Sorry," I smiled.

"You really look incredible," Mrs. Reynolds smiled. "Bippy told us about your transformation and said you gave our head designer, Meghan all of the credit?"

I just love how they refer to Meghan as *their* head designer and not *my* friend. I also love how they refer to my newfound sense of style as a transformation—as if I were the ugly duckling who magically turned into a swan.

I nodded, "Meghan is amazing. You're so lucky to have her designing Bippy's line."

"How are your parents?" Mr. Reynolds asked.

"Great," I said. "They were sorry to miss your Christmas party this year. Dad had a huge case."

"You should have come still. You're always welcome," Mrs. Reynolds smiled.

"Thank you, but I had finals."

"Oh sure, are you still pre-law?" Mr. Reynolds asked.

"No—I'm at a visual arts school in Boston," I explained.

"Visual arts?"

"Photography."

"Oh, interesting," Mrs. Reynolds said tightly. "Like family portraits at the mall or weddings?"

"Not quite," I said, knowing to them that meant I would be hired help. "My area isn't focused yet, though my major is editorial & corporate photography with a double minor in creative imaging & fine art."

They stared at me as if I were speaking another language and for some reason I pointlessly continued talking.

"I've been working with some record companies to photograph their bands for things like album covers and their websites."

"Oh, well, that's exciting," Mr. Reynolds said.

"Ah, there she is..."

I peered out of one eye to see Chuck Ashton coming at me. He wrapped an arm around me, reeking of alcohol. He was known for getting sloshed at parties and acting inappropriately. Apparently, Coryn was a waitress at a party Chuck attended in the Hamptons without Maggie, and he hit on her while drunk.

"It's rude to not say hi to the host of the party, don't you think, Haley?"

I looked at him uncomfortably and cringed as I tried to speak while he was squeezing my shoulder. He was a tall man with heavy hands. His arm around me felt as if it would coil me like a snake and try to squeeze the life out of me.

Jordan has very few of Chuck's physical features. Aside from them having the same hair color—which Chuck is going gray now anyway, they also have the same nose. Other than that, Jordan looked like Maggie, though her skin was darker than his and her hair was jet black courtesy of her Native American background.

"I—I'm sorry, Mr. Ashton. I was..."

"Busy preventing my son making an ass of himself as usual?"

Mr. and Mrs. Reynolds looked a little confused.

"He's just worried about Andrew," I explained to Chuck, knowing he had spoken about the boarding school already.

"When are you going to wake up and realize you made a mistake by choosing Charlie over my nephew?"

My eyes widened.

"Never," I said, annoyed. "Your nephew is not as perfect as you think. And as for your son, he's the most amazing person I have ever known."

Chuck laughed heartily. He looked at me as if he could never take me seriously.

"You must not have known many people then."

"Not many good people," I shot back.

As intimidating as Chuck is, I couldn't let anyone talk badly about Jordan.

"Wait, Haley, you're dating Charlie?" Mrs. Reynolds asked.

"Jordan," I nodded. "Yes, for a while now."

"Oh no, that boy—and excuse me Chuck for saying this—but that boy is nothing but trouble. He's selfish and reckless."

"With all due respect Mr. Reynolds, the Charlie Ashton you knew is not the Jordan Walsh I know and love," I said, looking into Mr. Reynolds' eyes, hoping he sees how sincere I am.

I know Jordan says he doesn't care what people think. I know it really doesn't matter what these people think. However, I want the world to know that Jordan Walsh is genuine and down-to-earth. I'm sick of these rich brats thinking Jordan is so terrible.

"Haley," Mrs. Reynolds sighed. "I know he's got an edge and the looks, but he spends most of his time with white trash, wasting his life away playing dive bars, and he hurt our little girl."

I laughed. Not only did they think Jordan's best friend, Danny was white trash—simply because he wasn't rich—they obviously didn't get the caliber of success Tortured was now having, and to top it off, they think Jordan broke Bippy's heart? Oh please!

"Jordan hurt Bippy?" I asked. "She hurt him with her *decision*."

The way I emphasized the word made them understand I knew what had happened.

"He was young and talking out of his ass about being there for the baby and Bippy," Mr. Reynolds said, now getting angry. "I'm sure he made us all out to be awful but neither one of those kids were ready to raise one. You, my dear, better be careful or you could end up in the same predicament."

Chuck sighed, "And if you think Charlie is going to put his dreams on hold for you, well...that's not going to happen."

I looked at him and then at Bippy's parents. Why were these people so antagonistic? Why did they all want to attack me and Jordan? Was it because we didn't live life according to their guidelines? We mixed with the poor. We followed our own path and not our parents. We had fun. Are they just jealous?

They should be. Nothing they have is real—with deep feelings and love. Everything with them comes down to money and status.

"I wish you saw who I saw," I said to the Reynolds before looking at Chuck. "You're missing out."

I walked away, not caring to speak to anyone else but Jordan and Andrew. I didn't want Jordan to know anything was bothering me. It was bad enough the Reynolds tried to talk me out of dating him, but his own father, too?

The rest of the night, I had to pull Jordan onto the dance floor—not that the music was much we could dance to—since he was angry and was never much into dancing. He did it more to humor me. I was highly disappointed in the musical selection, though. Besides Michael Bublé, most of the music was from the rat pack—not really music to shake to.

"We leave at midnight, okay?" Jordan asked as we slowed danced.

I smiled and wrapped my fingers in his hair, "Okay."

We kissed and when I opened my eyes, Chuck was staring at us from the bar. He raised his glass to me before he walked away. I wished we could leave before midnight, but I knew Andrew would be upset if we did.

December 31st

My father's New Year's Eve party was just as I expected it to be. Stuffy and boring. And I fought with my father, even though I promised myself I wouldn't for Andrew's sake. Oddly, enough I was fighting *FOR* Drew.

After finding out from Coryn that my brother would be attending boarding school, I made my way through the crowd of people—some of them saying surprised hellos to me—in search of my father. I didn't offer many hellos in return, which I'm sure, just made my bad rich kid image worse. I was too angry to make small talk with people I barely knew or liked.

Finally, at the bar, standing there with two other attorneys was Chuck Ashton—lawyer, adulterer, millionaire, and all around dickhead. He was drinking bourbon, his favorite.

One day when I was kid, I dumped the entire bottle of bourbon down the drain just to spite him for fighting with Mom. He assumed I drank it and threw me against the wall, and punished me for a month—I was only eight.

"Is that little Charlie?" Grant Reaser, Dad's mentor asked.

"Well, the big rock star decided to show," Dad laughed, tipping his glass to Grant. "Who wouldda thought those guitar lessons I signed him up for would pay off?"

Figures he'd take credit for anything I did well. There was no one more self-absorbed than Dad.

"I told him to work hard and chase that dream—"

"You told me shit. What's this about Drew going to boarding school?"

Dad's colleagues quietly stepped away.

"You want to make a scene?" Dad walked close to me, getting in my face.

"I will have you arrested. Do you want that? I'm sure your groupies won't think you're so cool when you're sitting in a cell."

"I know a good lawyer," I taunted him. "Richard Foster has a great track record."

Dad's jaw clenched and I took satisfaction in my low blow. Dad and Haley's father were always in competition and never really liked each other.

"If you think for one second Foster is happy you're banging

his baby girl, you're kidding yourself."

"Why are you doing this to Drew?" I turned the conversation back on what really mattered to me.

"Andrew *wants* to go to Wedgewood."

"He wants to make you proud—I just wish he knew that would never happen. Nothing will ever be good enough for you."

Chuck sighed, "Are we really having this conversation again, Charlie?"

"Yeah, because you still don't get it. You're making the same mistakes with Andrew that you made with me."

"I never enrolled you in prep school. You weren't exactly a go-getter in school," he smirked, trying to make me feel dumb. "Now, Andrew has a real chance to make something of himself. And I'm not talking about some musician who's going to be washed up in five years."

I was good at hiding my emotions. I was used to Dad trying to hurt me with words by now.

"Andrew is *my* son, Charlie. Not yours. Wedgewood was his idea."

I looked at my father, not sure if I could believe him.

"Please, let's just have a good time? It's a party. How's your mom?" He always asked how Mom was every time I saw him.

"The same."

"Does she ever ask about me?"

"No," I said quickly.

The truth was she did from time to time. Some days she completely forgot what happened, and wanted to see him—reliving happier times. Times I really couldn't remember.

"I will always care about her."

"Right—and that's why you tortured her for so many years."

"Tortured?" Dad looked at me. "I tortured your mother?"

"You treated her like a piece of furniture!"

"Calm down, have a drink..."

"I don't want to drink with you."

I walked away from him, pushing through the crowd once again. I found Haley and Andrew. His hands were a little low around her waist for my taste—young hormones. I asked to talk to him alone and Haley understandingly walked away.

Drew explained to me why he wanted to go to prep school.

He told me my dad wouldn't let him look at schools in Boston, but that's where he really wanted to go—to be close to me. My heart broke for my brother. He is a pretty tough kid, who despite his home life, lets things roll off his back. Brother like brother, I guess. I hated seeing him like this, though. It made me realize how much he hurt inside.

I patted his back, "Do you really want to go away for school?"

He nodded, "You know you can't run away from Dad, right?"

"You do."

"I'm a grown man, and I still have to face him," I sighed.

"I don't want to live there, Jordan."

"I'll see what I can do about getting Dad to let you go to Boston, but I'm not there all that much."

"Haley is, though, right?" he asked, his eyes bright and a smile forming.

I laughed, "Kid, she's my girlfriend, remember that."

"I know, I know. But she's going to be my sister someday, right?"

I looked at him surprised.

"What?"

"When you guys get married."

"Who says we're getting married?" I asked, wondering if Haley was being a typical girl and imagining her wedding day, expressing those visions to my brother.

Drew shrugged, "I just thought since you guys are in love and all..."

"Marriage isn't the only way to express how much you love someone."

"You mean like sex?" he asked, grinning.

I pushed him, "Drew!"

"What?" he laughed.

"You are asking for it," I shook my head at him.

Great, so now my brother wants me to marry Haley, too? If I were to ever ask anyone to marry me, I would want it to be because I'm sure and comfortable with the idea; not to make everyone else happy.

-J

Chapter 5

The next morning, I lie awake. Jordan was surprisingly sound asleep. He was really tired when we arrived back at the hotel last night. I'm sure his father wore him out.

I was feeling lightheaded and nauseous; it was worrying me. I wasn't someone who got sick often. The pregnancy thoughts kept creeping back into my mind, and I decided I should take a test just to be safe, especially since my period is somewhat nonexistent today. I imagined myself heading into a drug store and awkwardly purchasing a home pregnancy test. And then to pee on a stick and wait—those few moments would feel like forever—and then, to wonder if the test was even accurate? Ugh. What if it was a false positive or a false negative?

I wouldn't put myself through that. I sat up in bed and called Meghan. I needed someone to hold my hand—preferably a girl and preferably not Jordan. I didn't want him to know anything until I knew for sure.

"Hello?" Meghan's voice asked softly.

It was obvious she just woke up; I've never heard her answer the phone without a million exclamation points attached to her greeting.

"Hey, sorry I woke you," I whispered.

"Haley?"

"Yeah... Can we meet for an early lunch?"

I realized if I rushed out of here too early, Jordan would be suspicious. He was having lunch at his father's, reluctantly of course. I was invited, but the less I'm there the better. Jordan was even more defensive toward his father when I was around. He thought Chuck talked down to me and made too many digs about my father. I didn't care half as much as he did. I hated how Chuck put Jordan down the most. The only reason Jordan agreed to lunch was to help Andrew out with his schooling arrangement.

After hanging up with Meghan, I stood up.

"Where are you going?"

I turned to see Jordan rolled over on his side, hugging his pillow.

"Meghan's free for lunch. I hope you don't mind."

"No—I don't blame you. I wish I could skip out on my dad, too. We'll leave right after lunch, okay?"

I nodded and leaned down to kiss him.

"Are you alright?" Jordan asked.

"Fine—couldn't sleep really," I shrugged.

About an hour later, I was standing outside of a clinic I had seen advertised in the phone book of thc hotcl. I didn't want to go through my insurance; afraid of the questioning that would come from my parents if they were to ask.

I spotted the tiny and stylish Meghan crossing the street looking concerned. It was the first time since I've known her that she greeted me with anything other than a grin.

"What's wrong, Haley?"

"Nothing, I hope," I plastered on a smile. "I just needed someone to come with me."

"Are you sick? Where's Jordan?" Meghan wondered.

"He's with his family," I explained. "I might be pregnant," I blurted out.

To hear the words come out of my mouth was surreal. I realized I was almost sure of the results now. All of the signs were there and I was denying them out of fear. I felt nausea building in my stomach from nerves or maybe morning sickness.

"What?!?!" Meghan screamed, causing a few people walking by to stare.

"I'm really scared," I said, my throat going dry.

Meghan seemed to regain composure. She gave a small smile before hugging me.

"Don't be scared. You and Jordan will be fine."

I squeezed her tighter and took a deep breath. She was right. This was Jordan's child—if any child—inside me. He wouldn't let this shake him or us. He would be happy he gets another chance at being a father. I took a deep breath and pulled away from her.

"I'm ready."

Meghan smiled at me, and though I appreciated her being there with me, part of me wished I would have told Jordan my suspicion after all. I would have loved him to hold my hand through this process. I imagined the smile on his face when the doctor told us we were expecting.

In reality, my ready-to-freak-out expression was glued on from the time I walked into the clinic until the time I walked out. It was all a blur now, even though while I was inside, everything was going in slow motion.

Every sound had echoed in my ears. The teenage girl sitting in the waiting room looking more frightened than me seemed like an image I would never forget. Then, the doctor with his calm smile confirming what I already knew...

Those words rang through my skull the entire taxi ride back to the hotel. Meghan could barely get me to speak to her.

"I'm pregnant," I said.

"It'll be fine, Haley. You're graduating college in five months. Jordan's making money. You two won't even have to go to your parents," she said amazed.

I looked at her. Jordan still had his career, but would I still have mine? Could I pursue a photography career and take care of a baby at the same time? Jordan would be traveling so much. What if our baby didn't remember him when he came home?

"Jordan's going to be a daddy," I whispered.

The tears fell from my eyes and I smiled. He would make it work somehow. He would surely calm me down and help me realize this child is our little blessing.

All of the fear that I've been having about mine and Jordan's future was nothing compared to a baby.

The taxi stopped at Meghan's apartment.

"You'll be okay," she smiled. "Call me anytime."

I nodded and she hugged me.

"I'll see you next month."

Fashion Week was a month away, and though, I wouldn't be showing, I imagined my large belly staring Bippy Reynolds in the face. She would hate me, but maybe it would show her how much she screwed things up. I would have the man and the child she probably regrets giving up.

I stepped into the hotel and Jordan was sitting in the lobby with our bags. I had lost track of time, but there was no way I had been gone that long.

"What time is it?" I asked.

I wondered if he could see the word "pregnant" written on my forehead.

"Let's get out of here," he sighed, not even looking at me.

He reached for the bags and I gathered what I could of mine. I suspected lunch with his family didn't go well. He was usually tense after getting into a fight with his father, but now, I was tense as well. I needed one of us to be at ease. We had a five hour drive ahead of us, and there was no way I would last that long in the car without telling him what I just found out.

I was terrible at keeping secrets. I was even more terrible at pretending nothing was on my mind. Worse yet, Jordan knew me too well to get over on him.

We picked up the car at the parking garage in silence. This wasn't odd behavior. I always gave Jordan a cooling down period after he saw his father. He would calm down soon, and then I could tell him. Maybe I should make him pull over first. I wouldn't want him to crash over the surprise.

Jordan was walking too fast for me to catch up. When I walked into the parking garage, he had already pulled out of the spot and was coming toward me. I got settled into the passenger seat and strapped myself in.

Manhattan driving always made me nervous. Jordan was beeping at everyone, and it was aggravating me. I couldn't bring myself to say anything, though. It was as if I was frozen there, and the first thing I would say—the only thing I could say would be three words: I am pregnant. Absolutely nothing else could come out. Even while Jordan was furiously beeping in midtown Manhattan traffic, I felt the words ready to tumble out. I was biting my tongue so hard; I thought I would draw blood.

I needed this to be over. I needed him to know and I needed him to kiss me and tell me how much he loves me and how ecstatic he is to share this baby with me.

When we made it out of Manhattan, I sighed with relief. I looked over at Jordan, and I managed to swallow back the basketball-sized lump in my throat.

"Can you pull over?" I asked, hoarsely.

Jordan didn't react.

"J-Jordan?"

"What?"

His voice was vacant, as if he was on autopilot.

"Pull over?"

"Why?"

"We need to talk."

"I'm not in the mood. I just want to get home quick."

I burned a hole into his head.

"This is important," I said, but he cut me off.

"Haley, what don't you get?!?!" he yelled, only then turning to look at me.

As soon as his eyes could even connect with mine, they were back on the road. I glanced at his knuckles clutching the steering wheel; they were white from the grip he had.

"What's wrong with you?" I asked.

Just then, the car stalled.

"Shit!" Jordan yelled, smacking the steering wheel.

I jumped. I was somewhere on the edge of crying, yelling or curling up into a ball at this point. At least now, we'd have to pull over, though.

Jordan started the car again, but he didn't pull over. He kept driving along the highway!

"We're going to get stuck!"

"We'll make it," he insisted.

"Pull over, Jordan."

"Haley, it's fine."

"Pull over now," I said through gritted teeth.

He sighed, and started to pull over on the shoulder. The car stalled again just as he did so. He cursed under his breath and immediately got out of the car. He lifted the hood and the car was overheating.

I pulled the zipper up higher on my coat before getting out of the car as well.

"Don't say I told you so," he said, slamming the hood

down.

"I wasn't..." I shrugged. "I have something else to tell you."

I walked around to him as he was running his hands down his face. I grabbed both of his hands and looked into his eyes.

"Haley, I—"

"Jordan, I'm pregnant."

I said the words and waited for him to process them. He stared at me looking like he was either going to vomit or pass out.

Instead, he pulled his hands out of mine.

"Whoa, what?"

"I'm pregnant. I went to the doctor today. That's why I've been sick," I explained.

Jordan stood up straight and walked a few steps before turning around. He laughed—almost nervously.

"Is this one mine?"

"Huh?" I asked. "Is that supposed to be funny?"

It was not funny.

"Are *you* trying to be funny, Haley?"

I looked at him blankly before glancing at the passing cars on the highway. I didn't know what to say to his reaction. I expected he would be happy at best; shocked at second best and at the very least, worried and scared—like me. But angry and snarky? No.

"I can't believe this shit," Jordan mumbled, pulling at his hair.

My mouth opened a bit; my lips trembling as I tried to speak.

"This shit is," I said motioning to my stomach, "*your* child. I didn't get myself pregnant, you asshole!" I half yelled, half cried.

All at once Jordan charged at the car screaming. He

began kicking it. I moved out of the way and stared at him like he lost his mind. He hopped on top of the car and started stomping up and down causing the roof to dent in certain areas.

"Stop it!" I yelled. "Jordan! What the hell is wrong with you?"

He finally stopped jumping on the car and sat on the roof with his legs dangling over the windshield.

"The baby..." Jordan said, looking at me. "It wasn't even mine."

I didn't get it. Why was he questioning our baby? Of course it's his!

"What are you talking about?"

"Bippy's baby. It wasn't mine."

Finally, what Jordan had been talking about made sense—well, somewhat. The baby Jordan fought to keep alive was not even his. Bippy had cheated on him?

"Jordan, what...she cheated—"

"Yes," he said, standing up again. "My father knew. He knew and he kept it from me," he said angrily.

"He was probably just trying to protect you—"

"Protect me?" he laughed, jumping down from the car. "By letting me think a child he helped kill was mine?"

"Why did he tell you now?" I wondered.

At that moment, I was being selfish. I don't want Jordan to worry about the past. I have his future inside of me and that should be more important.

"You don't want to know," Jordan rolled his eyes and took his cell phone out of his pocket.

I bought him a new phone for Christmas; not a prepaid one he rarely refills, but a *real* phone with a monthly service plan. Funny how now of all times, he wants to talk on the phone!

"Who are you calling?"

"Triple A."

That seemed logical. When you're stranded on the side of the road, Triple A is certainly the place to call. However, when your girlfriend just tells you she's pregnant, I would think that overrides car trouble.

I stared at him before looking around. Maybe I was dreaming? This felt like an anxious nightmare! Jordan irrationally wanted to make a phone call when I just told him life altering news. He cared more about Bippy cheating on him than me carrying his child. And his stupid car broke down!

I looked down at my winter coat. I was fully clothed. Damn, I was usually naked in nightmares like these. What could be worse than my nightmares starting back up? The fact that this isn't a nightmare; this is my reality.

When Jordan got off the phone with Triple A, I was staring at him; probably looking like a mix between an angry mother and a helpless child—I could relate to both at this moment.

"They'll be here in twenty minutes."

"That's great," I said with a sarcastic tone. "So how do we get back to Boston?"

"We wait for the car to be fixed."

"I want to go home."

"We will go home—tomorrow."

Shaking my head, I protested.

"I want to go home now, Jordan. I feel like I haven't been there in forever."

"What would you like me to do, Haley?" he asked, rubbing between his eyes.

I didn't say a word. I just looked at him funny; no, worse than funny. I looked at him with disappointment written all over my face. I turned away from him and opened the car door to get my purse before I began walking down the highway. All logic was gone at this point. I needed to get away from Jordan. I needed to be some place familiar.

"Hey, where are you going?" Jordan called out to me. "It's freezing!"

"I'm going home—with or without you."

"Haley!" he yelled, but I ignored him and kept walking.

Suddenly, I stopped and stretched my arm out toward the traffic. The reality of what I was doing didn't hit me. I couldn't think of any other way to get home while I was stranded on the side of the road with someone I didn't want to be with.

"You're hitchhiking? Are you fucking insane?!?!" Jordan screamed before running toward me.

"No, I'm not insane!" I yelled back as I continued to try and get a ride from a stranger—praying to God that some nice old woman would pull over.

"You're pregnant!"

"Oh gee, so you did hear me?" I asked as he walked up to me.

I shoved him away.

"I'm not letting you hitchhike."

"You can't control me, Jordan. I'm not your wife—I don't have to consult with you."

"What's that supposed to mean?" he asked. "Did you think I was going to propose just because you got pregnant?"

I could have sworn my heart stopped. It's not that I expected Jordan to marry me now or anything, but did he really find it necessary to tell me he didn't want to at this point?

All I could do was look at him and laugh as I wiped a tear from my eye.

"Wow... I never knew—who would have thought me getting pregnant would prove you to be the biggest ass on the planet?" I asked. "Maybe you've been spending too much time with your father. He's starting to come out. Is this what I have to look forward to?"

I guess I pushed him too far by comparing him to his father, but I was insanely angry and hurt.

"Shut up, Haley!" he yelled and grabbed me by my jacket roughly.

I screamed, a bit shocked by the force he grabbed me with before tugging against him. He quickly released me. I looked at him as if he were a stranger.

Jordan wasn't the man I loved at that moment and I couldn't believe how easily he could turn on me.

"We're done," I said, tears coming to my eyes.

I turned away from him and stretched my arm out with my thumb pointing up. I couldn't control my soft cries.

A car stopped right in front of me, startling me. The window rolled down.

"Where ya going, sweetie?"

The man was in his fifties with gray hair and he spoke out of the side of his mouth.

"Vermont," I said.

I'm sure that surprised Jordan. Bakersfield was usually the last place I'd want to go to.

"Can you take me to the airport? I'll pay you."

"Sure, hop in," the man waved me into his car.

I once again felt like hitchhiking would be the stupidest thing I have ever done. Then again, I thought running off to New York with a stranger was stupid two years ago—that had proven to be the best thing I have ever done, so...

"Haley..." Jordan called, sounding like he choked on my name.

I couldn't even look at him before getting into the car.

"Haley, don't..." he pleaded, and for a split second I

wanted to run back into the safety of his arms, but then I remembered the way he was acting and the things he said.

Jordan walked closer to the car, but I slammed the door in his face. Finally, I looked over at him through the window with one last cold glare before the car pulled away. I couldn't figure out his expression exactly; it was somewhere between furious and worried.

January 1st

I'm not sure how it all started. I went to have lunch at my father's penthouse for Andrew's sake. My goal was to have a civilized conversation with him and discuss where my brother would go to school and live.

"I think Drew should go to Boston," I said in a calm, serious tone.

Dad looked at me and glanced at Andrew.

"Did you put your brother up to this?"

"Dad, I told you I want to be close to him," Andrew explained.

I saw the fear in his eyes. He knew as well as I did that this would turn into a fight.

"He left us, Andrew. I keep welcoming him back in and he disrespects me every time."

"And you disrespect me," I spat back at him.

"Andrew, go to your room."

"We're talking about his future. Don't you think he deserves to be part of the decision?"

"He might, but you don't."

Coryn spoke up, "Come on, Andrew. Let your father and Charlie talk alone."

She stood up and escorted Andrew out of the dining room—her heels irritatingly clicking against the marble floor.

"Dad, don't do this to Andrew. If he's going to be away from his parents, don't you think it would be nice for him to have family nearby?"

I thought I had a valid point.

"Charlie, you travel a lot."

"I travel to New York a lot, you know? I could bring him with me—this way he doesn't have to come home alone."

My father stared at me, surprised.

"You would have to see me more then. You would subject yourself to that for your brother?"

"I would do anything for him. Besides Haley, Mom and the band, he's all I've got."

Dad laughed.

"Haley...she's a lovesick puppy," he rolled his eyes. "Look, I get it—she's cute and naïve—and a Foster, whom you know I don't like. You know this thing you feel for her will wear off, right?"

"I don't think love wears off so easily, Dad," I said, smirking as I cocked my head to the side.

"Oh love. I'm sure if you proposed—she'd say yes. But you—well, you two remind me of me and your mom," he said.

I narrowed my eyes.

"Your mother was bright-eyed and youthful. She was in love with love. I was infatuated with her, but I wasn't ready for marriage or kids, Charlie. I was a shitty husband and father because I wasn't ready. Your mother got pregnant and I married her because I couldn't disgrace our family. I did love your mother—I grew to love her, but...part of me died."

I just stared at him. This was the first time my father ever opened up to me about anything in life. I didn't know whether to curse him out or tell him I understood. The strangest thing was I could understand. I'm terrified of marriage because of what I grew up around. When I thought I was going to be a father years ago, I accepted it and made the best of the idea—but I was terrified. I wondered if my life would be over.

"I was young—" Dad went on.

"What's your excuse now?" I asked.

"My excuse for what?"

"For being a lousy father to Drew and constantly arguing with Coryn around him?"

"He told you that?"

"Just let him go to the school in Boston. I'll be able to keep an eye on him for you."

"I'll think about it," he said, and I actually smiled at my father for the first time in years.

"Thank you."

I stood up and Dad decided more needed to be said.

"Do you understand now why I was against you having that baby with Bippy?"

I looked at him.

"Yes, but it was my decision to make. My feelings should have been considered—especially from Bippy."

"Charlie, there was more to it. These girls with money—they're worse than men. I was lucky I met your mom and not some debutant who slept around. Your mother was loyal at least—"

"And you weren't."

Dad sighed.

No wonder why Dad always found women who were broke. He found them to be more genuine. And some of them were, but there were always exceptions. Coryn was broke and is in no way genuine. However, Haley is wealthy and is nothing but genuine.

"Keep your eye on Haley—a girl like that...you're her first love and...well, she's going to want a ring or she'll walk."

"You don't know Haley," I said, turning to walk out of the room.

"And you didn't know Bippy. That baby wasn't yours."

I turned quickly and looked at him.

"You don't know shit. Of course the baby was mine."

"Charlie, Bippy told me herself. She was ashamed. She was sleeping around on you. Like I said, these rich girls...they'll take what they want."

I glared at my father.

"Why the hell would you keep this from me?!?!"

"I didn't want to hurt you."

"Bullshit! You let me believe my baby was killed!"

"Would you rather have known the truth?"

"Yes!" I yelled. "Either way I broke up with Bippy! Do you know the pain and remorse I felt for that child? The betrayal I felt by you and her?"

I was livid. I was yelling out of control and my entire body was shaking. Now, not only was I disgusted by Bippy aborting a child, but that she didn't even tell the real father most likely—and while I thought she was the love of my life, she was screwing someone else!

So many years I spent wondering how my life would be if we had the baby. So many years I felt the guilt and the hate for the loss. And now, I feel utter betrayal and even more hate.

"I was protecting you!" Dad stood up now. "If the baby was yours, you were both too young. Hell, you're still too young, Charlie. You want to travel the world and play guitar? Fine. Live like a low-life college dropout a few more years—when you're ready to settle down, I'm sure we can find you something and then you can apologize for hating me so much, okay?" he asked and patted my back.

I shrugged him off me hard.

"It's not fucking okay, Dad!" I screamed. "Do you ever take me seriously? Do you ever consider my feelings? I'm serious about my music career. And I'm serious about Haley. I was serious about Bippy and that baby, too...and you let me believe it was mine and then watched me desperately try to save its life..." I said.

My voice was starting to waver.

"Charlie, it was a fetus. You weren't ready."

He didn't get the emotional struggles I had at that time. I was being raised by a man I hated while my mother was having a mental breakdown in a hospital five hours away. My girlfriend was my only saving grace—the baby felt like a gift; some sort of sign. And that baby was destroyed—and so was any feeling for Bippy. Now, to find out that "sign" really was to tell me that I had the worst taste in girls back then, I wanted to lock myself in a dark room and not talk to anyone.

"Fuck you, Dad."

I just walked out after that. Unfortunately, I couldn't lock myself in that dark room like I wanted to. I had to meet up with Haley—who was very much filled with light. She was good at giving me space when I needed it though. When I calmed down and processed everything, I would tell her and she would wrap her arms around me.

But that didn't happen.

Instead, Haley was insisting we talk. I didn't take well to that. I didn't care about hurting her feelings at this point in time. I wanted the world to shut down until I could handle it again. However, the world kept speeding around and my car was the only thing that shut down.

And then she said it. The last thing I wanted to talk about or even think about fell from my girlfriend's lips. Haley was my new saving grace—much more than Bippy was. Bippy was great for a party. Haley was great for everything. She is phenomenal at showing me love in every way.

I expected Haley to just know what I was going through. She should have known it would be a terrible time to drop a bomb on me, but she didn't. How could she?

She just spit it out.

Haley is pregnant. How the hell can that be? I couldn't deal with it—not now. All I wanted to do was drive, and I couldn't. I needed to get my car fixed before I could fix anything else in life. That was all that went through my mind.

Haley didn't care about my car. I always thought she hated my car, and now I was sure of it. She just wanted to go home. It had been over two weeks since we were in Boston. Somehow though, that didn't feel like home to me right now. Nothing did.

I had never seen Haley look at me the way she had this afternoon. It was as if she was disgusted with me—not the same disgust when we met, but like I just slapped her across the face. I couldn't control myself after hearing her words. I tried to step outside of myself and look at me from Haley's perspective right now. I couldn't, though. Not when she told me I was acting like my father.

I was a stranger. I didn't know what the hell was going on anymore. I closed my eyes—trying to compose myself. Somehow I *had* turned into my father after lunch.

By the time I could process everything, things had gotten out of hand. Haley was trying to hitchhike and I was as lost as ever.

I thought about what I could say to Haley to make her

forgive me. Just as I was about to say some sort of an apology to her, a car stopped. Panic shook me. Haley broke up with me. Haley is pregnant with my baby. Haley just got into a car with a stranger while she is pregnant with my baby. Did this just happen?

Suddenly, this was overriding everything else: Bippy lying and cheating on me, Dad keeping that from me, the abortion; even my whole fear of marriage. Losing Haley was my worst nightmare and it may have just come true.

-J

Chapter 6

My plane landed in Burlington around six-fifteen at night. I was thankful Tasha was still in town, and that she had her own car with her. She and Christian spent New Year's Eve with a bunch of his friends. I didn't explain much to Tasha over the phone. She knew it was bad just by the sound of my hoarse voice that kept cracking throughout our brief conversation.

The man who gave me a ride to the airport must have thought I was having a nervous breakdown. Maybe I am. It was stupid of me to hitchhike on the side of the road after just finding out I am pregnant. However, I was desperate to get away from Jordan and his stupid car that he had refused to get fixed sooner.

I am thankful the stranger was harmless. Under normal circumstances, I would have been panicky the entire ride on whether he was going to kill me or rob me. I am already panicking over the rest of my life to have even felt anxious over the old man driving me.

I was still in shock as I saw Tasha's convertible pull up. I didn't have any bags with me; they were in Jordan's car. I can't believe how much the day spiraled out of control. I can't believe the man I am in love with reacted the way he did.

It makes me wonder if he responded similarly when Bippy told him she was pregnant. Maybe that was why she wanted the abortion in the first place. I know better than that, though. Bippy was and is a self-absorbed cheating bitch, who somehow continues to hurt Jordan still to this day with her betrayal.

"Haley, what's going on?" Tasha asked as I got into the passenger seat.

It has been so cold outside. I was grateful the heat was blasting in the car. My lips were even chattering.

"Just drive. Give me a minute," I said, trying to keep my voice calm.

I knew once I began to talk my voice would start cracking again. Tasha looked at me with the amount of worry my parents would look at me with. From her, that is surprising. I must really look like crap to alarm her this much. I guess the sheer fact that I made an unexpected trip to Bakersfield, when I didn't have to, is reason for caution.

It is no secret that my hometown is not my ideal destination. I honestly don't know why I am here, either. Was I planning to tell my parents the news…so soon? Maybe I was. Deep down, I know no matter how disappointed Mom and Dad will be, they will give me the comfort I need right now; the comfort I so desperately hoped to get from my boyfriend.

I began to cry as Tasha pulled onto the highway going toward Bakersfield. I didn't know where to begin. The baby would make the most sense to start with, but my heart was breaking over Jordan right then. The baby is not a baby yet—it is a growing change that I will adapt to. I am confident of that.

I am confident that even though my parents will hate the idea of me having a child at this point in my life that they will love their grandchild unconditionally.

Sure, I am scared, but I took such comfort in facing my fears with Jordan—my loving, warm and go with the flow boyfriend. I thought with him holding my hand throughout this pregnancy, I would be able to overcome fear and worry.

Then suddenly, that boyfriend turns into a hotheaded jerk that can't even react normally to the news. He didn't say much about *our* baby. He said a lot about his nonexistent child with his ex-girlfriend. He spoke about his ass of a father and his piece of crap car. Oh, and he spoke about how he does not want to marry me. But he barely mentioned the child we made together.

"Jordan and I are over," I said, closing my eyes.

I meant that. Maybe I was hormonal, but I couldn't bear the thought of being with any man who would react the way he did.

"Haley," Tasha laughed. "What stupid fight did you get into? Do you have your period?" she rolled her eyes.

I looked at her warningly.

"What did he do?" she asked, turning serious remembering the severity of my emotional state.

"I'm pregnant."

Tasha stopped short on the highway causing the car behind us to screech and swerve around us—honking its horn as it did.

"Can you please not kill me and my child?" I asked, looking at her horrified.

"You're pregnant?"

"Yes. I just found out today."

"And this is why you and Jordan broke up?" Tasha asked surprised.

"I don't know. I guess so."

"Haley, what the hell is going on?"

"He was pissed off at his father and Bippy…and he—it was like we didn't matter. Like me being pregnant was nothing compared to his past."

"I'm sure he was just upset. Maybe you should have waited to tell him until he had calmed down," Tasha sighed.

She was right, but I couldn't wait. And I didn't know the severity of the fight with his father. And now… Saying we're over seems a little hasty.

I took a deep breath before beginning to cry all over again.

"Haley, it'll be fine," Tasha reached over and rubbed my back.

"I shouldn't have come here. I need to talk to Jordan and I can't face my parents like this."

I was a mess—plain and simple. My emotions were all over the place and I had no control over them. I saw the exit for Bakersfield and I panicked.

"Don't take me to their house!"

"Where should I take you then?" she laughed, incredulously.

Christian still lived at home—the big mama's boy, so his place was out. Not that I would even want to be near Christian right now.

"Take me to the ski lodge," I said.

"I'm not driving all the way to Foster's and stranding you there," she groaned.

"We're only forty-five minutes away. You'll stay with me."

She laughed, "Oh gee, how nice of me to offer."

Tasha was already pulling off the highway and heading toward Killington. Best friends were great for times like these.

A minute later, my cell phone rang. It was Jordan. I smiled and looked at Tasha.

"It's him."

I was ready to forgive him. I was ready to tell him I'll meet him back in Boston tomorrow, and we can make up, and discuss our future.

"Hi," I picked up the phone, but was immediately cut off.

"Are you okay?"

"I'm fine. I'm with Tasha—we're heading to the ski lodge."

"You're insane," he said.

His tone was harsh and angry.

"Do you know how much danger you put yourself in by hitchhiking?"

"I know—I'm sorry."

"You are always so careful and then you go off with a total stranger?"

"That's how I met you, remember?" I reminded him.

"That was a little different, Haley," he blew that comment off. "You just ran out on me! You need to grow up and realize that life isn't always smooth."

"Uh, excuse me?" I asked.

"I had a really difficult day, and you were insensitive and impatient and..."

"Me? You—me..." I stuttered over my words. "You had a difficult day?" I yelled. "My stomach has been in my throat all day and I needed you to be there for me. You're the one who is insensitive! I'm so sorry to hear that Bippy is a bitch, but we knew this. We know your father is an asshole. I just wish you would get over it already, Jordan," I breathed.

I never had to talk to Jordan like that before. I am not going to allow him to blame me for telling him news that affected both of us all because of Bippy and his father, and something that happened almost six years ago.

"I can't deal with this right now," he said, coldly. "Call me when your hormones aren't in an uproar."

Jordan hung up on me and I literally stared at the phone for five minutes.

"What did he say?" Tasha finally asked.

"He can't deal with *this* right now," I mumbled.

Tears filled my eyes and I heard Tasha sigh. I couldn't tell if her sigh was sympathetic toward me or annoyed with my dramatics. I have to say, Jordan and I had a lot of stupid, little fights that made us laugh by the end of it—but this was just ridiculously out of hand. It was like neither one of us knew how to calm down.

By the time we made it to the ski lodge, the temperature had dropped and the sky was pitch black. It fit my emotions—cold and scary. Tasha and I walked into my family's cabin—it felt so much emptier than I'm used to. I took one look around and decided I was finished with the day. I wanted it to be tomorrow already.

"I'm going to bed," I announced.

"Haley, call Jordan and end this."

My eyes widened when I turned to look at her.

"End it?"

"I mean the fight, not your relationship," she rolled her eyes.

"I already did end it. We're done."

A few tears rolled down my cheeks. I broke up with Jordan this afternoon. I still can't wrap my head around that, let alone anything else that had been discovered today.

"Call him and tell him you didn't mean it."

I wanted to call him, but I couldn't be sure it would be the guy I love on the phone. Right now, he is Charlie Ashton, III—the boy at the bus station who resented me for who I am—this time though, he resents me for who I have growing inside me. That shocked me; hurt me deeper than I thought it could. I was sure if Jordan knew nothing about the truth of the paternity of his lost child, he would have reacted warmly. Now, maybe he sees this entire thing with Bippy as a chance to let go of that mourning he went through, though the truth did hurt him.

How ironic that I wound up pregnant the same day he found out he never impregnated Bippy Reynolds.

"Good night, Tash," I said solemnly, dragging myself

upstairs.

I didn't have any clothes with me, but I wanted to get out of my jeans especially. I undressed in front of the mirror as I watched myself cry. I imagined my belly swollen. I wanted so much to just accept the news and smile about it.

I just couldn't—not tonight when my baby's father is brooding over his messed up life. I lay down in bed, under the covers and thought about the whole marriage thing that was expected of me when I graduated college. I had wanted it—there would have been nothing holding me back. I am in love with Jordan. Why would we wait any longer? By then, we would have been dating for two years.

Now it seems two years didn't mean as much as I thought. There are still secrets you find out about a person, like how irate someone becomes when he finds out unexpected news.

I cried myself to sleep.

Hours later, I was startled awake. I couldn't remember my dream, but I'm sure it was something terrible. My entire body was tense. I checked the time and it was almost five am. I had an insane craving for hot cocoa. I suppose I was in the right place. I sighed to myself. I always rebelled against Frosty Foster's Famous Hot Cocoa. I hated to admit that is the best hot chocolate I had ever tasted. It is a part of my family, and for a while, I was sick of being a part of it all.

Now, I am bringing a baby into this world, though and I want to surround myself in comforts from home. I will not suppress my child's individuality and own thoughts to suit my wants for him or her, like Mom and Dad did to me, though. My parents will spoil the kid rotten, which would be okay, as long as at home, Jordan and I are a little more humbling.

Listen to me... Jordan and I... at home.

I am delusional sometimes. I'm trying to tie my life up

into a pretty bow when it has just been turned upside down. My parents could completely disown me. Jordan could continue this mood he's in, and I could lose him forever.

My breathing became shallow and I ran to the bathroom, not caring that I was half naked. It was just Tasha and me here anyway. As I was hurling everything I had eaten today, which consisted of a few saltines and some chocolate covered peanuts, I thought I heard knocking on the door.

I tried to speak, but I was too busy with my head facing down in the toilet. Next thing I knew, someone was holding my hair back. I assumed it was Tasha. When I was finally done, I looked up at the person who came to my rescue with swollen, teary eyes.

That person was not Tasha. It was Christian. Here I was in my bra and panties, crying my eyes out and barfing bile out and Christian was holding my hair, with his hand on my back.

"Are you okay?"

"Get out," I shoved him away, and did my best to cover myself with my hands.

I felt incredibly weak and disoriented. The day had spun out of control entirely too fast. I hadn't eaten real food all day and I was profusely puking out what felt like everything inside of me.

I closed my eyes, hoping when I opened them I would be fully clothed and Christian would be long gone. No such luck.

"Let me help you," he said, grabbing my hand and pulling me up. I tried to fight against him, but I felt insanely dizzy and almost fell back down.

Christian swooped me into his arms and I seriously wished I was able to fight against him. I just felt so lifeless. I didn't like how close his right hand was to my breast or how the fingers on his left hand were subconsciously tickling behind my knee.

I was placed on my bed and I immediately snatched the blanket over myself and turned away from him.

"Can I get you anything?" he asked.

"I'm fine," I said as I surveyed the room for any sign of my clothes.

"Don't lie to me, Lee," he sighed.

"You can get me my clothes," I said, looking him in the face with a serious glare.

"Tasha put them in the wash before she went to bed. I'll switch them to the dryer for you in a bit."

"What are you doing here anyway?"

"Tasha asked me to stay with you guys for the night. I woke up when you ran to the bathroom. What's wrong?"

"I'm sick," I answered automatically. "Can you get me some hot cocoa?"

I figured it would give me some time to figure out how to lie better. Plus, despite my gag reflex, I still craved the stuff.

I wiped my face on some tissues on the nightstand. I felt exhausted, but wide awake at the same time.

A few minutes later, Christian was back in my room with a mug. He sat down on the bed.

"Sit up," he said, refusing to hand me the hot chocolate until I did.

I grasped the top of the blanket and pulled it up as I moved into a sitting position. Holding the fabric shield against my chest with one hand, I reached for the mug with the other.

"Thank you. You can go now. I'm fine," I said, taking a sip.

The thick liquid warmed my insides, feeling like someone just gave my heart a hug.

"Haley, I know you pretty well. You don't look so good,

babe," he said, brushing my cheek with the back of his hand. "You were just sick last week..."

"It's all the junk I've been eating from the holidays," I shrugged, also pulling away from his touch.

"Where's Jordan?"

"In New York. His car is stuck there."

"And weren't you heading back to Boston?"

"Change of plans," I explained.

"Right—you just had to come to the lodge because you craved Frosty Foster's cocoa?" he asked with a raised eyebrow.

I sighed, "Would you stop being nosy? I didn't invite you here. Tasha did."

"You know, you really do hurt me when you treat me like this," he said.

"Chris," I sighed, cocking my head to the side and setting the mug down on the nightstand. "I'm fine. Believe that, okay?"

"If Jordan hurt you, I'll—"

"He didn't hurt me," I said, blatantly lying.

I was very much hurt by Jordan yesterday. I felt my face crumbling when I said the sentence. I couldn't help it. It is impossible to lie successfully when your emotions are out of control.

"Haley, what did—my God...," he gasped as if he had some big epiphany. "You're pregnant. That would explain the constant nausea and sleepiness and Jordan staying behind in New York..."

I wiped my tears as quickly as possible and tried to deny it, not very convincingly.

"N—no, I—"

"Shit, the jackass got you knocked up and he skipped out on you?"

I lay back down and turned away from him, not being able to pull the blanket completely over me due to Christian's ass sitting on top of part of it.

"Just go, please," I begged.

I felt his hand on my shoulder.

"Haley, you're a wreck. Tell me what happened or else I'm going to find the son of a bitch and make my own conclusions."

"Leave Jordan alone, Christian," I ordered, turning to look at him.

"Shh," he pulled me into a tight hug, which I fought to break free from at first. "Just tell me."

He rubbed my back and I closed my eyes allowing him to comfort me. I felt my body go limp against him. My crying subsided as Christian continued to rub my back, lulling me into a calmer state.

I forgot he was Christian. I forgot I was in my underwear. And for a split second, I forgot I was pregnant and that my heart was breaking.

"Haley!"

I snapped my eyes open and pulled away from Christian to see Jordan in the doorway. I was incredibly happy to see him, but then I realized how bad this looked to him. Here I was in my underwear and in bed with Christian! The thought grossed me out and I could only imagine the disgust Jordan must have felt seeing this sight.

Suddenly, I remembered everything that had slipped my mind just a moment ago. I struggled against Christian; he didn't seem to want to let me go.

"Get your hands off her!" Jordan stormed toward us and practically threw Christian off of me.

"Would you get a grip?" Christian asked, looking up at Jordan like he had no right to flip out.

"Jordan, this isn't—"

"Get your clothes on, Haley," he sighed, before turning

and walking out of the room.

"The guy is an animal," Christian sighed.

"Can you get out?" I asked, holding the blanket tighter against me.

"Haley, this is what he does…" he said, getting up off the floor. "He's a heartbreaker. I hoped he wouldn't hurt you, but now he's gotten you pregnant, too?"

I didn't deny or confirm the question.

"He didn't get Bippy pregnant," I mumbled.

"Bippy?" Christian asked.

"The girl who he supposedly got pregnant…that you think he's a terrible person for…" I rolled my eyes. "It was Bippy. They dated for two years, remember? She decided to get an abortion against Jordan's wishes. Well, turns out—she was cheating on him. The baby wasn't even Jordan's," I explained. "Do you still think he's such a bad guy?"

Christian looked at me blankly before walking out of the room. I found a pink robe in the closet I hadn't worn since I was fourteen. It was a little tight, but it covered me mostly.

I walked downstairs and Jordan was sitting on the couch, brooding. I walked toward him and sat down in his lap, surprising him.

"Before you say anything," I began. "I did nothing with Christian. I would never do that to you or Tasha."

"I know," he sighed, putting his arm around my waist. "It was just a little alarming to see you in his arms half-naked."

"I didn't… My clothes are in the washing machine. I had the blanket over me most of the time—he wouldn't leave me alone until I told him why I was upset."

"Did you tell him?" Jordan asked, looking into my eyes.

"No—but he has an idea."

He sighed, "That's great."

"What are you doing here?"

"I came to apologize," he said, brushing my hair back. "I'm sorry. I got way out of hand."

I smiled, "I'm sorry I was a bit of a hormonal mess."

He laughed, "You hitchhiked to get away from me!"

"That was stupid."

"Incredibly stupid," he agreed. "You have our child to think about now," he said.

I had to smile at that.

"Are you okay with this?"

He nodded, "It's a big change, but I can't think of anyone I would want to raise a baby with more than you. I'm just worried about you."

"Me? I'll be fine."

Just then, I felt another wave of nausea. I quickly ran to the bathroom.

"Haley?" Jordan called after me.

After I threw up whatever I had left in my system, I lie on the cold tiles of the bathroom. I hope the rest of my pregnancy won't be like this.

I felt a hand on my back, and I looked up to see Jordan, thankful it was him this time instead of Christian.

"Is this normal?" he asked.

The worried look on his face was endearing. I sat up and put my hand on his cheek.

"For the first few months," I nodded.

"I didn't even get to ask... How far along are you?"

Jordan helped me stand up.

"Two and a half months," I said, wobbling a bit. "I'm due July 12th."

"Easy," he said, supporting my weight against him.

"I just need to lie down," I sighed.

He helped me back upstairs and I insisted on brushing my teeth before getting into bed. He was waiting by the bathroom door when I opened it up, nearly scaring me to death.

"What are you doing?" I whispered.

"I wanted to escort you in case you were still woozy," he explained.

"I'm fine," I laughed, but he took my arm anyway and led me to the bedroom.

I locked the door behind us, not wanting Christian wandering into my room any more tonight—not that he'd dare try anything like that with Jordan here.

Sometimes I wonder if I should advise Tasha against marrying him. I've dropped hints, but I have never outright told her she is making a huge mistake. The sleazy things Christian does to get me in an awkward situation, like earlier for instance have been going on since I was a teenager. Now, he is engaged—shouldn't that have put an end to it?

I guess I never wanted to upset Tasha. Besides, she isn't one to take advice from anyone on men. I used to try with her ex-boyfriend, but she never listened. She would probably accuse me of being jealous if I explained Christian's flirtations are a little much. Plus, she always knew how I felt toward Christian. She has to know my ill feelings didn't disappear.

I turned to see Jordan kicking his jeans off. I knew I was exhausted, but he looked pretty tired himself. I took off the tiny robe before getting into bed next to him. I looked at his dream catcher tattoo and smiled, knowing me and my baby were safe in his arms.

"I love you," Jordan said after he turned the light out.

I found his lips in the dark and kissed him softly.

"I love you, too."

January 2nd

It's 7am and I've been up all night. I know I already made an entry about yesterday, but too much has been on my mind to leave it at that.

After Haley hitchhiked away from me, I dealt with the tow truck and made my way back into Manhattan by taxi. I found myself at Carney's that night with the guys.

Chugging a beer back, I watched Sebastian and Darren play pool. Danny stood next to me, looking at me expectantly.

"What do you mean the baby wasn't yours?"

I hadn't been able to tell him the entire story at once; he was getting a shorter version in between interruptions from the other guys. The rest of the band didn't know much about my past—not the way Danny did. He was my best friend throughout high school, even though he was lower middle class and I was a rich kid. That never mattered to us like it did my father and Bippy.

He probably hates Bippy just as much, if not more, than I do. They never got along and she tended to be a whiny brat most of the time.

"Bippy lied to me, man," I sighed, exhausted from repeating those words in my own head all day.

"So, you were all broken up over a baby that wasn't even yours?" Danny asked. "That slut screwed you over in so many ways."

"I almost feel sorry for the guy. He didn't even know about the baby."

"It's probably better that way," he said. "If you hadn't known about the pregnancy, you would have never gone through—"

"I would have never broken up with Bippy," I reminded him.

"I'm sure her true colors would have come out, J," Danny laughed. "I mean, they already were, you just didn't see it…There's no way you would still be with her."

"I was so lost back then," I sighed. "It was difficult for me to make sense out of things—and now, I almost feel like I'm right back there. Nothing makes sense. And Haley…"

I could hear the way my voice sounded when I said her name, like I yearned to talk to her. I was just too angry to be near her. I was too upset to offer anything to her, and I know it's wrong. I can feel how much the day spun out of control. I just couldn't stop.

"Where is she? I thought you and her were going back to Boston."

"She's in Vermont."

"Oh, and you're still here..." Danny looked at me, waiting for me to tell him more.

"We had a fight."

"A fight?" Danny smirked. "Come on, you two fight like sitcom characters. You make up in twenty minutes."

I shook my head, "Not this time."

He rolled his eyes, "If Cami and I can be okay after our fight, you two will be married by next year," he laughed.

I groaned.

"What's with everyone bringing up marriage, huh?"

"It was a joke, Jordan."

"Like I told Haley today, I'm not marrying her. I don't want to get married."

"Whoa—did you say it to her just like that?"

"I don't know. I said a lot of things today that came out wrong."

"Sounds like you were being a jack ass," he said, taking a swig of his beer.

"She's pregnant," I spat out.

Danny almost choked on his beer

"Haley is pregnant?"

"That's what she says," I said finishing my beer.

"She wouldn't lie to you," he smacked my chest.

I didn't realize how much he likes and trusts Haley until now. Danny has been fairly protective of me ever since I broke up with Bippy. He is not always easy to get along with—mostly because he is always brutally honest, but he is a brother to me. I know I could never get rid of him. He always has my back even when I am being a jack ass.

"I know," I nodded in response to Haley being honest with me. "And I know that the baby is mine this time."

Even I had to crack a smile at that. I also know Haley would never want to get an abortion, especially if I don't want her to.

"I just didn't expect her to say that, and literally right after I found out about Bippy. It's like history is repeating itself, and I'm freaking out."

"Who wouldn't freak out, bro?" he asked. "Your father drops this bomb on you, which he's a total douche for doing that now and not five years ago. Then Haley tells you this..."

"She broke up with me."

Danny laughed, "She broke up with you because you were an ass. She's probably crying herself to sleep thinking you hate her."

He was probably right. Haley can't stand to see other people upset. When she saw me last, I was beyond upset—and I directed all my anger at her.

"Go to Vermont. Apologize to her and tell her you'll work through this and love that baby like I know you will."

"My car is in the shop."

Danny laughed again, rolling his eyes.

"I thought you were going to fix it up?"

"I was, but... I've been busy."

"If I loan you my car, will you promise to be careful with her?"

"Wow... You trust me with your baby?" I teased him.

He shook his head hesitantly.

"Your baby and your girl are more important than my precious car, but please take care of her," he said, pulling the keys out and handing them to me.

"Thanks, man," I smiled at him and patted his back.

"I better be Godfather," he warned.

I laughed, "I think that can be arranged."

Suddenly, it hit me—I mean really hit me. I am actually going to be a father! I have never loved any girl the way I love Haley, and I will be sharing something amazing with her.

I always wondered what my life would have been like had Bippy kept the baby. I couldn't imagine being tied to her forever, or her being a very nurturing mother.

Maybe yesterday was one of those days of revelations. Now that I know the truth about Bippy's baby, I'm free to completely move on and put my heart into my child with Haley.

I offered a quick goodbye to the guys before taking off toward the garage where Danny kept his yellow Porsche. I realized flying would be a lot quicker, but it was already after midnight. Haley would be asleep by the time my flight landed. By driving, I arrived in the early morning. Besides that, I needed the drive to sort out my head a bit.

The novelty of Bippy cheating on me is starting to wear off. I am still pissed off, but not so much about her—because I am over her—but the fact that she and my father allowed me to believe that baby was mine. Even while I fought for her to keep the baby, she didn't have any remorse? No sign of guilt even? I am amazed that a person can be so good at lying. Between Bippy and my father, I am really beginning to question the good in humanity.

How can you hurt someone you claim to love so deeply?

As Danny's Porsche handled the dark highway with incredible ease, I smiled thinking about the purity of my beautiful girlfriend. I am a complete sap for her, and it killed me that she was up in Vermont thinking God knows what about me.

We still have a lot of figuring out to do, but at least I know we'll do it together.

-J

Chapter 7

I grabbed my decaf vanilla soy chai tea latte and took a sip as I glanced outside the café for Jordan. The liquid was soothing going down; warming my insides. I missed my regular vanilla lattes from Starbucks, but even decaf coffee is giving me acid reflux now. I am trying to be a good mother even while my baby is still in the womb.

I am becoming slightly neurotic about it. If someone was smoking on the sidewalk, I crossed over to the other side. I avoided stairs if I could. I wasn't always the most graceful person, and I constantly have nightmares of me falling down the stairs and losing the baby.

The past month, I hadn't gotten much sleep at all. I usually throw up every night around two am. School started a week ago and I feel like I'm behind already. I can't focus on anything; not even a camera lens ironically. My first photo project of the semester was a B-. I always get A's. I'm usually so alert in class, especially when I'm actually learning about camera techniques. My mind has just been anywhere but school.

I still haven't told my parents and that is causing me way too much worry. My birthday is coming up. I plan to tell them then, figuring they won't be too hard on me on *my* day.

Jordan has been quiet lately. I guess he'd probably say the same about me, though. When we're in bed together, we lie there in silence—both staring at the ceiling for hours every night.

During the day, we act like those nights don't exist, like

we both had a decent night's sleep, like I wasn't puking my brains out for almost an hour, and like he didn't go outside to smoke.

We hang out with our friends and go for walks and smile like nothing has changed.

Everything has changed, though. I change every day. I look at my body and I can see my boobs swelling. I see my stomach beginning to round out. I see the bags under my eyes and the worry lines in my forehead.

Suddenly, I'm not turning twenty-two. I'm forty with a career I left behind, raising a teenager who wants to get their tongue-pierced and rebel against me while their father is across the world performing for eighteen-year-olds flashing their breasts to him while he's on stage.

Jordan walked into the café, wearing a black jacket, his hands tucked inside. I almost didn't recognize him. I don't know why, but it took an extra moment for me to grasp that this guy is my boyfriend. He holds himself differently; he isn't light and carefree anymore.

He actually *is* the angst-ridden person he comes off as in songs like "Detonate" and "Break The Mold". I wonder if he didn't recognize me either. I'm sure I no longer look like the girl in love with the moon. In fact, I can't remember the last time I noticed the moon.

"Hey," he smiled, and pecked my lips.

"How'd it go in the studio?"

"Good. James thinks we can be done by the end of the month."

James Manzello is producing Tortured's album. Jordan says he's incredibly talented, and Darren has formed a nonsexual crush on him.

"Awesome," I smiled. "I had a few minutes until I had to

go to Lincoln Center, so I thought I'd see how you were."

I was in New York for Fashion Week while Jordan was in town to finish the album.

"I'm good. I was actually wondering... Does Meghan still have that pass for me?"

"Yeah..." I nodded, unsure of why he cared.

Maybe Cami wanted to go. She didn't strike me as the kind of girl who would want to go to a fashion show. She is a sensible dresser, who usually wears baby doll t-shirts with a band logo on it, some skinny jeans and Converse. Then again, she was also broke until recently. Maybe she wants to upgrade her style.

"Good. I want to go."

I laughed; a genuine laugh.

"Seriously," Jordan smiled, but that wasn't genuine.

There was something extremely wrong with his smile, like this one was forced.

"Why?"

"I want to be there for Meghan and to be with you."

"What about Bippy?"

"I can handle Bippy," he said.

His voice was thick when he said her name. I imagined if stirring fudge brownie batter had a sound that would be it. I just nodded, but I wanted to say so much.

I know he deserved answers. I know he had every right to lash out at Bippy and clear the air. However, doing it at a public event was something I wanted to avoid. I just want him to move on. I am his pregnant girlfriend now, and I love him, and am not getting rid of our baby. Shouldn't that make all the difference? Shouldn't all that hate and guilt dissolve into happiness and love for me and his real child?

We took a taxi uptown. The ride made me nauseous not

surprisingly. I couldn't tell if it was from my claustrophobia of being stuck in a car crushed in Manhattan traffic or because of the baby. Or maybe I was making myself sick with anxiety. I have always been good at that.

"Are you okay?" Jordan asked me.

"I'm fine," I sighed.

"You don't seem happy I'm going."

He was staring out the window as if he were a tourist. I realized he hasn't been looking me in the eyes very much lately. Jordan was fantastic at eye contact. I missed those gorgeous green eyes with the specks of gold staring into mine.

I pulled his chin toward me. He still looked different to me. His eyes met mine briefly before he took my hand in his.

"I'm not happy you're going," I admitted to him. "You're coming to see her," I swallowed mucus back.

The taxi stopped and the driver muttered a price to us in a thick accent that I couldn't place. I grabbed money from my purse and handed it to the driver before Jordan could reach into his pocket. I was out of the car just as quick.

"Haley..." Jordan called from the other side of the car as he walked toward me.

"Don't," I shut my eyes. "Please? I can't talk about this now. I will lose it and I want to be happy for Meghan. I really do, so just do what you have to do."

I walked ahead of him toward the Fashion Week signs. I kept telling myself to just get through today. I reminded myself things will go back to normal—whatever normal is now.

I ran my hands over my navy blue dress designed by Meghan, of course. She says navy is the new black this season. Luckily, it wasn't a form fitting dress like the one she sent me for New Year's. Though my belly didn't show I was pregnant, my clothes were starting to get tight on me.

When I got to the entrance, I presented my pass and felt Jordan come up behind me. I absently handed him his. We went through a security check and made our way over to the area Meghan told me her show would be in. It wasn't hard to miss.

Above the runway was a huge lit sign that read "Bippy" in script with a heart instead of a dot for the "i". *How original*, I thought as I rolled my eyes. I almost hated myself for getting Meghan involved with Bippy Reynolds. Not only did she drive Meghan crazy, but now, I am forced to support her clothing line in order to support my friend—and I will have to see her more.

Jordan and I found our seats. The area was packed with photographers and buyers. Suddenly, I saw flashes of light. Did all of the photographers decide to test out their lighting at the same time? I was blind!

I then realized they were actually capturing a celebrity in the crowd: my boyfriend.

"I probably should have dressed better," he snickered.

Under his coat, he wore a white thermal shirt which was tattered on the bottom and black cargo pants with holes in each knee.

"Maybe you should have thought of that before deciding to cheer on your ex-girlfriend."

Jordan looked at me and groaned.

"I am not supporting her any more than you are. I'm here for Meghan."

"Bullshit," I murmured. "You're here because... you know, I'm not sure why anymore."

"Can we not do this here?" he asked, looking around at the reporters. "You said you wanted to talk about this later, remember?"

I just sat back in my seat and tried hard not to look miserable. Tasha and Christian walked into the room and were making their way over to us. Even though I hated being around them as a couple, I welcomed the distraction.

"Hey!" Tasha cheered, loudly.

She hugged Jordan and me. Christian kissed my cheek and ignored his cousin. I talked with Tasha for a few minutes as a reporter approached Jordan.

"How's the album coming along, man?"

"Great. I just came from the studio," Jordan said, enthusiastically.

"Oh yeah? Any new songs recorded?"

"Yeah—we did one today called 'I'm OK'. I wrote it this morning on a whim."

I listened in to Jordan's impromptu interview. Jordan wrote in his notebook quite often lately. I wonder if he wrote more than just song lyrics in there though. I used to keep a journal, but I stopped about a year or two ago. I used to write journal entries because I felt I had no one else to talk to about all of my fears and dreams.

When I met Jordan, that all changed. I looked over at him and thought maybe I should start writing in my journal again. Lately, it was hard to talk to him, and maybe he felt the same way about me.

"I'd say with the quick rise of Tortured, you're more than okay," the reporter laughed.

Jordan laughed, too, "I guess I am."

"Haley?" the reporter called me and I looked.

"Yeah?"

"How does it feel to have a song about you in the top ten on Billboard?"

"Amazing," I said honestly. "And a little weird," I admitted. "It's something personal to Jordan and me, but at the same time, I'm so flattered he wants to share it with the world."

I looked over at Jordan and he smiled. For that instant, we were those people again—smitten with each other; our biggest conflict was allowing ourselves to fall completely.

As soon as the reporter left us, the bright "Bippy" sign began flashing red as if it were a huge traffic light telling me I was stuck in this moment. I was abandoned in the debris left behind from her relationship with Jordan.

I felt his arm slip around my shoulders as the show began. I appreciated the gesture despite our hostility, and I put my hand on his thigh, allowing myself to relax into his body.

Models began to strut their stuff down the runway, cameras flashed, people clapped. The designs were incredible like I knew they would be. Tasha would "ooh" and "ah" over every ensemble to pass us.

Bippy's friend and model, Lila Stoltz charged down the runway as if she owned the room. I am not a fan of hers. Her personality ruins any beauty she has—that and her insanely thin figure. Each time I have seen her, it seems she loses another ten pounds. I'm sure to her I look like a cow, especially now with my body starting to change from the pregnancy.

The last "model" to grace the runway was who else, but Bippy Reynolds herself. Her long dark brown hair bounced down her back as she strode across the stage in a red dress with an interesting black sash belt. The look was '60s retro with a modern New York club flair. The entire line fit into this theme, and it was downright gorgeous.

The room stood up to applaud Bippy. I looked at Jordan and he rolled his eyes before standing, but refusing to clap. I did the same. Bippy ate the attention up. I glanced over at Tasha, who was clapping along with Christian. I scowled at her.

"I'm sorry—she's one of Chris' friends," she shrugged.

I wouldn't call Bippy and Christian friends. He has

always been pretty close to Bippy's best friend, Leslie Tyler. Bippy is too into the party scene for Christian to get close to her.

Bippy grabbed a microphone and her annoying voice boomed over the sound system. She blabbered on about her dream coming true before introducing the designer who helped her achieve it. Meghan came walking out looking like an excited child—she is one in many ways. Jordan and I clapped and cheered her on.

After the show was over, Meghan sent me a text message telling me to move into the press area. I paid close attention to the photographers stepping on each other to get a good shot of Bippy as she posed like an airhead. I don't want to be one of those photographers. I don't want to give fame whores like Bippy Reynolds a spot in US Weekly for being stupid. I also didn't want to post scandalous photos of some rock star, like Jordan, to make a few bucks.

Now that "Haley's Letter" is number two on the Billboard charts, photos of Jordan and I are popping up in tabloids more frequently. From what I hear, paparazzi get a nice chunk of change for a photo of us.

I am not sure what area of photography I wanted to go into still, but I knew it wasn't photojournalism. Sure, it was exciting seeing celebrities, but that gets old. Besides, I had the opportunity to work with some music artists, and I much rather work for them—like I have done—than fight to get to them like these photographers who wait outside celebrity homes and hotels.

I looked away from the photographers and Jordan wasn't next to me. He was being interviewed again.

"Champagne?"

I turned to see Christian with an outstretched hand.

"Oh, I forgot," he said, taking a sip from the glass.

I sighed, "I never said I was pregnant."

"You never denied it, either," he countered.

I just looked at him.

"When are you going to tell your parents?"

"My birthday."

He laughed, "Smart."

Christian's eyes glanced over at Jordan.

"Is the rock star prepared to give up his life for you and this kid?"

"He doesn't have to give up anything."

"Oh, but you do?"

"We'll work it out," I said turning to look at Jordan, but he was gone.

"Where'd Bippy go?" Christian asked. "I wanted to congratulate her."

I just walked away.

"Real nice, Haley," he called after me.

I made my way through swarms of people, trying to search out Mcghan.

"Haley! Over here!"

I smiled, seeing Meghan's bouncing blonde head waving me over. She hugged me, ignoring the people surrounding her for a moment.

"You are so amazing," I commended her.

"Thank you. You look beautiful," she said, pulling away from me.

"Only because you designed my dress," I rolled my eyes.

"Well, you look gorgeous in it."

I had a hard time believing that. I felt queasy all around.

"Thanks," I forced a smile.

"Where's Jordan?"

"I don't know."

"I'm happy he came."

"He wanted to support you."

"I'm sure the press was all over him," Meghan giggled. "I had a couple of reporters asking me about him and if I was going to be working with Tortured on any projects."

"Now, that's an idea."

I was trying to focus on my conversation with Meghan and not on where Jordan went off to with Bippy. I couldn't help it, though. I tried incredibly hard to forget about Jordan's encounter with his ex-girlfriend. I tried hard to forget about my rapidly increasing nausea. I just wanted to enjoy Meghan's moment in the spotlight with her. However, once my chai latte from earlier began to rise into my throat, I had to rush off to the bathroom.

After hurling for twenty minutes, I decided to get some air before I looked for Jordan. I put my coat on and walked around outside, feeling the cold air against my cheeks. It helped somewhat, but I still felt sick. I stopped short when I noticed in between two tents, in a fairly discreet area, were Jordan and Bippy about fifteen feet away. I wouldn't have noticed them except for the fact that I was looking for them. They spoke to each other calmly—Bippy with an apologetic expression and Jordan with sympathy written across his face. Maybe I was hallucinating—was that a side effect from pregnancy? When Jordan pulled Bippy into a hug, I was about to have a heart attack. How could he hug someone he hates?

Maybe Jordan didn't hate Bippy after all. Maybe he was still trying to mend his broken heart. I couldn't help but think the worst of the situation. I know Jordan loves me, but maybe he still loves Bippy, too. I didn't know how that was possible, honestly. Aside from her beauty, she is vapid and lacks any knowledge outside of her own existence.

Is Jordan's disgust of her all this time just to cover up underlying feelings?

That was my last thought before it was there again—the nauseous feeling. I dry heaved once, then twice before vomiting right there on the ground. I quickly ran to the bathroom before anyone noticed it was me. I didn't want humiliation added to my list of ailments at the moment.

After I finished up in the bathroom for the second time, I realized I had a text from Jordan asking me to meet him outside of the main entrance. I tried my best to freshen up before walking outside toward Jordan. I still felt sick and I was sure I looked it; he looked a little green as well.

"Are you okay?" he asked.

"I've been throwing up for the past forty minutes," I sighed, feeling completely out of it.

"Let's get back to the hotel and you can rest before tonight's show." "Oh, the show..."

I rubbed my forehead thinking about making it through a night of live music and crammed groupies feeling the way I do.

"You don't want to go?"

I could tell he sounded surprised and maybe a bit offended by my reaction. I suppose I vomited so frequently now, it was natural to Jordan, not cause for me to stay in bed the rest of the night, which is what I truly wanted to do.

"It just slipped my mind," I explained.

We got into a taxi and took it to the hotel. I practically had to run to the room from the elevator. I burst into the bathroom and the now familiar sound of my vomiting was filling the room.

Jordan walked into the bathroom and I immediately waved him off with my hand. I know he wanted to comfort me, but when my head was practically in the toilet—I just wanted to be alone. It isn't something I wanted my boyfriend to see. No one wants to date the girl from the Exorcist. I know women get morning sickness, but I don't feel well for more than half the day almost every day. This baby does not understand the cut off time for morning.

When I finally walked out of the bathroom, Jordan was laying on the bed. I turned my back to him.

"Unzip me, please."

He sat up and did as I asked. I took the dress off and slipped into a long t-shirt. Jordan stared at me while I changed. I wondered if it was because he finally noticed my slightly rounded belly that I started to see weeks ago.

Weeks ago…

That was also the last time we made love. I wasn't used to that. Unless Jordan was on tour for a while, we had a very active sex life. The pregnancy is taking a lot out of me, so thankfully he didn't push. I felt bad, though. It isn't that I don't want to, but I am so tired and sick lately that I fear I'd puke on him in the middle of it.

I lay down next to him, with my back toward him and he wrapped his arms around me. I didn't sink into his body like I usually did, nor did he pull me closer like he normally did. There was some distance between us, and it was extremely noticeable.

"What's wrong?"

He asked this question a lot, even more than I asked him.

"I feel like crap."

He kissed my shoulder, "I'm sorry."

"For what exactly? For getting me pregnant or for hugging Bippy?"

I turned around to look at him accusingly as if he had cheated on me. "You were spying on me, huh?"

"I walked outside to get some air, and yes, I did wonder

where you ran off to…"

"I needed to confront her."

"I figured there would be a little more yelling and a little less affection."

"Are you really going to be jealous?"

He sounded angry and I honestly didn't think he had a right to be.

"Jordan, I don't know what I should feel," I sighed, tears immediately falling down my face.

"Great, and now you're crying."

"I'm pregnant—get used to it," I snapped.

"Oh, so that's going to be your excuse for everything from now on?"

"You are so…" I clenched my teeth, frustrated, "insensitive."

"Maybe you're the one being insensitive. If you would just ask me what happened with Bippy, I will gladly tell you."

"Oh, okay. What happened?" I asked, flashing a sarcastic look.

"We had a serious talk and there's a lot more to the story."

"Like?"

"It's something Bippy really doesn't want people to know."

I narrowed my eyes, "You just said if I asked, you would tell me what happened."

Jordan sat up and ran a hand through his hair.

"She was raped."

I held back a laugh not because I think rape is a funny topic, but I have a hard time believing it is true. It seems too ironic that when Jordan is pointing a finger at Bippy; she is trying to point it at someone else.

"What?" I asked, rolling my eyes. "And you believe that?"

"Haley," he sighed. "Why would she lie about that?"

"This is Bippy we're talking about. She's been lying to you all along, remember?"

"Yeah, well, I know Bippy a lot better than you."

"Right, because you two were in love. Jordan," I said, my tears renewing. "What is going on?"

"I don't know," he said, honestly.

It wasn't comforting.

"Do you still love her?"

He looked me straight in the eye and touched the side of my face.

"I love you."

"That's not the question," I said, feeling my jaw tighten under his touch.

"I don't love Bippy—I care about her."

"You just found out a bunch of new information about this girl, and..."

"Listen to me, I am not leaving you."

"This is too much on us, isn't it?" I asked.

He didn't give an answer. We both know it is too much. We are barely floating in this relationship lately. It is scary and sad and I don't want to lose him, but I am not sure what is for the best anymore.

"You should get some rest. If you don't want to come to the show tonight, I understand."

He slid off the bed and went into the bathroom. I felt completely alone, abandoned even.

February 2nd

In a heartbeat your life can change
Fall apart then rearrange
Another minute explode
Then an hour passes and you're on the mend
Standing still
While life spins out of control
And falls back to the ground
I'm barely alive
But I'm still breathing
I don't want to be found
Then I see the world without taint
An infant child, the love of a saint
And music pumping my veins
And I'm OK
Yes, I'm OK
Oh-oh-oh-kay

I wrote those lyrics before I went to the studio with the band and our producer, James. He thinks we need a few more songs to round out the album, so I presented this song.

I always had a song in the works, that's why when James called Cami earlier to explain this issue—she wasn't worried in the least. She and the guys had such an unwavering confidence in my songwriting ability that it worried me sometimes. What if one day I woke up and it was gone? My mind was just blank. A white page with no music notes; no lyrics. No inspiration.

But then I thought about the rush I got from being on stage, the creativity flowing through my fingers when I pick up my guitar, or even looked at the 1963 Eastwood I had won from a bet with Sebastian.

I thought about my mother, and the pain I feel for her. And the love I feel as well. I remember the imperfect world that I equally hate and love, which would always provide me with topics for songs.

And of course, I thought about Haley, too. The way she looks at me—like I am her world. Lately, I thought about our baby and how he or she would be our world soon enough.

In fact, when I began writing the song this morning, the baby is what inspired it. I feared what kind of father I will be if I am always on the road.

That is why as soon as the baby is born, I'm taking a break from Tortured. I just don't know how to tell the band yet. Danny is the only one who knows Haley is pregnant and I swore him to secrecy.

"That's great stuff, man," James smiled, hunched over with his fingertips touching.

James Manzello is in his mid-twenties like me, but the guy is amazingly seasoned already. As far as producers go, he is on the rise and we are lucky to get him to make our album now. In a few months, he will be working with some of the biggest names in the industry, and I'm sure we wouldn't have been able to nab him.

The first song James produced for us was "Haley's Letter", which he did on recommendation from my favorite band, Landry.

Danny and I worked on finishing a song together in the studio today. Danny figured out most of the instrumentation while I focused on the rest of the lyrics. Four hours later, I was recording the vocals for the song. The name of it is "I'm OK", and like "Haley's Letter", it is a little out of character for Tortured. We kind of like that about it, though. We don't want to be labeled as an angry rock band or a sappy one for that matter, either.

"Perfect, Jordan," James said, over the microphone.

I stepped out of the sound booth and everyone was knocking fists with me. Cami hugged me, surprising the crap out of me.

"What was that for?"

"For being so amazingly talented and giving me this opportunity to be part of something so huge."

Her pale blue eyes actually twinkled at me.

I looked at her like she was crazy. It's not that Cami never expressed her gratitude before. It was that she usually didn't do it in such an emotional way. She is the only girl I never saw cry. I glanced over at Danny and he winked at her.

"Thanks. Is something going on with you?"

"Why do you ask that?"

"Uh, the sudden need to get sentimental on me, maybe?"

She laughed and shoved my shoulder kind of hard. Now, that's the Cami I'm used to.

"I'm just trying to tell you how excited and grateful I am to manage such an awesome band."

"Sounds like Danny's giving you a little something extra before recording sessions," Sebastian teased, nudging her arm.

Danny laughed arrogantly while Cami scowled. After we finished up some things with James, I pulled Danny aside.

"You told her, didn't you?"

"Tell her what?" Danny asked.

"About the baby?" I whispered.

"I'm sorry, bro. It just slipped out."

I groaned, "Nice. I thought she'd be pissed?"

"Oh, she was. She was sure you were going to ditch the band to be a stay-at-home daddy, but I told her that you were still devoted to the band and Haley totally wouldn't want you to give up your dream."

I just nodded. Instead of being angry, Cami is sucking up to me. I feel guilty. I don't plan to give up the band completely, but I know that's an option that I might have to face. A baby changes everything, no matter what anyone says. Having a child is not the end of the world, but it sure as hell can turn your world upside down.

"So, that's the reason for her good mood?" I asked.

"Yeah, right," Danny laughed. "It's because I asked her to move in with me," he shrugged casually.

I looked up at him surprised.

"Excuse me? You what?"

"I'm sick of living with my mother, but I really don't want to live alone. Cami's been talking about moving out of her shit hole apartment, so..."

"Whoa, this is a big step, man. You know that, right?"

"Bro, it's cool," Danny said, sounding like a member of the cast of "Jersey Shore".

We always tease him that he should be on that show. I'm just grateful he never wanted to be called some ridiculous nickname like "The Situation", though he is fond of Haley's "Danizzle" nickname for him. I just call him Dick, usually. He calls me other profane names. That is how we express our love for one another.

"It's cool? You and Cami fight like crazy as it is. Do you think living together will change that?"

"We're stupid, but we love each other. Yeah, we fight, but

it's just how we are. You know we don't mean half the shit we say about each other. She's the one, J. And I plan to marry her someday."

I just stared at him, trying to keep my jaw from dropping. My best friend is talking about marriage? How can he be so comfortable with the idea? His parents are divorced. He cheated on his last girlfriend. She cheated on him. How does he know any marriage he's in won't be the same messed up crap?

Why is it that I feel like I'm the only one with serious hang-ups? Why is it so hard for me to want to commit entirely to my girlfriend whom I do want to spend the rest of my life with?

After we finished at the studio, I walked around the west village like a zombie. I needed to be alone. It has been a month since Haley found out she is pregnant, and we still haven't told her parents or mine, not that I cared to tell my father.

It still doesn't feel real, even after I saw the first sonogram. We haven't discussed our plan for the rest of this child's life. It is occurring more and more to me that we will both have to make serious changes—more than I initially thought.

Cami and the record label basically want the band to tour

for two years straight. Now, that can't happen. I can't be missing from over a year of my child's life.

And Haley...she will need my help. I can't expect her to give up her career while I still have mine.

Our lifestyle, right now, is exactly the wrong environment to raise a child in. With me always traveling and Haley going back and forth from school, home and New York, it's chaotic. I am beginning to panic about the entire situation.

As I sat on a bench near NYU and smoked a cigarette while I started to write this, another overwhelming feeling came over me.

This used to strictly be my song book. I never used to keep a journal. I always thought diaries were for girls to gush over how much they loved their crush. Lately, I feel like I need to unload my thoughts beyond songs—so here I am.

I keep thinking... Was my father right almost six years ago?

I was out of my mind at eighteen to think I could raise a child! And with Bippy of all people! Either way, abortion is just something I can't support. I know it's a personal choice, and I respect that, but Bippy and I both come from wealthy families. We would have been able to provide financially, and we supposedly loved each other...

Then again, I wasn't the real father. I guess Bippy didn't see any other way out. I suddenly want to confront her. I avoided her for so long. I need to face this before I can completely move on. Or maybe I am looking to distract myself longer from the reality I am having trouble facing. Worrying about a child that never came into this world seemed easier now than worrying about *my* baby who will be here in several months.

When I met up with Haley before she went to Fashion Week, I suddenly felt the need to be there—she seemed pissed about it, too. She just didn't get me lately, and I know that's because I haven't exactly been inside my body; it feels like I've been floating above it for the past month. I don't know how to talk to Haley without hurting her.

At Fashion Week, I didn't realize I would be such a paparazzi magnet. The publicist at Struck Records will probably thank me immensely for attending this event.

"Is it true you dated Bippy Reynolds?" a female reporter asked me.

"Uh..." I stammered, wondering how that had gotten out.

"Bippy told us you were high school sweethearts and you're still good friends."

I didn't know whether to laugh or smear her name. I saw Bippy flipping her hair a few feet away.

"I wouldn't say we're friends or that we were sweethearts," I answered the reporter. "Excuse me, please."

I hurried over to Bippy, fighting my way through people to get to her. Unlike the crowd surrounding her, I was not interested in getting her picture or sleeping with her.

"You know who my favorite band is?" Bippy said, making eye contact with me as I approached her.

She was talking to a girl, who was obviously excited to meet her.

"Tortured!"

"Oh my gosh!" the girl gushed. "Mine, too. Jordan Walsh is so hot."

I blushed somewhat as Bippy smirked at me devilishly.

The other people surrounding them laughed, realizing who I was. The girl turned beet red and I smiled at her.

"Thanks sweetie," I winked at the girl. "Can I talk to you?" I then looked at Bippy.

"Sure," she smiled, and motioned me toward the exit.

I followed her until we were standing outside on the side of Lincoln Center. It was a little cold out, but we didn't bother with coats.

There wasn't anyone around, and that's what I wanted. I didn't want Bippy to play up anything for the media. I wanted her to be real—as real as she is capable of being, that is.

"I'm really glad you came, Charlie," she smiled.

"Don't think this has anything to do with you."

She laughed, "Oh, okay. So this is about Haley then? I have to admit I'm surprised you're still with her. I mean—she cleans up nice, but she was always kind of dull."

"Not everyone can be a drunken table dancing queen, right?" I shot at her.

"If this has nothing to do with me, why are you with me right now, alone?" she asked stepping closer to me.

"Who was he?"

"Who was who?" she looked at me confused.

"The father of the baby."

She looked serious for a moment and then smiled as if I were kidding.

"You really have to move on. I have."

"I knew you could be cruel, but I never thought you could be that heartless."

"Charlie, we were so young..."

"Was that it? Or was it because the baby wasn't mine?"

"What are you talking about? Why are you doing this to me now?" she asked, getting annoyed.

"My father told me... You were cheating on me?"

Her face remained serious and I knew she couldn't deny it anymore. The color drained from her cheeks and she stepped back from me slightly.

"I felt stupid and so ashamed," she sighed.

"You should be!" I raised my voice. "You saw how hard I fought! To just let me believe the baby was mine was inhumane!"

"Charlie, calm down..." she said, putting her hands on my arms and I shrugged her away.

"Don't touch me," I snarled. "I cared about you and you

were sleeping around on me?"

Bippy sighed, "You didn't love me. You convinced yourself you did."

"Is that what you think?"

I know I don't like Bippy. Even back then, I didn't like the way she acted which was much better than she acted nowadays. However, I did have feelings for her. When it was just the two of us, she revealed a different part of herself. She is smart, but was treated like the airhead her parents make her out to be. She liked the attention—any attention she could get. She knows how to manipulate any situation to get what she wants.

"I loved you—maybe not a forever type of thing. But you were my first everything, Bippy."

She looked up at me with teary brown eyes.

"I'm so sorry, Charlie. I was messed up."

"Was there more than one guy?" I asked, trying to remain cold—no matter how much she cried.

"Just one," she sighed, closing her eyes.

"Do I know him?"

"What does it matter?" she sighed, wiping under her eyes

to make sure her make-up wasn't running.

"It doesn't, but I feel like you're still keeping something from me."

I am sick of being lied to. I want to move past this for good. I want to do it for Haley and for my child. I want to do it for me—and maybe even for Bippy. This hatred I hold for her—though she may deserve it—is just like a big stop sign whenever I run into her. I'm tired of avoiding her.

"Why are you doing this now?" she asked, her face crumbling into distress. "This is supposed to be my day."

"I need to know. I'm going through so much and my dad dropped this bomb on me..."

"He always was an asshole," Bippy shook her head. "I wanted to tell you the truth, but he convinced me not to. He wanted to protect..." she sighed, and turned away from me. "I was drunk—really drunk. It was Leslie's eighteenth birthday party. You had gone to visit your mom, remember?" she asked, but I just listened instead of responding.

"I was dancing and having fun—like I always do. Next thing I knew, I was upstairs with him... I told him no, but he was even drunker than me, and..."

"Wait, he raped you?"

My fists clenched in anger. How quickly my fury was switching gears from Bippy now to this unknown guy.

"I don't know if it can be considered rape—I wasn't very good at pushing him off me."

"Bippy, if you told him no—it was rape. You should have reported it."

"I didn't know what to do," she cried. "I told my parents, but they just wanted to sweep it under the rug."

"Are you kidding me?!"

She nodded and cried harder.

"I hate you right now, Charlie!"

She went to walk away, but I grabbed her hand and pulled her into a hug.

"I'm sorry I'm doing this here—"

"You avoided me for so long and I just wanted to tell you everything, but I didn't want to hurt you anymore."

"You should have told me back then," I rubbed her back.

"I wanted to—your dad told me you would never forgive

me. I didn't expect you to be so angry about the abortion," she cried harder. "You wound up hating me anyway."

"Bippy, what happened wasn't your fault. This asshole... Who is he?" I asked.

It had to be someone I knew, I figured. Leslie had many friends, and I've met most of them—not that I was close to any of them, though.

"I can't tell you," she whispered.

"Why are you protecting him?" I asked, looking at her.

"I have to go," she said, pulling away. "I have to get back in there," she wiped her face and headed back into Lincoln Center.

I sent Haley a text message before walking inside the building. I just wanted to get out of there. Part of me felt relief after speaking to Bippy, knowing she wasn't as callous as I thought. Yet, I felt uneasy knowing she had gone through that experience alone. I wanted to punch my father in the face for convincing Bippy to lie to me and not report the asshole who forced himself on her.

When I met up with Haley again, she was not understanding about my talk with Bippy. She also looked like she wanted to die when I reminded her about the Tortured show tonight.

Haley always wanted to come to our shows. Is she that upset with me? I know she doesn't feel well, though, so I am trying to be understanding. But I am tired and annoyed that my girlfriend is being petty and accusatory.

-J

Chapter 8

I must have dozed off, crying myself to sleep. Next thing I knew, I woke up and it was pitch black in the room. The heat was pumping to the point that it was stifling hot in the room. I didn't feel nauseous anymore, but I had a headache. I sat up and turned on the lamp before making my way to the windows. I unlocked one before pushing it open.

I relished in the cold February air in contrast to the stale, heated room. I looked up at the sky, but I didn't see anything of significance. No stars; no moon. It seems any time I look for the moon lately, I can't find it. I had bad timing with the phases—I hadn't been paying it much attention.

I miss my relationship with the giant nightlight. The moon was a catalyst for my relationship with Jordan; for finding myself, and now that I'm lost—it feels like the moon is too. Even worse, my relationship with Jordan is vanishing as well.

I just didn't think it was possible. I never thought Jordan and I would get weird on each other; that we would get spooked over a baby. Then again, it's more than just a baby—it's Jordan's past that's entwining itself with the news of our child. I never felt threatened by Jordan's ex-girlfriend because I knew how much he hated her. Now, with this sympathetic side of him coming out toward her—she is in fact a threat.

I took a warm shower and felt a bit better, so I decided to go to the show after all. It was still early enough. I wanted to salvage the day somehow; to let Jordan know him and the band meant something to me, in case he doubted it for whatever reason. We were both fairly sensitive toward each other lately.

I have seen Tortured perform hundreds of times, and I know some girlfriends would get bored seeing the same show, but not me. Jordan is incredibly entertaining on stage, and he gets bored easily himself—so he usually tries to change things up by adding a couple of cover songs or a verse of a new one he is working on. It keeps things fresh and Tortured's fans wanting more.

The show was at a brand new venue that opened in midtown; it was close enough for me to walk to. It wasn't too cold out, thankfully. I just threw on a jacket instead of my winter coat.

I waited in line with a dozen of people still outside. I could hear the opening act playing, and knew that once I was inside, I'd be shoved in between people. Just great.

"Ticket?" A deep voiced bouncer asked me.

"I should be on the list," I said, though I had no idea if I actually would be.

Usually, I arrived with the band—I didn't need to be on the list.

"Name?"

"Haley Foster."

"You're not on here."

"Oh my God... Haley?" A girl from behind me shouted. "This is the girl from the song!"

I smiled at her awkwardly.

"That's not her," a curly haired teenage boy laughed. "Just because her name is Haley..."

"No, it's her," the girl insisted. "I saw her with Jordan before. There was a picture of them on some website earlier today."

"It's nice to meet you," I said politely, shaking the girl's hand before turning back toward the bouncer. "I'm just going to buy a ticket."

"If she's her, why is she buying a ticket?" the boy asked.

"I'm trying to support," I shrugged, with a smile.

The box office was at a window a couple of feet away. I stepped up to the window and asked to purchase a ticket.

"Sorry ma'am, we're all sold out."

I groaned, "Seriously?"

Of course, I was happy the band was playing for a packed house, but there couldn't be one ticket left for me? I didn't want to disturb Jordan before the show, but I had no choice now. I called him and received no answer.

There wasn't a line any longer and I walked up to the bouncer at the door once more.

"I know this sounds like I'm just a fan trying to get in, but the lead singer is my boyfriend."

"You're right, it does sound that way," he rolled his eyes.

"Thanks a lot," I gave him a dirty look before walking to the side of the building and trying to call Jordan again.

A couple of photographers walked by.

"You're sure you saw Bippy Reynolds go into the Tortured show?"

"Yeah—she said she was a guest of the band and walked right into the place. Do you think she has something going on with Walsh?"

I didn't realize Jordan's phone had gone to voicemail as I listened to the paparazzo's conversation. I just hung up. I didn't want to think the worst, but I couldn't help it. I pictured Bippy backstage with my boyfriend like she was his groupie, and Jordan buying into her sob story from earlier.

I don't get it. He's told me stories himself on how Bippy conned people and how easily she can turn on someone. How can he be so gullible when it comes to her?

I thought to call Cami or the rest of the guys, but now I

just wanted to go back to sleep—hoping today was just a nightmare.

I looked down at my phone and saw I had three text messages. One from Tasha and one from Meghan—they were both at the show and hoped I felt better. The last message was from Christian—asking if I needed anything or wanted to hang out. I should have known he wouldn't go to the show.

I didn't respond to anyone. I just walked back toward the hotel, looking up at the sky the entire way. It was blank. As I stared off into space, I bumped into someone as I approached the hotel.

"Haley... I was just coming to visit you."

It was Christian, of course.

"I'm fine, Christian. I just want to be alone."

"What's going on with you?"

"I'm just not feeling well."

"You shouldn't be alone," he sighed. "Have you eaten?"

I shook my head.

"Let's grab a bitc and talk."

I agreed because I knew I had to eat and because I needed something to get my mind off Bippy and Jordan. I wanted to get along with Christian for Tasha's sake.

There was a brief moment in time when I actually started to think I could be friends with Christian. It was the summer I began dating Jordan. While my parents were angry with me for lying to them about where I had been and who I was with, Christian offered me comfort. I thought maybe with him being with Tasha and me being with Jordan, things could be different. I hoped we could actually have a normal friendship without him trying to force me to feel something for him.

We walked down the block to a pizzeria. I only ordered a plain slice while Christian ordered three slices of the chicken cutlet pie.

"I thought pregnant women eat more?" he asked.

I sighed, "I haven't had much of an appetite."

"I guess Jordan's not stepping up to the fatherhood role, huh?"

"If I'm going to have a conversation with you, I need you to stop judging him. He's your cousin and I love him. Please?"

"Fine," Christian nodded. "Talk to me."

"I never imagined something like a baby would make us freak out, but... it does. I'm scared and sick most of the time."

"Well, that's natural," he nodded.

"I'm afraid I'm going to lose him," I sighed.

"Look, I know I say a lot of crap about Jordan, but he does care about you and I don't think he'd run away from his mistakes."

I looked at Christian, hurt by the words. I hope to God Jordan would never call our child a mistake.

"This baby is not a mistake," I stared at him.

He held his hands up in defense, "Sorry. That came out wrong."

"Maybe Bippy looked at her child that way—but with the way she got pregnant—I almost can't blame her."

"What do you mean?" Christian asked, leaning forward curiously.

I sighed and looked down at my half-eaten pizza. I don't know why I felt the need to tell Christian any of this. I just thought maybe if someone in Jordan's family knew what he was going through, maybe they could help him instead of knocking him down all the time.

"It's not the baby so much that I'm having trouble with. It's Jordan's inability to let go of the past. Ever since his father told him Bippy's baby wasn't his, he's been lost. He confronted

Bippy today and she told him why she got the abortion…"

Christian looked at me intensely.

"Why did she get it?"

I sighed, "I can't say. I'm not even supposed to know."

Christian stared at me—not the way he usually did. He looked concerned, and I don't think it was for me.

"Do you think Jordan still cares about her?"

"Yes, but he loves me," I said to him, knowing what he was trying to do now.

"I'm not debating that, but Bippy was his first love," he shrugged.

I didn't say a word. I stared down at my pizza.

"Haley, you deserve so much better."

"Oh yeah?" I laughed. "Better as in you?"

Christian smirked, "I'm taken, remember?"

"Then why do you still do this?" I asked, frustrated.

"Do what?"

"Flirt with me."

"I don't know how else to be around you."

"Chris, do you love Tasha? With all of your heart?"

He played with a string of cheese on his plate, taking his time answering.

"We have that whole opposites attract thing going on," he gave a sly smile. "I love her, yes," he nodded.

"Good," I smiled.

"Will I ever love her like I love you?" Christian asked, taking me by surprise. "No…"

I was caught completely off guard that I didn't even notice he placed his hand on top of mine.

"If you would just open your eyes, Haley, and see that it has always been us—"

I pulled my hand back.

"It has never been us, Christian," I groaned. "You are hurting Tasha. I won't lose my best friend because of you."

"Is she who you're really worried about?"

"Yes! Regardless, I never wanted you. Never. Not before Jordan and definitely not now."

Christian sat back in his seat. Maybe what I said sounded harsh, but I didn't know how else to get through to this guy. He looked at me before snickering.

"You're such a fucking little tease," he said scathingly as he shook his head.

"Oh, I'm a tease?" I laughed in disbelief.

"Yeah, you are. All those years, you led me on—acting like this innocent little princess. I paid my dues, Haley… I took you to dances—I worshipped the ground you walked on, and you spread your legs for my cousin who doesn't have an ounce of class and treats you like shit."

I gasped, "How dare you talk to me that way! Jordan respects me way more than you ever have, Christian. I love him and you have to accept that."

I wanted to say more. I wanted to say how Jordan treated me incredibly; maybe not recently, but we were both guilty of neglecting each other.

I wanted to tell Christian how much he grossed me out when he touched me. I wanted to call him names. I wanted to tell him I would never see him again. I couldn't be sure of that though. With my parents constantly keeping the Erikssons around and Tasha—my God, she was going to marry him! I didn't know how to stop it. I was kidding myself thinking things could ever change between Christian and me.

Christian shook his head at me; mockingly.

"Well, that guy you love so much… What's he doing cozying up to his ex-girlfriend backstage? Have you seen Bippy's

Facebook status lately? She's not very discreet," he rolled his eyes. "I quote," he continued using his fingers as quotation marks before reading Bippy's Facebook status from his phone. "Backstage with Tortured. It's just like old times for me and Jordan."

I am not friends with Bippy on Facebook, and now I wanted to know what else she was saying about Jordan in her status, but I didn't want to indulge Christian by asking. I didn't know what to say to him. I didn't have an answer for why Bippy was backstage at my boyfriend's show.

"You can't compete with her, Haley. Bippy Reynolds always gets what she wants. You may dress the part, but you'll always be the socially awkward girl who doesn't fit in."

I stared into Christian's eyes. He always bugged me, but now, I can see he is spiteful and vindictive. Not only is he relentless, now he is taking my insecurities and displaying them on the table. I don't want him anywhere near me or Tasha. I will no longer hold my tongue about him to her.

"And you will always be the jackass who never had me," I said, standing up.

I almost spit in his face, but instead I walked out of the pizzeria quickly. I felt like my life was spiraling out of control. It is almost as if I am all alone in this. Meghan and Tasha are both preoccupied. And Tasha is still blinded by Christian for me to talk candidly to her.

Jordan was always good for comforting me. He calms me down and puts things into perspective. He is the biggest part of this whole mess, though. I always knew who Christian was—losing him from my life will be a blessing. It's Tasha I am concerned about.

As for me—I am terrified of where things stand. I don't know exactly where my boyfriend stands; if he will break my heart. I don't know where I stand. Will I ever finish school? Will I ever become this notorious photographer I want to be? Will I even be a good mother?

When I got back into my hotel room, my phone rang. I hoped it was Jordan. I hadn't heard from him in what felt like forever—though it was merely several hours. Instead, it was Luke. I debated on answering his call or not, not really in the mood for small talk. It is getting harder to pretend like everything is okay. It is harder to keep my pregnancy a secret and even more difficult to pretend I am happy about anything. I hit "ignore" on my phone and received a text from Luke a couple of minutes later.

"Hey! How's NYC? I feel like we haven't hung out in forever. Give me and Laney a shout when you get back. We want to take you out for your birthday."

I smiled to myself. Luke is sweet. I sent him a message back and told him I was going to bed before actually doing just that—not very successfully, though.

February 3rd

I'm sitting in the lobby of the hotel writing this. After the show tonight, I told the band about the baby. I told them I needed to be practical. I basically told them the future of the band was unsure. And they basically told me they hated me for it.

Haley is always willing to sacrifice for others, and this is a sacrifice I needed to make for her. I just wish my sacrifice didn't affect my best friends so much. Each one of them looked at me with such disappointment and confusion.

I can't blame them. We are on the verge of fully making it big—we kind of already are big. By the end of the tour, if things kept progressing as rapidly as they already have—our debut album is sure to be in the top 10 on Billboard. We already have 2 songs in the top 10. With the response of "Haley's Letter", our label is predicting that to go to #1 next week.

Ironic, isn't it? Haley will be the reason for our first #1 and she'll be the reason for our demise. That's terrible to say. I'm the reason for it, not her.

All anyone kept asking me was: Why? Why do I have to

give the band up? Why can't I be a father and a rock star? I didn't have a solid answer. Just a bunch of excuses.

1. I can't expect Haley to be alone with the baby all the time while I toured.
2. I can't focus on being a good father and give my all on the road.

Maybe that is all bullshit, I don't know. Mostly I feel guilty for wanting Tortured over a baby. My baby. I feel like a terrible person.

I also know there is more to it. I am afraid of the band's success. Afraid that we will change—that I will change. I don't want to be some glamorous rock star that wears sunglasses in doors and has a fake-looking chick on my arm.

I saw a glimpse of that person within myself tonight. I'll admit I had a few beers. I usually don't drink before a show. I don't believe in getting smashed in order to put on a good show. I want to be completely aware and in the moment.

Tonight, though... I needed something to take the edge off. Everything is crashing down on me now... Finishing up the album... Haley and me barely being Haley and me. How are we supposed to raise a kid together if we're miserable?

When I think about becoming a father, my own dad comes to mind.

There's always my dad and my fears of being like him.

I am on my way to being like him...

I resent Haley. I can feel it growing inside me as much as I try to fight it. I always thought I was a carefree person. I thought I didn't allow things to bother me, but I don't know myself at all. I just hold onto all of this pain; all of this anger and I'm going to spit it back out on the wrong person.

Then there is Bippy. She got backstage somehow after the band left me alone. I don't know what to think of her anymore. I don't know whether to hate her or... There is no or. I hate her. I didn't kick her out of the dressing room like I should have.

After I told the band my decision—they didn't want to be near me. The look on Cami's face when I told her I was taking an indefinite break from Tortured reminded me of the same look she had when I broke up with her. I hated doing this to her again; I hated doing it to all of them. I was breaking up with the band;

with the love of my life basically—aside from Haley.

"So, we're just supposed to go on with this big album release and tour—create a future for ourselves before destroying it?" Danny asked.

I looked at him surprised; he'd been supportive throughout this whole ordeal thus far.

"You will regret this decision," he sighed.

My best friend walked out of the door and I wondered if he walked out of my life as well. This band was everything to us both for so long.

By the time Bippy walked into the dressing room—uninvited, I was chugging down a whole beer. I was a complete mess—feeling like I just lost everything. Somewhere in between texting Haley and trying to avoid telling Bippy what was going on, she was comforting me.

"Are you sure you're okay?"

"Fine," I said before she pulled me into a hug.

"I'm so sorry that I lied to you for so long. I've missed you so much, Charlie—I mean Jordan. That takes some getting used to," she smiled.

She looked like she was drunk herself. I wouldn't be surprised. She drank a lot in high school, and from what I've seen in the news—that hasn't changed.

Her head was on my shoulder and her breath hit my neck. Next thing I knew, her lips were on mine. And I couldn't respond fast enough. I was frozen there—allowing her to kiss me like the jackass I am!

I finally pushed her away and I didn't say much to her. I just asked her to leave before I left myself. As I walked from the venue to the hotel, I just kept picturing that rock star image of me. Then I pictured me as my father: a liar, a cheater and selfish. I looked up at the sky and it was blank. Is that a metaphor for my future?

I don't know how I can face Haley. The more I sit down here, the worse I feel.

-J

Chapter 9

When Jordan came back from the show, I was in bed with the lights off. I debated on talking to him or pretending I was asleep. I just lie there motionless listening to him rustling around. I had gotten his text message saying he hoped I felt better, but I didn't respond. I felt the mattress give, but that was the only sign of him getting into bed. I didn't feel any brush of skin as I normally would since we slept fairly close to each other.

He must have fallen asleep right away. I heard his breaths getting heavier. He also smelled of alcohol and cigarettes. I turned on the bedside lamp and looked over at him.

He was fully clothed. He usually slept in his underwear or nude. His mouth was open, squished into the pillow. I got out of bed and noticed Jordan's backpack was open and thrown on the floor.

I sighed and bent down to put the things that fell out back inside. I took a hold of Jordan's song book. I ran my fingers over the cover of the book and I wanted to read what he had been working on. I needed something to help me understand him better. He spoke through music when he couldn't find any other way.

I opened the book and saw the scrawled lyrics to "You Make Me Hate Me". The next page had scribbled out lyrics that were restarted and scribbled out again. The page after that had the lyrics to "Break The Mold". Song after song, I read the lyrics to—though I knew most of them already.

Seeing the songs down on paper on top of whatever thoughts he had jotted down for lyrics made me realize something. Jordan is full of anger. I knew that to an extent. He always hid the anger well, aside from his music, though.

I flipped further through the book to see what Jordan had written recently. In between song lyrics now, there were paragraphs written with dates. They looked like journal entries. When did Jordan start keeping a journal?

I turned to the very last page. The entry was from tonight. I read the top paragraph.

Next thing I knew, her lips were on mine. And I couldn't respond fast enough. I was frozen there—allowing her to kiss me like the jackass I am!

I couldn't read further than that. My eyes were glued to those two lines. I knew the "her" mentioned had to be Bippy Reynolds. She was backstage while I stood outside, shut out from the show. He is shutting me out of his life, too.

I felt the tears running down my face. I wanted to slap Jordan awake. I wanted to slap Bippy. I wanted to hit something! My chest felt insanely tight and I felt dizzy.

I let out an involuntary gasp as I sat on the floor crying. Jordan began to move. He turned to the left and then rolled to his right, now facing me. His eyes fluttered open and were about to close again before he sat up, looking at me.

"Haley, what's wrong?" he asked, and then he noticed his notebook. "What are you doing with that?"

"You can yell at me for reading it, but I just... I wanted to feel connected to you again," I sniffled, trying to steady my breath in order to speak. "I didn't know you kept a journal."

"I started it when I began having the nightmares," he sighed.

"What nightmares?"

I knew he was having trouble sleeping, but he never mentioned nightmares.

"It's not a big deal."

"I came to the show tonight," I said as he slid to the floor next to me.

"Where were you?"

"They wouldn't let me in—Bippy got in no problem," I said, looking into his tired green eyes.

"I did not invite her or put her on any list, Haley," Jordan sighed. "I swear."

"Why did you let her kiss you?"

Jordan looked at me. His expression looked remorseful.

"I had a few drinks."

"You told me I had nothing to worry about," I reminded him.

"And you don't," he groaned, running his fingers through his hair.

"Obviously I do if she kisses you and you just let her."

"I'm sorry. It was stupid and I did push her away—if you would have read further down, you would see that."

I looked back down at his journal.

"What other stuff do you write in here?"

Jordan shrugged.

"Stuff."

"Stuff you can't tell me?"

"I tell you everything," he said, picking at the carpet instead of looking me in the eyes.

"No, you don't," I whispered, staring at his journal. "I know you resent me and the baby, and I understand... I just wish you would talk to me about it instead of ignoring it."

I stood up and got into bed.

"You mean so much to me," he said softly, not moving from his spot on the floor. "I would give up anything to make you happy."

"I'm scared," I said hoarsely.

"So am I," he whispered.

I felt his arms wrap around me a minute later. I felt comfort for the moment and turned around to look at him.

"I know you love me," I told him. "I know you don't want to marry me and you are going through a difficult time."

"Haley, if you want to get married—we'll do it."

Jordan looked sincere, but I don't want to get married right now. I don't feel ready. I don't feel we are ready as a couple. And I certainly don't want to get married when my boyfriend just wants to please me.

"Jor," I swallowed. "We need time."

"I know. I just thought it would make it easier on you with your parents."

"I mean—we need time apart."

I have never been cut so deeply by my own words. I had thought about this all night, and it is the only solution I came up with. We both need space to get our heads together. We are smothering one another with the pressure of being happy. Instead, we are both feeling dejected and guilty about not being able to make each other happy.

"Haley, don't say that," Jordan sighed. "I know you're upset about Bippy, but... I swear—"

"This has nothing to do with Bippy," I said, running a hand through his hair affectionately as a tear ran down my face.

"This is about you and me, and our baby."

"You're breaking up with me?"

He looked incredibly hurt and slightly surprised.

"No—I am not breaking up with you. I just feel like when we're together... We're not really together. We're missing something. Take time for yourself and think about things."

"Oh, so this is on me?" Jordan asked.

"I didn't say—"

"I'm not the only one who's not all here, you know? You are constantly pushing me away."

"I'm not pushing you away—I feel like shit half the time. I'm sorry if that comes off cold when I don't want to be touched."

Jordan pulled away from me.

"Time apart, Haley..." he shook his head and rubbed his eyes sleepily. "That's just a shortcut to breaking up."

"It's not like we can have such a clean break," I said. "I'm carrying your child. It's not like we won't have reasons to speak to each other."

I took his hand and placed it on my stomach. I silently prayed we would feel the baby's first kick at that moment, though I know logically, it would be too soon.

Nothing. Jordan sighed and removed his hand—maybe he was hoping for the same thing.

"I'm connected to you," I said to him. "Every part of me loves you and that will never change. I just hate that I'm making you miserable."

Jordan turned toward me and I could tell he felt terrible. His face showed remorse.

"Hale," he sighed. "I'm just... You don't make me miserable. I'm making myself miserable."

"Why?" I asked.

"Because I'm not as strong as you are."

I laughed, "Jordan, you're the strongest person I know."

"I put on a good show," he said, running a hand over his face. "That guy everyone sees on stage—the guy you fell in love with... He isn't me. I wish he was, but really I'm just harboring all of this hate on the world and... I don't want to raise our child with these feelings inside me."

I wrapped an arm around him and pulled him close to me.

"Get it all out—whatever it is eating at you—just work on getting rid of it. If that happens to lead you to Bippy... If there are unresolved feelings..."

It killed me to say that to him. Bippy would be the last person I'd ever want to see him with. The thought made me sick to my stomach.

Jordan just looked me in the eye. I know he wanted me to believe Bippy had no hold on him, but she was his first love—there had to be something there still. I couldn't be naïve about that.

"Just promise me you'll find the guy I know you are—he's not a façade."

He nodded before kissing me softly.

"This is not over," he said, placing his hand on my jaw.

I smiled, "It better not be. Just breathe. I'll always be here for you."

February 6th

Haley went back to Boston and I don't know where I am going. I stayed in bed the past couple of days and when I did go out, I walked around aimlessly. I feel numb. I don't know who I am or where I'm going.

I decided to visit Andrew today. He knew something was wrong right away. I refused to tell him. I didn't want him upset over Haley—he'd probably hate me if we ever broke up. I would hate myself if I lost her.

Drew seems down, though. He decided against Wedgewood Academy until next year in hopes that our father will allow him to go to Carlton Crest, which is in Boston. After my last argument with my father, I really don't know how to face him anymore.

Bippy has been calling me. I'm not even sure how she got my number. I keep hitting ignore. I still have unanswered questions for her, but I am afraid of being sucked in by her. She has this insane ability to make people feel sorry for her somehow.

If her story is true, I do feel sorry for her but I still don't get why she would go to my father and not me. It is still hard for me to take in everything I have learned the past month about her and the baby.

Haley thinks I may still have feelings for her. I guess I thought I might, too, for a little while. I realize now I just still have a lot of pain left over from that time in my life.

I'm at the airport getting ready to go back to Boston now. I will only be in Boston for a few days before I leave to promote "Haley's Letter" to various radio stations and talk shows across the country for the next few weeks. Spending the next three weeks with the band will not be easy. Sure, I'm used to getting attitude from Cami, and I've had my fair share of arguments with the guys, but nothing like this. I think they hate me.

Haley's birthday is next week, and I want to take her out. I will be back in town that morning. I know she said we need space, but I'm not going to miss her birthday. I'm hoping Haley and I can work things out by the time I get back.

Originally, I planned to take Haley for her tattoo—she keeps chickening out. Now, she's using the pregnancy as an excuse, which I can't argue. I thought about getting her an engagement ring. I know I don't believe in marriage. I feel we are too young even if I did believe in it, but I know it will be what her parents expected us to do.

Maybe my nightmares are trying to tell me something. I began dreaming of Bippy—and she came back into my life. I dreamt of a baby and Haley wound up getting pregnant. I also dreamt that Haley broke up with me and she sort of did.

I know I pushed Haley away. Why? I keep asking myself that. It's not because of the baby. It's because I'm afraid to trust in people. I'm afraid somewhere down the line Haley will let me down just like everyone else has.

I couldn't bear that. I couldn't take that kind of blow.

An even bigger issue might be that I'm afraid to trust in myself. I'm afraid I will mess her up the way I was messed with. Breaking Haley's heart would be like breaking the moon.

We haven't just stared up at the moon in a while. Haley usually photographs the full moon every month. She completely missed it last month—so did I. The moon is symbolic of so much for us. It's ironic that it's gone from our lives right now. ~~Things are so~~

I don't remember what I was going to write. This girl at the airport just recognized me. She was telling me how my music helped her deal with her parents and life. She thanked me, and I hugged her. If only she knew what a poser I turned out to be.

I'm not bad-ass. I'm not this cool guy who plays guitar and lives on dreams. I'm a stupid rich kid who hates his dad and can't even face his girlfriend when life gets tough.

What would that teenage girl think if she knew I just quit the band? I crushed so many people's dreams in one shot. And I am taking away that girl's escape.

All I want to do right now is see my mother. I miss her. I wish I could talk to her and have her understand everything.

-J

Chapter 10

I was almost falling asleep as slides flashed by of Luke's fine art project on the projection screen; not because it was boring, but because I was exhausted—emotionally and physically.

My birthday is tomorrow and I will be heading to Bakersfield with Tasha. I have been trying to find a way to voice my concerns about Christian all week to her, but I just didn't know how to. How do you tell your best friend that her husband-to-be makes you cringe? How do I tell Tasha that he makes inappropriate comments to me without making her feel inadequate?

A minute later, Luke sat down next to me and nudged my elbow. I snapped out of my comatose state and managed to smile at him.

"How'd I do?"

"Great," I nodded enthusiastically.

"Did you like the one of you by the tree?"

"Yeah, the shadow came out really cool," I complimented him.

I could see his cheeks turn red and he smiled. Something about Luke reminds me of myself a few years ago. I wasn't used to compliments and didn't know how to accept them; just like Luke. I used to not be comfortable around the opposite sex, either. With the only boy constantly hanging around me being Christian, no wonder why.

After class was over we slowly walked to Luke's car. We got inside his trusty Honda Civic and he looked at me oddly.

"Are you okay?"

"Fine," I smiled.

"Haley, I know I haven't known you that long, but I've known you long enough to see something has been up with you."

"I'm an easy-read, huh?" I laughed, picking at a thread on my messenger bag.

"You can talk to me, you know? I'm a good listener."

"I know you are, Luke."

He's one of those sweet guys you see in movies who gets walked on all over by the main female character. Jordan calls him my Duckie from *Pretty in Pink*. For her birthday last year, Tasha had a brat pack party where we had to dress up as our favorite '80s movie character. Jordan and I went as Molly Ringwald and Judd Nelson from *The Breakfast Club*, of course. Jordan teased that Luke should come as Duckie.

Thinking of old memories makes my heart ache. Will things ever be like that again?

"Is it Jordan?" Luke asked.

He didn't sound hopeful like a guy with a crush normally did. He truly was concerned for me. I have been more withdrawn than usual; not just because of Jordan, but because I am still in shock over being pregnant.

"It's a lot of things," I sighed. "I just—I really can't talk about it right now. I have to get home and get ready for tonight..." I told him.

Laney insisted on getting a bunch of people together from school to go out drinking tonight. I didn't drink much anyhow; no one would notice anything weird about that.

"Okay. I'm always a phone call away."

"Thanks, Luke," I looked over at him. "I'll see you

tonight."

He is much more attractive than Duckie. With impossibly blue eyes and a crooked smile that makes you smile in return, I'm sure he has no trouble getting girls—if he was confident enough to put himself out there.

When we pulled up to my apartment building, I was surprised at who was standing outside waiting for me.

"What's he doing here?" I muttered.

"Who is that?" Luke asked.

"Jordan's best friend."

Danny stood there, with his hands in his pockets. He held his hand up in a wave, almost as a sign of peace. I took my seatbelt off and looked at Luke.

"Thanks for the ride."

"Happy Birthday," he leaned over and kissed my cheek.

I stepped out of the car and approached Danny.

"That guy..."

"Just a friend," I sighed.

"Just wondering—I may be pissed off at Jordan, but I still am protective," he shrugged, making his 6'3" frame look childlike for a moment.

"Did you come all the way up here just to see me?"

"Sort of. We're promoting here in a couple of days. Cami and I came up early. Jordan had to stay behind for a magazine photo shoot. You know how the front man gets most of the attention," Danny rolled his eyes.

I couldn't tell if he was joking or serious. Danny sang lead on one song and backup on almost every other song for Tortured. Plus, he wrote most of the music with Jordan. All of the members of the band received attention from fans and the press. They never seemed bothered by that extra notoriety

Jordan gets.

"Come on," I nodded toward the building and he followed me. "It's freezing—were you standing out here long?"

"About ten minutes. I tried calling you."

"I turn my phone off in class."

"What a good student," he chuckled.

We took the elevator up to my apartment. I unlocked the door and Tasha was lugging her over sized suitcase down the hall.

"Tash, we're only going for a couple of days," I rolled my eyes.

She shrugged before noticing Danny.

"Hey…" she smiled.

"What's up?" Danny nodded at her.

After making small talk for a few minutes, Tasha made an excuse to go to her room. It was obvious Danny wanted to talk to me alone. I offered him something to drink and instead of answering me, he asked a question that caught me off guard.

"Is this what you really want, Haley?"

I turned away from the refrigerator and looked at him.

"What?"

My first thought was the baby. Is the baby what I really want? I had never thought about it. I never thought if I wanted my baby. I don't have a choice—well, no other choice I feel comfortable with. The baby is growing inside of me. It was a question I couldn't answer honestly without feeling guilty. I wanted a baby, sure. I just didn't want one now.

Does that make me a horrible person? A horrible mother? I hate the feelings I have inside of me. I hate the fact that I haven't once celebrated the news of my baby. Even when Jordan and I agreed to make it work, we were just happy to not be fighting and to have calmed down.

I pray my feelings would change soon.

"Jordan..." Danny directed my train of thought.

I expected him to say something about mine and Jordan's "break". Maybe Jordan had sent Danny to convince me to reconsider this whole time apart thing. And maybe Jordan wanted to be with me tomorrow to tell my parents the news. I want him there, too, but I feel we do need some time to ourselves.

"He doesn't know I'm here," he sighed, guessing what I was thinking.

"Danny, I'm flattered you care this much about my relationship with Jordan, but I want him to focus on—"

"Do you honestly think I don't want him to focus on being a good father?" He asked; looking at me annoyed.

"I didn't say that. I'm not blaming you or the band for any of this. Jordan and I are just going through a rough time. We need time apart," I explained. "I would hate to be that person who's making Jordan feel trapped."

Danny looked at me, somewhat confused and he walked over to me.

"You know I love you like a sister, right?"

I nodded and hugged him. I needed to be hugged and Danny is great at giving hugs in spite the foot of height difference between us.

"I just didn't think you'd let him make this decision," he sighed, with his chin resting on top of my head. "I know how much you love Tortured. Before you, the band was all that kept Jordan going..."

I pulled back a little to look up at Danny's face.

"What decision?"

Suddenly, something sunk in to Danny. He sighed as he closed his eyes.

"He didn't tell you, did he?"

"Tell me what?" I asked.

"After the album is released and once the baby is born, Jordan is taking an indefinite break from the band."

I stared at Danny—the one person who is as close to Jordan as I am. This is hurting him. This decision hurt me. I thought about the end of a dream; the end of Jordan's dream; the end of my dream for him... I couldn't imagine what this would do to him and his friends. He would lose them; he would lose part of himself—such a beautiful part of himself.

This was the reason for the hostility in Danny's voice when he mentioned Jordan getting more attention for the band. Danny feels without Jordan, there is no Tortured.

"He can't," I shook my head. "I never—" I swallowed. "I never asked him to do that. I would never want him to do that!" I practically yelled.

"That's what I thought. Apparently, it's what he wants then."

"You don't believe that, Danny," I sighed as I paced my kitchen for a moment. "Jordan is doing this because he doesn't know what else to do. He is freaking out and I don't know how to calm him down," I cried.

"Hey, hey," Danny pulled me into another hug. "Everything will be fine."

Danny didn't stick around for long. I invited him and Cami out to the bar tonight, but they had tickets to a show. It is probably best anyway. Danny is a little overprotective. I feared for Luke if he even smiled at me.

That night, as I listened to various stories my friends were sharing, all I could think about is my own story—the only story I care about right now; the one with an uncertain ending. My poor friends were trying to celebrate my birthday with me, and I was practically a slug on a stool.

I looked down at the Buffalo wings in front of me. The smell was bothering me. I used to eat wings with Tortured at Carney's all the time. Now, everything about them is turning my stomach.

"Excuse me," I said, standing up and hurrying to the bathroom.

After I vomited in the stall, I hesitated a moment to make sure I was finished. I began carrying a toothbrush and toothpaste in my purse for the past few weeks. I brushed my teeth and washed my hands before leaving the bathroom. Luke stood outside the ladies' room with his hands in his pockets.

"Are you okay?"

"I must have eaten something bad," I lied.

He nodded, though I don't think he was convinced. We walked back over to the table. My friends were all pretty much drunk and laughing loudly.

"So, what does the birthday girl want to do next?" Laney asked.

"She's not feeling well," Luke spoke up for me.

"Oh no," Laney pouted.

"I'll be fine. You guys have fun. I'm going to catch a taxi."

"I'll drive you," Luke offered. "I didn't drink."

After goodbyes were exchanged, Luke and I put our coats on and walked toward his car. I went to open the passenger side door and Luke leaned against it.

"We're friends, right?"

"Yes," I said, looking into his very serious face.

"I feel like you hold back from me," he sighed. "Like you want to be closer to me, but there's something... Is it Jordan?"

"Luke..."

"I understand. I'd be jealous, too, of any guy that came near my girlfriend."

I felt nauseous again. This time, it was because of the topic of our conversation. Luke was going to make me hurt him, wasn't he?

"Jordan is fine with our friendship," I explained.

"But you're not," he nodded. "You can tell me."

"I just don't want to give you the wrong idea about us."

Luke laughed, "Do you think I'm stupid?"

I looked at him; not sure what he was getting at.

"Haley, I like you. I'll admit it," he said; his timidity returning a bit. "You're the only girl I feel comfortable around, but..."

"But?"

I found myself wondering what is preventing Luke from trying to tear me away from Jordan. Even though I am not condoning Luke's kindling for me, it is still a compliment.

"But I know you're not into me—"

I cut him off, feeling terrible.

"Luke, I think..." I stammered. "You're perfect."

He raised his eyebrows at that and laughed. Now, I blushed along with him.

"Thank you, but I'm not *him* to you," he explained.

He referred to Jordan as Him just as a religious person would refer to God. I know that has to be his interpretation of my feelings toward Jordan. He is my everything, but I don't want to be defined by my boyfriend.

"I see the way you look at him, and how much he means to you."

I clenched my teeth and my eyes squeezed shut. At that moment, I hated Luke for thinking Jordan was my world. I hated him for being insanely understanding, and for not just kissing me like any other competitive, hot blooded American male would. I can deal with that much better than him pretty much saying I am "Jordan-whipped".

What if it is true? What if Jordan is the only thing that matters to me? The only man I could ever love? That realization cut me. I never wanted to count on anyone for happiness. What if this is it for Jordan and me? What if we really are finished? I'd be unhappy for the rest of my life? I'd never love again?

I couldn't allow this to happen. I wasn't thinking straight anymore. All I saw was this incredibly sweet and understanding boy in front me who cared about me. Without thinking it through—just like the first time I kissed Jordan—I pressed Luke up against his car, and kissed him. He kissed me back, wrapping his arms around me, and pulling me closer.

Luke wasn't a bad kisser, but he didn't compare to Jordan. I pulled away and I was in tears. I wish there was no such thing as hormones sometimes. They are really messing me up.

"Haley, it's okay," Luke hugged me.

"I'm sorry."

"Do you mind telling me what's going on now?"

"Jordan and I," I breathed out as I pulled away from him. "We're on a break."

I didn't tell him about the baby. I'm not ready to spread the word yet. My first priority is to tell my parents—once I mustered up that courage, I can tell anyone.

Luke wrapped an arm around me, and I sighed, leaning into his shoulder.

"I kissed you."

Luke laughed, "I know."

"I'm sorry."

"I know that, too."

He opened the car door for me and I slid inside. We were silent on the way home. When he pulled up to my apartment, he turned to me.

"Things will be okay. Have a happy birthday, okay?"

I nodded, "Thanks."

Feeling like a total idiot, I walked into my apartment defeated.

The next afternoon, I was in Tasha's car listening to her go on about hers and Christian's engagement party in a couple of weeks before she went back to discussing the wedding. I didn't know whether she was trying to distract me from my problems or she is just oblivious to what I am going through.

I suppose I wouldn't care half as much about hearing wedding plans if she was marrying a good guy. I couldn't hold my tongue any longer. Part of me just wanted to selfishly shut her up and another part of me just wants her to be happy with someone worthy of her.

"Tash," I said. "Don't do it."

"You don't think we should have the salmon as an option?" she asked. "Is this that whole vegetarian thing again?" she rolled her eyes. "I already took the veal off the menu."

"I'm not talking about the menu. I'm talking about the whole wedding," I said, looking at her.

It was dark outside, making it so I could only catch clear glimpses of her face when the reflection of a street lamp would shine into the car.

"What?" Tasha laughed. "That's not funny, Haley."

"I'm not trying to be funny."

"Haley, I know you get annoyed with Christian, but I

love him."

"And he doesn't love you, Tasha," I said, and I know that sounded harsh, but I didn't know how else to say it. "Not the way you want him to," I clarified.

"I can't believe this," she shook her head to herself.

"I'm sorry, but you need to hear this. I can't allow you to make the biggest mistake of your life."

She laughed, "Oh, because you're the expert on mistakes, right Haley?"

Just then, we passed a street lamp and I could see her eyes glance at my stomach. Like Christian, she referred to my child as a mistake. And like before, I felt my insides tighten at that thought.

I knew then the answer to that question from yesterday when I misunderstood Danny. Do I want my baby?

Yes—no question about it anymore. I love my baby. In spite of all the confusion and all of the panic that is surrounding my pregnancy, I love my baby and I suddenly am overwhelmed with the thought of holding him or her. I sighed deeply—content with something for the first time in months.

I wanted to tell someone about this feeling. I wanted to tell Jordan. I wanted him to feel the same way, but I didn't know if it worked like that for men.

"Are you listening to me?" Tasha asked, in a raised tone. "I don't know what it is about Christian that irks you, but you better get rid of it if you want to be my maid-of-honor."

"What irks me about him…? Tasha, what doesn't irk me?"

"Just because you don't like him doesn't mean that everyone else—"

"He keeps making passes at me," I spat out, not knowing how else to convince her that he will make the worst husband.

I might very well lose her friendship over this, but I couldn't live with myself if I didn't try to stop this wedding.

She was silent for a moment before pulling over quickly.

"Look," she sighed. "I know you've been going through a lot. And I know as much as you've hated Christian, it was nice having the attention from someone, but... Think about what you're saying, Haley," she said, pleading with me. "Think about what you're doing. You're ruining my relationship because things are going badly for you."

I looked at her truly hurt that she would think I wanted to tear someone down just because I am upset.

"I'm sorry if I've been preoccupied with the wedding..."

"Tasha, things are not going badly for me."

Okay, so maybe they aren't going well, and maybe I am in denial.

"I saw Bippy at the concert," Tasha sighed. "I didn't want to say anything to you."

I suppose she thought something happened between Bippy and Jordan. She is right, but it isn't as bad as she assumes. At least I hope not. I wonder if Bippy's kiss felt as wrong to Jordan as Luke's felt to me.

"Speaking of that concert," I said, focusing once more on Tasha. "I saw Christian that night."

"He told me. He said you were really upset."

"Did he also tell you that he hit on me? Again. Did he tell you that while I was puking my brains out in my underwear at the ski lodge he put me to bed and refused to leave my room?" I asked, crying now. "He makes me feel uncomfortable, Tasha. He says things he shouldn't say. He does things he shouldn't be doing."

"Haley, he was just being a good friend to you during a hard time. You need to stop thinking you're his world."

"Tasha, please. I would never intentionally hurt you," I wiped a tear.

"If that were the case, you wouldn't have said this to me."

Without another word, she pulled back onto the highway and just kept driving. When we got to my parents' house, she wouldn't speak to me. She dropped me off and sped away.

I looked up at the house and sighed, dragging my suitcase behind me.

February 13th

I had another nightmare. I was at a wedding. I didn't know whose. I was sitting down holding a black rose. I felt a hand on my shoulder and I looked up to see my father. I had never seen him look so human.

"I'm sorry," he said.

Water droplets were on the rose and I realized they were from my tears. I looked up at the altar and Haley was standing there, smiling—looking beautiful as always. She was the bride, but I couldn't see the groom. He obviously wasn't me and that hurt.

I woke up this morning wanting to visit Haley for her birthday—that was my original plan all along since I knew I'd be in town for the next day or so. I haven't spoken to her since she left New York—which isn't even two weeks ago, but it feels like a lifetime. It is the weirdest feeling in the world. I miss her, plain and simple. I miss the band, even though I've been around them the past couple of weeks. They've kept their distance. I definitely felt a cold shoulder from everyone. Danny and Cami opted to go up to Boston a day sooner than me for some promotion we're doing here. I had to stay behind for some additional press. I think they did that so they wouldn't have to travel with me.

I miss the way things used to be. I miss my mom. I always missed Mom. Even after I visit her, I still miss her. I went to visit her late this morning, and she wasn't feeling well. She caught bronchitis, which brought on severe asthma. She's also been having panic attacks, which wasn't helping her illness. On top of all that, her seizure medication isn't working and they are trying a new one. What else could go wrong with her?

She always asks about Haley. She often asks about Dad, too.

After leaving the nursing home, I took a drive to Haley's apartment. She wasn't there. I guess I shouldn't be surprised. She did say she was going to spend her birthday with her parents.

I remembered Tasha and Christian's engagement party is in a couple of weeks—Haley has already RSVP'd that I am coming. I have about a week off at the end of the month. I don't know if I should make a trip to Bakersfield or not. I called Haley but it went straight to voicemail. I hope she isn't avoiding me.

I had a text message from Bippy when I looked back down at my phone.

"I want to be friends. I miss you."

I sighed, not sure how I feel about that. Do I miss Bippy? Do I want to be her friend? I think back to high school and I don't remember feeling much. I was numb. Bippy and me dating was automatic. It was natural for us since our families were close and we were both popular.

It was kind of like Haley and Christian—though it wasn't natural for Haley. The way she described high school—nothing was natural to her. I think about what is natural to me now...

It's not Bippy... at all.

It's definitely Haley.

I just need to get my head together.

-J

Chapter 11

The cold tiles below my knees were uncomfortable as I hung over the toilet. My sickness was almost nonexistent at the beginning of the week. I thought I was finally past it. Last night had started it up again apparently.

"Haley?"

I heard my mother calling me from my bedroom door. I quickly closed the bathroom door so she wouldn't see me if she came into my room.

"I'll be right out! I'm in the bathroom!" I called back.

"Dinner is ready, sweetie."

I stood up and steadied myself, rubbing my knees. I looked at myself in the mirror.

"We can do this," I sighed, rubbing my belly.

Suddenly, I felt something. I wasn't sure if I imagined it or not. It wasn't exactly a clear movement, more like a flutter. I was still early on in my pregnancy, so other than the slight changes to my body and the vomiting; there was no sign of life inside of me until now.

I laughed aloud at the feeling. I pressed my fingers around my belly.

"Thank you," I whispered.

I fixed myself up and went downstairs to have dinner with my parents. Elsa rubbed my back as she passed me.

"I made you something special."

I sat down and saw a beautiful array of vegetables

with roasted potatoes. I was grateful for two reasons. I am really trying to eat healthy and try vegetarianism out. The second reason is I don't think my baby enjoyed meat too much. The few times I did have chicken, it came right back up.

During dinner, my parents discussed graduation plans with me. They wanted to throw me a party, which I didn't know if I really wanted one. I didn't care for too many of the people that my parents would invite. I rather have something more intimate with my real friends. It is weird to think that my entire life I didn't have anyone.

Now, I have quite a few close friends. I wonder if I can count Tasha as one of them anymore. That hurts, especially if Christian is the reason for our friendship ending.

"Have you given any thought to jobs after school?" Dad asked.

"Well, I'm hoping my internship will want to keep me on full-time after graduation," I smiled, though I still haven't thought about what I will do after the baby is born.

I have been interning at a publicity firm as an in-house photographer for the past month.

"What about Jordan? Have you two thought about the future?" Mom asked.

I looked at both of my parents. I wasn't sure what they wanted to hear or expected. Do they want Jordan and me to have a future together? I know Mom liked Jordan. Does she think he is good for me, though? I'm still not sure if my parents wish it was me marrying Christian instead of Tasha.

"We talk about it once in a while," I shrugged.

This was the perfect opening to tell them.

I swallowed, "I don't think we're ready for marriage yet."

"Look, we can see how much you love him," Dad said.

"And how much he loves you," Mom smiled.

"But with his lifestyle—we don't want you to take a backseat to his career," Dad sighed.

I had told them he was working, which is why he couldn't be with me on my birthday.

"Dad, I don't. Trust me. Jordan would give it all up if I asked him to."

After speaking to Danny, I am sure of that. I still don't know whether to scream at Jordan for making that decision or hug him for wanting to make me happy. I am leaning more toward screaming since he should know me well enough to know him giving up the band would never make me happy.

"I have something to tell you, though."

For some reason, I wasn't scared anymore. I felt empowered. I finally felt like a woman and not an unsure little girl. I know who I am. I am not ashamed of getting pregnant. I am happy that mine and Jordan's love is so purely obvious in the form of a baby.

I am proud of myself for taking this time apart from Jordan. That takes a lot of strength that most girls my age would not be able to muster. I know there is a chance Jordan and I didn't last—as much as we love each other—sometimes it isn't enough. He is my first love and though the story goes, "you never forget your first love", it's usually not your last love.

Luke's thoughts on me and Jordan last night opened my eyes. I never wanted to be one of those girls who depended on a guy for everything. That wouldn't be fair to Jordan, and that would leave me helpless. Jordan taught me the world and I will forever be grateful. He is my best friend, but I know in my heart if it were to come to us being just friends—I would be okay... eventually.

I pray though. Every night since I decided on this

break, I prayed we would be together forever. I prayed we'd make love again. I prayed I wouldn't have to set up custody days for our child. I prayed we'd look at the moon together again.

"Tell us," Dad said.

He hates beating around the bush. I wonder what he thought I would say. He tends to think the worst.

"I'm pregnant."

The words fell from my lips so swiftly. Maybe it was because I finally accepted the idea. My eyes closed and I smiled. When I looked at Dad, he seemed to be in shock. I looked over at Mom and her mouth was hung open.

"Now, I know you might be disappointed in me—and you might hate Jordan—but just know we were very careful and—it's not like the circumstances are terrible. We love each other and I'm not asking you for help, just support. I need you both to tell me it's going to be okay."

I have no idea where my ability to communicate came from. I guess since I have spent so many years suppressing my thoughts, it is now easy to just keep spouting out things. It was so freeing. My fear was there under my words. My parents could call me irresponsible and disown me, but regardless, I had to tell them.

"Jordan is willing to give everything up for us, but I'm not letting him. I don't know how yet, but we're going to make it work. So please, just... say something," I said, looking at my mother and then my father.

"Well, you haven't shut up for two minutes," Dad said.

I couldn't tell if he was being funny or serious.

"I'm just...in shock," Mom said.

"Are you sure you're pregnant?"

"Positive. I went to the doctor and everything," I

nodded.

"This is...unbelievable," Mom mumbled.

She looked over at my father with tears in her eyes. It was as if they shared something I didn't know.

"Is Jordan too much of a coward to face us?" Dad asked.

"No—he wanted to be here. I made him stay away."

"Haley, we're not going to lecture you. You're twenty-two now and as long as you're happy, that's all we care about."

I was shocked. That was it? No yelling. No disappointment.

"Daddy," I cried, getting up and hugging him.

He squeezed me tightly.

"Congratulations, Pumpkin."

"You too, Grandpa," I laughed, wiping tears before going over to Mom.

She was in tears as I hugged her.

"I love you so much," she whispered. "Are you feeling okay?"

"Aside from all the morning sickness, yeah, I'm fine. Just tired," I shrugged.

This moment was the first time I felt pure joy over my pregnancy. A weight had been lifted seeing the slightest bit of happiness in my parents' shocked faces.

A little while later, the Erikssons and Christian came over for cake. Tasha wasn't there. I didn't even bother asking Christian where she was, knowing she is avoiding me.

I walked into the kitchen to get a glass of water. As I took a sip, I saw Christian's reflection through the large window on the far wall of the kitchen.

I turned around and looked at him.

"What did you say to my fiancée?" he asked.

"I told her to stay away from you," I said, putting my water down and pressing my hands against the counter behind me.

"Haley," he sighed, walking closer to me.

He walked around the island in the middle of the kitchen and placed his wine glass down next to me. He had been refilling his glass steadily all night. I got the impression he had been drinking before he even got to the house. He stood in front of me, pretty much backing me into the counter further.

"This rebellious phase you're going through is cute, but..." he flipped my hair off my shoulder. "It isn't you."

"Move," I said, trying to push him away.

"Why can't you just accept that I'm marrying someone else?" he asked. "You're a terrible best friend."

I rolled my eyes, "You're not right for Tasha. Why don't you stick with the girls in your circle? Like Leslie maybe?"

"Or Bippy?" he smirked. "To keep her away from Jordan?"

I pushed past him finally.

"I've already been there, you know?"

I looked at him and crossed my arms.

"Been where?"

"Bippy. She's not all that," he laughed and came closer to me. "She's too controlling and dramatic."

It sounds like he and Bippy have a ton in common. Christian trailed a finger over my collarbone and I smacked his hand away, starting to get freaked out by him.

"Stay away from me or I'll scream so loud," I threatened.

Just then, the kitchen door opened and Elsa stood there. Christian backed away from me.

"Everything okay?"

"Dinner was wonderful and so was the cake, Elsa. Thank you," I walked over and kissed her cheek before walking out.

I said goodnight to my parents and the Erikssons before going to bed. I locked my bedroom door and changed for bed. As I lay there, I wondered how I can convince Tasha that Christian was a sleaze ball.

I reached for my cell phone and checked my voicemail. Jordan's voice made me smile. He explained he wanted to see me, but didn't know how I felt about it. I called him; excited to speak to him. Hopefully my excitement answered his question about whether I still wanted to see him.

"Hey," he answered. "Happy birthday."

"Thank you."

"How'd your day go?"

"Good... The baby moved."

"Moved? Like you felt it?"

"Yeah, it was weird, but really cool."

"I wish I could have felt it."

"I'm sure it'll happen again," I laughed.

"I miss you."

"I miss you, too. I told my parents."

"Are you okay?"

"They were insanely calm."

"Wow... Do they hate me?"

"No, I don't think so."

Jordan laughed, "Was Tasha there for support?"

"We got into a fight, sort of."

"About what?"

"Christian. I told her not to marry him."

"You just have to accept that she has rotten taste in men."

"I can't accept it, Jordan. He has serious problems and I'm afraid for her."

"Haley, did he do something to you?" Jordan asked, sounding worried.

"He makes me uncomfortable. I don't want to be around him anymore."

"Did he touch you?"

"No—he just...he says things and..."

"Do me a favor, okay?" Jordan asked. "Don't ever be alone with him."

"Jordan, he's not going to—"

"Just please."

"I don't plan to be alone with him—ever," I said disgusted. "How are you doing?"

"I'm okay."

"Why did you quit the band?" I asked.

"Who told you?" he sighed.

"Danny."

"I did it for you."

"But I didn't want you to do it. I'm angry you did. You would just blame me for the rest of your life," I sighed.

"No, I wouldn't. Besides, I'm not quitting. I'm taking a break."

"Jordan, you know if you leave now... Who's to say your label or anyone else will give you another chance? A break just means you're giving up."

"Like you're doing with us?" he asked.

I was furious at that statement.

"I am not giving up on us!"

"Good."

"Don't give up on me, okay?" I asked.

"Never."

"And you'll tell the band you're not giving up on them either?"

"Will that make you happy?" Jordan asked.

"Will it make *you* happy?" I returned the question.

"Yes."

"Then it makes me happy."

"Thank you," he said and I smiled to myself, wishing I could kiss him.

After I got off the phone, I thought to call Tasha, but I knew she wouldn't answer. Instead, I sent her a text message.

I love you. I want you happy. This has nothing to do with me. Just think things through.

I closed my eyes and heard my phone beep a moment later. I looked at Tasha's reply.

You're still my best friend.

I am happy Tasha still wants me as a friend despite my opinion of her fiancé, but I secretly hope the engagement party won't happen. And I really hope the wedding will be called off.

February 27th

For the first time in a while, I woke up content even though it's been almost a month since Haley and I have been on a break—it's been that long since I've seen her, too. I think I had such a good night's sleep because I am looking forward to this weekend. I am planning to go to Tasha and Christian's engagement party tomorrow.

I didn't tell Haley I am coming. Partly because my work schedule has been up in the air and I didn't want to get her hopes up. I came back to Boston later than expected, which upset me because it means I have yet to see Haley.

Luckily, the band didn't hold any grudges against me. I apologized for almost quitting on them and they forgave me in a heartbeat. For the next week, we're promoting in Boston, so it's nice to finally be home for a little. These guys are my family and Haley is right. I need them.

Another reason why I'm looking forward to this weekend is because I'm going to tell Mom today about the baby. I just hope she will understand what I am saying. I imagine her holding her grandchild and seeing the joy on her face that she always has when she looked at me. I just wish my kid could know her outside of the facility and that she would know who he or she was all the time.

I need Mom more than ever.

-J

Chapter 12

The coat check area was crowded with arriving guests for the swanky engagement brunch in Bakersfield. I followed my parents into the grand ballroom somewhat self-consciously. In the past couple of weeks, my belly was beginning to show. My black dress hid it well, but still, I wondered if everyone could tell. Mom kept telling me it was in my head.

Christian and Tasha were posing for photos with their parents. I hadn't seen Tasha's parents in a long time. I wanted to go over and say hello, but I didn't want to be near Christian.

A waiter passed by with mimosas, I refused politely as my parents each took one.

"Do you want some ginger ale or juice?" Mom asked.

"Juice sounds good."

Mom walked away and Dad wrapped an arm around me.

"How come you two are being so good about this?" I asked with a laugh.

"Would you rather we disown you?"

"It just surprises me."

"Pumpkin, it's all in the way you tell people. If you came to us with your head hung in shame, I'm sure we might have reacted differently. You've grown into this mature woman who knows who she is, and I think Jordan has helped you get to this point."

Dad is right. Jordan helped me find my own voice. I

want to return the favor by helping him overcome the people who hurt him.

I smiled and hugged my father. I spotted Chuck and Andrew walking in just then. I was surprised to see them. Then again, Christian is Chuck's nephew.

"Could you maybe convince Chuck Ashton that Jordan is a good guy?" I sighed.

Dad glanced over at Chuck.

"Like he would believe me."

Just then, Tasha walked over. We've been arguing on and off since my birthday. In fact, we had a fairly large fight yesterday about how her life was going to be controlled by Christian and his family if she went through with the wedding. A perfect example of the Erikssons' necessity to control things was this engagement party. Originally, this event was supposed to be a cocktail party, but Trisha Eriksson found it much more respectable as a brunch.

"There's my maid-of-honor," Tasha hugged me.

My father left a moment later.

"So, I'm going to chalk yesterday's little outburst up to hormones and everything you're going through," she said.

I narrowed my eyes, "Like I told you, this has nothing to do with me. You can't be this blind, Tasha. Call this all off before it's too late."

I would never be so adamant and meddlesome if Tasha was marrying someone else—even if I didn't like the guy much. However, this is Christian. As years pass, my gag reflex is set off more and more whenever he's around. I feel responsible for Tasha getting involved with him since I'm the one who introduced them.

"Just stay away from Christian and things will be fine," Tasha said before plastering on a big smile and walking off.

I couldn't believe it. Tasha Torres, the girl I had known to be free and wild was putting up with crap from a man because she was afraid of losing him. It was so obvious to me now that this had always been Tasha's downfall in life. I saw it with her ex-boyfriend Ricky and now with Christian.

"Haley!"

I turned and Andrew was standing there. I hugged him, happy to have some representation of Jordan with me, though part of me hoped he would miraculously walk into the party any minute.

"Hello," Chuck smiled.

"Hi," I said.

"Where's my son?"

"He's in Boston with the band. Where's Coryn?"

"She had a function," he shrugged. "Excuse me for a second," he said walking away.

"I begged Dad to let me take Coryn's place," Drew told me.

"Why?" I laughed.

"Because I knew I'd get to see you and Jordan."

I smiled, "I'm sorry he's not here."

"What's wrong with him?"

"He's fine, Drew. He's been busy promoting the upcoming album."

"Haley, I'm old enough to understand."

"I know," I nodded.

"Are you breaking up?"

"No."

Just then, a big fuss was being made by the doorway. Bippy and her parents had walked in. She was wearing the smallest dress in the world and eating up all of the attention.

Chuck walked back over.

"Here you go," he said offering me a mimosa.

"No, thanks."

"Haley, you can't have a drink with me? I know my son hates me, but you have no reason to..."

My mother apparently got lost getting me juice. At least, I could have passed the drink off as a mimosa. I reluctantly took the drink from Chuck and he clanked my glass, but I didn't take a sip. He watched me curiously.

"Andrew, why don't you get something to eat?"

Drew sighed, knowing his father was just sending him away.

"I'm staying here," he said protectively of me.

"Now," Chuck said sternly.

"I'm fine," I assured my twelve-year-old bodyguard.

Andrew walked away in a huff.

"Look, I know I come off as an asshole, and I can be one," Chuck told me. "I'm trying, Haley. Since my sons are so fond of you, what can I do to change things?"

I was surprised. Chuck was coming to me for advice? I folded my arms and just looked at him for a moment.

"For starters, let Andrew move to Boston."

"That school doesn't have a dormitory."

"So?"

"So, I'm going to send my son off to a school where he'll be homeless?"

"He won't be."

"Jordan will be traveling. You think leaving Andrew unsupervised will make me a better father?"

"I'll take care of him."

Chuck laughed, "You?"

"Is that funny?"

"I just—what's going on with you and Jordan?" he

asked. "Are you even together? From what everyone's saying... He's back with Bippy."

"That's a misunderstanding."

Chuck looked at my untouched drink and then back at my face.

"You didn't try your drink."

"I'm not thirsty."

"You're pregnant."

I sighed, "Just because I don't want to drink?"

"Don't deny it. Christian told me."

My eyes widened and I wanted to hurt Christian even more.

"He called me up to tell me that my son screwed up again," Chuck sighed and I wanted to tell him off. "First Bippy and now you..."

"Why do you look at Jordan like that?" I asked. "Don't you have any remorse for what you did to your family?"

Chuck was quiet for a moment.

"What Christian doesn't know is I know Charlie didn't screw up. He didn't get Bippy pregnant, Christian did."

My mouth hit the floor and I looked up at Chuck.

"What?"

"Bippy's baby... Christian was the father. That's why I didn't tell Charlie. I was protecting my angel of a nephew," he said with sarcasm dripping from the word "angel".

"Christian slept with Jordan's girlfriend?"

When Christian had told me on my birthday that he hooked up with Bippy, I assumed it wasn't while Jordan dated her. I also assumed he was lying, since he lied so frequently about me being his girlfriend.

"And Jordan slept with Christian's girlfriend—ironic."

"I was never Christian's girlfriend," I said hatefully.

"I know, Haley. Christian, I've come to realize, is a compulsive liar. I don't know why, but I believed everything he said. Jordan hated me so much that I wanted to believe it was him that was the bastard and not me."

I was trying to figure out what Chuck was telling me.

"So all the drug rumors..."

"Christian started them."

"I can't believe this. Why are you just now figuring this out?"

"Because I wanted to believe Christian. My sister always bragged about the perfect kid that he was. It wasn't until that last phone call he made to tell me you are pregnant and how Jordan abandoned you that I realized what he is doing."

"This is the person my best friend is marrying," I said, overwhelmed by this information.

Before I knew it, Chuck was hugging me.

"It's going to be okay."

"Aww, isn't this sweet?"

I turned and Bippy was standing there with a hand on her hip.

"Haley, what's wrong? Is it Jordan?"

I realized I was crying at that moment. I was frustrated with everything and upset for Jordan. Crying is how I release my emotions.

"Excuse me," I said, walking through the crowd to get to the bathroom.

My hands were shaking once I got there. This was too much. I've known Christian my entire life. He was always annoying, but to be as vindictive to feed lies about Jordan to his own family and to sleep with his girlfriend?

I put my head down on the sink and when I looked back up, Bippy was standing there.

"What were you and Chuck talking about that got you so upset?"

"Christian."

She walked up to the mirror and began to fix her make-up.

"I'm so happy for him," she said, shrugging her shoulders. "You should be, too, Haley."

She was acting like I was upset and jealous he was getting married.

"So, he raped you, huh?" I asked, casually.

My tears stopped. Now, I felt nothing but anger toward Bippy Reynolds. She tried to manipulate my boyfriend to feel sorry for her after she utterly betrayed him!

Bippy laughed, "What?"

"You told Jordan you were raped, but you told Chuck the baby was Christian's. Are you saying Christian raped you?"

"Jordan wasn't supposed to tell anyone."

"Well, he told me. Should I call the cops on Christian right now?"

"Haley, don't be ridiculous," she rolled her eyes. "We were drunk and things got out of hand."

"So, you and Christian just slept together once?"

Bippy didn't say anything. I grabbed her arm.

"Get off me, bitch! You're so weird! What do you care how many times I slept with Christian? Jordan could care less! He was always taking off whenever he wanted and whining about his crazy mother! So, I kept myself busy," she shrugged.

"You are such a—"

I didn't get to finish my sentence.

"Slut!"

The word came from the bathroom stall. The door opened and Tasha walked out with tears filling her eyes. She was ready to tear Bippy's eyes out, but I held her back.

"She is not worth it," I said grabbing Tasha's face.

She looked at me and nodded. Together, we walked out of the bathroom. Christian immediately found us.

"There you are. My dad's about to make a toast."

Before I could stop her, Tasha pulled her hand back and slapped Christian across the face so hard it felt like the entire room turned to look.

"What the fuck?!" Christian yelled, rubbing his cheek.

"That wasn't even for me," she said through bleary eyes.

"What did you tell her, Haley?" Christian asked as he grabbed my arm and yanked me roughly while Tasha ran off.

My entire body jerked forward and the pressure he applied on my arm hurt. I could feel his fingers digging into my skin and I involuntarily yelped.

My father immediately stepped in.

"Don't touch her like that," he scolded Christian, not even knowing the full extent of his golden boy's wrongs.

Christian let go of my arm and I rubbed it as I stared at him, hoping he gets everything that is coming to him. At that moment, I realized someone like Christian is probably capable of rape. I just don't think Bippy ever made it that difficult for him.

I never want to see Christian Eriksson again, and I hope Tasha feels the same way.

Christian fooled so many people over the years into thinking he was a respectful young man; one any girl would be lucky to marry. Most people always thought I was crazy for not giving into him. Now, I hope everyone will finally start to see how wrong they are about him. Jordan isn't the disgrace of his family—Christian is.

"I'm fine, Dad," I said, pulling my father back from

attacking Christian.

I looked at Christian, "I didn't tell Tasha anything. Bippy gave it away. You two deserve each other. What you did to Jordan is disgusting," I sneered at him.

"Haley—"

"Stay away from Jordan and me. Stay the hell away from Tasha."

I walked outside to comfort Tasha and all I could think about is how I am going to explain this all to Jordan. Part of me doesn't want to tell him how much Bippy and Christian really wanted to hurt him, or how much his father wanted to hate him.

Tasha's arms wrapped around me. She was hysterically crying and trying to apologize to me.

"It's okay," I soothed her.

"I feel like such an idiot," she sobbed. "I was horrible to you."

"If you would have told me that Jordan was no good—I wouldn't believe you either."

"Because Jordan is good," she said, wiping her tears and pulling away from me.

I nodded and just then, Tasha's mother was hurrying toward us.

"Baby, what's wrong?"

As Tasha asked her mother to get her out of there, I felt my phone vibrate in my purse. I missed the call. It was Danny. I had three missed calls from him, one from Cami and one from Jordan.

Panic washed over me. I called Danny back since he was the last person to call.

"Haley..."

"What's going on?" I asked.

I had a terrible feeling and I couldn't help but worry something had happened to Jordan. I was shaking and hoping I wouldn't hear he had been in a terrible accident or anything along those lines.

"It's Maggie," Danny explained.

"Oh God," I gasped. "Is she okay?"

"She hasn't been feeling well and one of the medications caused her to have another seizure..."

"She's okay though, right?"

"She hit her head while having the seizure and it sent her into a coma."

"No!" I cried. "I'll be there as soon as I can."

I felt like running directly to Boston—if only I had superhuman speed to match that feeling.

"Jordan's a mess," Danny continued. "I can't get him to leave her side. This is bad—I've never seen him like this, Haley."

After hanging up with Danny, I rushed back into the party. I wanted to tell Tasha, but she is going through a lot already and I know how much she cares about Maggie. I just didn't think she could handle this right now.

I walked over to my parents and interrupted them talking to whomever they were speaking with. I'm sure I know them, but I couldn't focus on making small talk or even on who they were talking to.

"I need to go to the airport right now," I explained.

"Haley, what is it?" Mom asked, wiping my tears.

"Jordan's Mom..." I cried harder. "Today is the worst day..." I said, feeling my insides crumbling.

How can so much pain come to the surface in one day? It wasn't even directly my pain. It was Jordan's and Tasha's, and in some way I felt responsible for a large portion of it. I'm the one who brought all of this Bippy and Christian crap out. I can't blame myself for Maggie, but I should be with Jordan, and I felt guilty for not being by his side.

"Her illness got worse?" Dad asked.

"She's in a coma."

I heard Mom gasp as I spotted Andrew and Chuck and I hurried over to them. Jordan needed people who loved him and would offer him comfort. I wanted to take Drew with me.

"Chuck, can Andrew come back to Boston with me? It's an emergency."

"What kind of an emergency?"

"Maggie is in a coma. Jordan needs him," I pleaded with him.

Chuck's eyes widened. He looked concerned. I have never seen him look that way.

"I'll go with you."

I didn't expect him to say that. I didn't know if I should object, but I couldn't stop him. I barely said goodbye to my parents before heading to the airport with Chuck and Andrew.

On the plane ride, Drew held my hand as I closed my eyes. I felt someone touch my other hand. I looked over at Chuck.

"Thank you," he said softly.

I just looked at him, wondering what he was thanking me for.

"For being there for my sons. You're going to make a great mom."

He turned away from me and looked out the window. I never felt close to Chuck. I've never seen kindness in his eyes let alone gratitude. Now, when his son is falling apart—he thanks me. I couldn't help but think I've only contributed to Jordan's sadness this year.

I looked over at Drew and he was falling asleep beside me. I couldn't sleep; I was just thankful it was a short flight.

Dear God,

I know you don't hear from me much. I guess I take you for granted. You know I'm grateful for all that you've given me. I just don't get why I got such a bad deal as far as a father goes.

Why was my mother cursed to love so deeply that it made her snap? How could my father take advantage of her the way he did?

How could you let Mom stay in a nursing home all these years and now this? I always hoped she'd get better. I imagined her living in her own home; dancing around the kitchen to the Bee Gees and Chicago like she always did.

Why can't I ever see that again?

This isn't about me, though. I'm sick of blaming everyone. I blame Dad and Bippy. And I blame Mom. Lately, I've even blamed Haley. And of course, I blame you.

Whatever—what doesn't kill us makes us stronger. I believe that. All I ask now is that Mom can be happy. I want her happy. I will always miss her, though.

-J

Chapter 13

Walking into the hospital gave me chills. I had never actually been in a medical hospital. When my grandfather was sick, he had a nurse take care of him at home. He could afford to have his personal doctor make house calls. I had only seen hospitals on TV and I hadn't planned on being in a real one until I was going into labor.

We got onto the elevator and I looked at Chuck. I don't think Jordan would want to see him—especially right now. When the doors opened, we walked down the hall and I stopped.

"Chuck, wait," I grabbed his arm. "Stay here. Andrew and I will go, okay?"

He looked at me confused.

"She was my wife. I want to see her."

"Do it for Jordan, please."

"Haley, he can't be this selfish."

"Please, you owe him," I glared at him.

He just sighed and yanked his arm away slightly. Andrew and I turned the corner.

"I don't know what to say," Drew sighed as we walked to the end of the hall where I spotted Danny and Cami.

"You don't have to say anything," I told him, putting my arm around him.

I didn't know what to say either. I wasn't equipped to help people through tough times like this. First, I tell him I want to take a break and now, his mother is in a coma! The poor guy.

And still, he doesn't know any of the information I found out today. I don't know if I can ever bring myself to tell him at this point.

Danny was leaning against the wall with his arms wrapped around Cami. He straightened up as he saw us approaching.

"Thank God you're here," Cami sighed.

Danny hugged me.

"Any news?"

"They brought her out of the coma," Danny explained.

I smiled and looked at Drew, who also smiled.

"That's great!"

Danny shook his head and kept his hands in his pockets as he looked down.

"She's gone," Cami said, her ice blue eyes looking like shallow puddles with the way they were welling up.

Cami never met Maggie. I'm not even sure if Jordan ever told her about his mother. She and the band didn't know much about Jordan's upbringing. I gathered her tears came from the state Jordan must be in, which worried me.

"Oh my God," I gasped, covering my mouth, in shock.

I felt Drew shrink away from me; he knew as well as the rest of us what the death of his mother would do to Jordan.

"She came out of the coma and she had another seizure and her heart kept stopping…" Danny told me.

I put my hand on top of my head.

"He won't come out," Cami sighed, wiping a tear. "He doesn't want us near him. He won't let them take her away."

I wiped my tears, but they kept falling.

"I didn't even get to say goodbye to her," I cried, putting my hands over my eyes.

Danny hugged me once more.

Maggie didn't deserve this. She didn't deserve to spend eight years in a nursing home only to pass away at forty-five.

I tried to pull myself together for Jordan's sake. I looked at Drew. He was just a kid. I didn't think he was ready to see his brother hanging onto a lifeless body. I'm not ready either, but I have to be there for Jordan.

Slowly, I approached the door to Maggie's room. I could barely make out that it was Jordan hunched over the hospital bed. I pushed the door open and he didn't even lift his head as I walked into the room.

"Get out," he grumbled.

"I'm so sorry," I said in a whisper.

Without even looking at me, Jordan whirled around and hugged me tightly. He never held me so tight, but I just let him—ignoring the cracking of my back as he buried his head into my chest. I ran my fingers through his hair as I imagined his mother would have done to him when he was a child.

I felt his tears on my dress; hitting my fingertips as I ran them down his jaw. In all the time I had known him, I had never seen him cry. Sure, I cried plenty around him, but even when his face showed raw emotion whether it was anger or pain—he never came to tears.

I'm sure that had something to do with his father. Jordan didn't always talk about the details of his childhood. He gave me vague looks into the abuse he took. He mentioned once that his father slapped him across the face for crying when he was ten. Jordan also told me Maggie was easy to tears and Chuck hated it.

I suppose Chuck saw crying as a weakness. I wondered if Jordan did too. Any time I had cried to him, he always asked me why I was crying as if he didn't understand the natural emotion. However, unlike his father—he was always quick to comfort me. Not that I had a lot to be upset about the past eighteen months, but I was a sap when it came to movies.

Now, here I was physically holding my boyfriend up. I didn't know what to say. I didn't know if he even wanted me to say anything, so I just held onto him, trying not to look over at Maggie's body. The last time I had seen her she was in such good spirits, I didn't want to ruin that image of her. Unfortunately for her son, it had already been ruined.

Jordan pulled away from me after a few minutes.

"I'm so sorry," I repeated.

He was barely looking at me as he tried to wipe his tears. I took his hand away from his eyes.

"It's okay to cry. You need to."

"I just—I can't believe she's gone, Haley," he said, pressing his fingers into his forehead.

"I can't either," I wiped a tear.

"I feel so gypped out of a mother."

Every word he spoke was said with clenched teeth. I had felt the sadness seep through my dress as he cried a few minutes ago. Now, this was the anger.

"I know you do, but she loved you more than anything."

He shook his head and turned to look at Maggie before looking back at me.

"Not more than *him.*"

"Jordan, don't do this now," I pleaded. "Let's just get out of here. Drew's outside waiting."

He looked at me surprised.

"What? How?"

"I know you need him."

Jordan looked at me gratefully.

"Thank you," he said, hugging me.

"I love you so much. I want to help you through this. Please let me."

"I love you too, Haley," he said, but it came out hoarse.

He was crying again as I rubbed his back soothingly. I was crying again, too. There was a knock on the door and two orderlies walked in. We pulled apart and Jordan turned back toward his mother. I took his hand gently.

"That's just her body," I said softly. "She is where she always was to you." I put my hand over his heart and he nodded as his tears fell quicker.

We walked out of the room and Jordan was trying to fight his pain as he faced his friends and brother. Drew ran to him and they hugged.

"I'm sorry, J," he whispered.

Danny gave my neck a comforting squeeze. I looked over at him and then at Cami. It's ironic. I never thought I'd be here two years ago. I went from having one friend and being fearful of life to being surrounded by this loyal close-knit group of people who are like family. I couldn't imagine going back to feeling incredibly alone or going through life as if I were in a fog with nothing to be passionate about.

Lately, I know I felt alone in many ways with the baby putting distance between Jordan and me. And Christian putting distance between me and Tasha. Somehow I knew I would never lose the people who really cared about me, though.

I know they were Jordan's family and friends, but they've all become my family as well—Drew, Danny, Sebie, Darren, and yes, Cami, too. I never would have thought I would see her as a friend. She truly had everyone in the band's best interest as far as business goes—and personally as well.

"Does Aunt Lacey know?" I asked as Jordan and Drew pulled apart.

"She was on vacation," Jordan explained. "She's on her way back."

As he finished the sentence, Chuck appeared from around the corner. I had almost forgotten he had come with me. Everyone sort of froze.

"What the hell are you doing here?" Jordan asked.

My body tensed at the tone in his voice. Chuck was definitely the last person Jordan wanted to see.

"Hey Drew, let's go take a walk, buddy," Danny said.

I could tell seeing Andrew standing in between Jordan and Chuck made him nervous. The entire air between Jordan and Chuck made me nervous. I was staying, though. Maybe it wasn't my place, but I felt responsible for putting Jordan in this position. I also felt protective of my boyfriend.

Drew sighed and eyed his father before following Danny and Cami toward the elevator. I took a step toward Jordan, wanting badly to take his hand. All he saw was his father at this moment, though. No one else was in the hallway in Jordan's eyes.

"Is she..." Chuck asked.

He looked at Jordan, but got no response; just a dead stare. Chuck looked at me and I nodded. His eyes closed and he squeezed the bridge of his nose.

"Charlie, I'm—"

"Don't," Jordan sighed, his breathing becoming shallow. "You killed her."

There was just silence for a moment.

"How dare you," Chuck shook his head. "You want to blame someone right now, fine. But you can't blame me for everything fucked up in your life, Charlie," Chuck sighed. "Your mother went crazy. I was a shitty husband, but her mental illness was not my fault. You want to blame me for your mother's genes? How about you getting your girlfriend knocked up? You want to blame me for that, too?"

That was it for Jordan. All at once, he charged at Chuck, slamming him into the wall. I screamed and as I did, I felt a sharp pain in my side.

Chuck shoved Jordan back into the other wall and I yelled.

"Stop it!"

I heard my scream echoing off the walls followed by my sobbing. They both froze as I cried out of fear they'd tear each other apart.

"*This* is what he gets from you, Chuck," I said wiping tears. "Holding in his anger and not knowing how to release it… All Jordan needs is you to hug him and comfort him. He just lost his mother for God's sake and you want to make him feel like crap?" I asked, with tears falling down my face. "What is wrong with you?"

"Why did you come here?" Jordan asked, pushing away from Chuck.

"To see her," Chuck sighed. "To be here for you. Haley, Drew and I… We came here for you."

Jordan turned toward me and looked at me through narrowed eyes.

"You brought him here?"

"Jordan, I—"

"You knew I would need Drew, but you didn't know this asshole would be the last person I'd want to see?" He asked, looking at me with such disappointment.

I did know Chuck would be the last person Jordan wanted to see, but I wasn't thinking clearly.

He practically ran down the hall and I tried to run after him, but I felt the sharp pain again and I winced.

"Are you okay?" Chuck asked, holding my arm.

"Just leave me alone," I said, hurrying to the elevator.

The doors already had closed. I waited for the next elevator. My body felt weak from the commotion of the day. The stress wasn't good for the baby.

When I got outside, Jordan wasn't there. Danny, Cami and Drew were, though.

"You left them alone?" Drew asked, worriedly.

"Jordan took off. He didn't come out here?" I asked.

"No," Danny shrugged.

We waited for Jordan for twenty minutes. Danny tried calling him, but he didn't answer. Chuck had left, taking Drew with him. I barely said anything to him. I don't know what I was thinking allowing him to come there.

Things just got so out of hand at the party that Chuck almost seemed like he could be normal. I guess I was wrong and now Jordan hated me for it.

Finally after about ten more minutes, Jordan walked out of the hospital. He stepped right up to us and didn't even look at me; just Cami and Danny.

"Thank you."

He hugged Cami and then Danny for a long moment.

"Let us know if you need anything," Danny said.

I just waved at them both as they walked away. I looked at Jordan, but he wasn't looking at me. He was staring off somewhere.

"Look," I began. "You have every right to be angry, at God, at your father, me, and yes, your mother. You have every right to be upset and I'm so sorry I came here with him, but I didn't know how... I thought he finally got it, you know?" I asked, sticking my hands in the pockets of my coat.

Jordan still didn't look at me. His face was stone. He finally turned to me and said something that meant so much.

"Can we go home?"

I nodded and Jordan reached his hand out to me. I took it gratefully and we made our way to his car. I didn't know where home was anymore. Would it be his apartment or mine? It didn't matter.

February 28th

It's 4am. I can't sleep. I am afraid to sleep. Afraid of what I'd dream. All of my nightmares are starting to add up. Haley apologizing. Bippy trying to blame Haley for the loss of "our" child. My mom sobbing. My dad yelling. The moon breaking into pieces. In some form, these visions came true. The moon was Haley and me and it was time we started to put the pieces back together.

I was angry with her for bringing my dad to the hospital. He didn't deserve to be there. I didn't want him at the funeral tomorrow either, but Aunt Lacey said to "let it go for now". I didn't know how to let it go when it came to Mom. I always saw her as the victim, but I do know she was at fault for allowing him to treat her the way he did for so long. She used me as a reason to stay with him. She told me it was for my sake. She told him they needed to make it work for me. Deep down she knew it was a selfish act on her part.

I still didn't think she deserved this life, though. She

was too young. I held onto every hope that she would get better. Now she's really gone and I'm an absolute mess. I stayed in bed with Haley for hours yesterday. We just lay there; sometimes I wouldn't even look at her, but knowing she was beside me was comforting.

Losing your mother is an indescribably terrible feeling. She was the one person who was there from day one of my life, and even though she didn't always know what I was saying to her, she always listened. She always smiled at me. She loved me even when she didn't know who I was.

Kind of like Haley.

I think about how I didn't see her for her birthday. By the time I got back from New York, she had gone to Bakersfield without me. I missed Valentine's Day, too—not that I even really buy into the holiday in a traditional way. Last year, Haley and I spent the day watching movies and making dinner together. I could use a day like that now: something normal.

I'm watching her toss and turn in bed. I feel like a shitty boyfriend—even if we are on a break. Aside from asking how she was feeling I haven't asked her much about the pregnancy or if she needed anything. I wasn't even there for the last sonogram. She e-mailed me the picture a couple of weeks ago and I felt horrible that I wasn't with her.

After the fight with my dad at the hospital, I walked around needing to be alone as usual. I saw this guy with balloons and a goofy smile on his face. He was a muscular guy with tattoos and he looked overjoyed to go see his wife and child.

I thought about what Mom said. One of the last conversations she had with me was kind of freaky. I figured she was going off on one of her delusions, but it was really weird that she asked about her grandchild before I even got to tell her.

"What grandchild?" I had asked.

"The little girl with the green eyes and blonde hair," she said with a smile. "I met her last night in my dreams. She has so much light in her heart."

I was dumbfounded. I stared at my mother not knowing whether to chalk what she just said up to her condition and medication or to some freaky spiritual shit that I never really believed in.

"Just love her, Jordy. That's all you can do."

And then, as focused as she was when she said all of that, she began talking about something else—nonsense as she often did. She didn't look at me like she knew me anymore.

I was so in shock by what Mom had said that I didn't even tell her that Haley is really pregnant. She wouldn't have known what I was talking about anymore anyhow.

I'm thinking so much about my mother and how her dreams were cut short because of love. I wouldn't allow the same to happen to me because of fear. Being a father was always a dream of mine—it was just coming true sooner than I expected. The truth is I am afraid to be completely open with Haley; with the world. I am afraid I will be too much like my father. It doesn't have to be that way, does it?

-J

Chapter 14

I felt like I have been asleep for a week. I could barely move; my entire body felt like it was weighing me down. I was in Jordan's bedroom and I was staring at a photo of him and his mother on the nightstand. Jordan looked about twelve—he had a guitar in his hand with a blue bow wrapped around it. Maggie was behind him, hugging him closely. They both had the biggest smiles on.

I had asked Jordan about the picture the first time I had ever seen it. It was taken Christmas morning. I assumed Chuck took the shot, but Jordan told me Aunt Lacey had. It seemed like a sore subject; not that I expected anything to do with his father to be anything but sore. Jordan merely summed it up by stating Chuck didn't have time for family—even on Christmas.

Next to that frame was a picture of Jordan and me taken this past summer. We were pretending to pick each other's noses. I smiled to myself. I missed that side of us.

When did life get incredibly serious for us? Jordan and I are still kids in so many ways. We still want things as individuals, but now we have to make life decisions for a whole other person as a team.

Nobody comes out of childhood unscathed. I fear what scars I will leave on my kid's childhood and I'm sure Jordan fears that even more than I do.

While Jordan and I are still trying to accept the baby news, there are these hateful people in our lives. I always believed in the greater good in the human race. Bippy, Christian and Chuck prove me wrong. They are selfish, manipulative, spoiled snobs who don't care who they hurt to get what they want.

It's funny because all of my life my parents protected me from bad neighborhoods and public school kids. Meanwhile, the people they encouraged me to spend time with were the real low class deviants that I needed protection from.

To top this complicated time in our lives off, Jordan's mother passed away so unexpectedly. I don't know that kind of loss, but I can only imagine what he must be feeling. He just stayed in my arms after we left the hospital. For hours I held him until we both fell asleep.

"How are you feeling?"

I turned away from the nightstand to see Jordan sitting by the window with his songbook slash journal in his hands. I offered him a smile as I sat up. Truth is I am feeling some discomfort lately. With everything going on, I haven't thought much of it—I know it's stress. At least I was throwing up a little less.

"Don't worry about me," I said. "I'm fine."

"I do worry."

"Why?"

He got up from the chair and slid onto the bed, putting his notebook aside.

"Because you're being strong for my sake, and though I really respect that, you don't have to."

"Jor, you have every right to be selfish. You don't have to fix us right now—I'm here no matter what," I explained, taking his hand and squeezing it.

He smiled down at our entwined hands and then looked into my eyes.

"The last conversation I had with Mom was bizarre," he said.

I just waited for him to elaborate.

"She asked about you, and I hated that I gave her a standard answer. I don't really know how you are doing. I don't like that feeling, Haley. I need to know how you and our daughter are doing..." he said, tears filling his eyes.

I looked at him funny. Our daughter?

"What makes you so sure it's a girl?" I laughed, but felt my insides flutter at Jordan making some kind of paternal reference to our child for the first time.

"You're going to think this is crazy," he sighed, his breathing a bit erratic. "Mom... After she asked about you... she—she asked about her granddaughter—the one with green eyes and blonde hair."

I was speechless. Could Maggie have said that out of pure coincidence?

"You didn't tell her about the baby?"

Jordan shook his head, "I was going to—yesterday, but... it was too late."

"She already knew," I said, wiping a tear from his face as a few drops fell from my eyes.

"She said she met our baby in her dreams. How can that be?"

I shrugged, "I don't know, but that's freakily beautiful."

I felt my face come alive at the thought of Maggie seeing our baby in her dreams. I prayed that the thought of being a grandmother brought her joy. I hoped it comforted Jordan in some way, though I already knew it had.

"So, honestly… How are you both doing?"

"Well, *honestly*, the baby seems to be good. I kind of feel little kicks now and I really want you to feel it," I said, taking Jordan's hand and placing it on my belly.

Jordan stared at my stomach, in awe of how firm it has gotten since the last time he had touched it. I just hit the four and a half month mark and the thought of a little baby growing inside me is starting to excite me more than just frighten me.

"I want to feel it too," he assured me, pressing his hand against my stomach.

I smiled, "It kind of feels like a flutter, so I don't know if you can feel it too well on the outside." I shrugged. "To finish answering your question, I'm okay. I know this wasn't planned, but I am happy to become a mom even if I'm scared at the same time."

"Bet you wish it isn't with an asshole like me…" he sighed.

"Jordan, you're not an asshole."

"Haley, I wish I could turn back time and…" he swallowed hard. "I'm turning into him, and that scares the hell out of me that I will do to this baby what he did—"

"You are nothing like your father," I said, scooting closer to him while keeping his hand pressed to my belly. "I know I called you your father when I first told you about the baby, but I was upset and things just got out of hand."

"I was out of hand," he sighed. "I reacted badly."

"Well, I shouldn't have gone off and hitchhiked, either," I smirked.

We both chuckled at that before I got back on topic.

"You'll be here for me. You'll be here for her…or him," I smiled, wondering about Maggie's premonition of our baby being a girl.

"It's a her," Jordan nodded. "I had a dream she was a girl, too."

"We'll see," I laughed. "Anyway, we both handled this awkwardly. It's a life altering thing that takes some getting used to."

Jordan nodded and eyed his notebook.

"I just feel like... Mom was the only person I could be completely open with about my life. Mostly because she was too out of it to understand. Even Danny—he doesn't know half the stuff that goes through my head. I just stopped trusting people, Haley. That's not fair to you. I do trust you with everything, and so I want to be completely open with someone for once in my life..." he explained, grabbing his notebook.

He handed it to me.

"Read it. This book has all of my fears and insecurities. You always say I hold back... No more," he said, looking into my eyes. "I just don't want you to get offended by anything in there."

I looked at his face and I could see how incredibly difficult this was for him. Sure, he shared his emotions with songs, but this was even deeper than that. In this notebook was all of Jordan's struggles within himself, which I'm sure, were amplified with the news of becoming a father and the latest in his Bippy and Daddy drama.

"Thank you," I said, hugging him.

"I'm going to go for a walk and pick up some breakfast. Any requests?"

"Pancakes?" I smiled.

"With chocolate chips?"

"Please."

Jordan walked out of the room and I heard him

talking with Aunt Lacey from downstairs. She sounded a wreck, much like Jordan did yesterday. I know there was more emotion to come from him, especially with the funeral tomorrow. Grief is such an unpredictable emotion.

I looked down at the book in my hand. I carefully began to thumb through the pages, skipping over lyrics I already knew. I came across Jordan's nightmares I guess that is what he first started journaling. Oddly enough, there was usually a baby in his dreams. Bippy was usually in them, though.

Jordan also had nightmares of losing me and that broke my heart being that we are technically still on a break, I guess... I'm still not sure where we stand. My heart never really took a break from Jordan, even though my mind tried to. I always knew our break was only temporary. I'm not sure Jordan had that same confidence.

I read through a dozen or so new song lyrics; I love them, of course. The journal entries, however, were hard to get through. Every emotion Jordan felt from before Christmas until now is displayed in those pages. Jordan filled this book with hatred for his father, his pain for his mother, and his resentment toward them both.

Then there is the topic of Bippy. He questions if he ever really had feelings for her on one page. On another, he wonders if he'd still be with her had she not gotten pregnant. That hurt. Does that mean he has been imagining his life without me in it?

He would dismiss these thoughts, though, saying how Bippy could never be real for longer than an hour. She always had a secret agenda, he stated. He would then say how much he loves me.

I was actually picking my boyfriend's brain for the first time. It was probably the hardest thing I ever had to do.

However, it was a relief to finally be allowed inside, even if he says I'm stubborn and mellow dramatic at times on December 27th.

On December 28th, he went on for a page about us making love in the shower. My cheeks burned red reading that page, but it made me miss his body tangled with mine. It made me want one of those passionate kisses we shared so frequently before the New Year. We barely spoke in a month due to our break; it didn't feel right. It feels like the world is out of whack, and it's good to know Jordan feels the same way.

After New Year's Day, Jordan's journal entries became more intense. He wrote about the baby and me. I was in tears. Even though I felt similar emotions to his at that time, it hurt to see his struggle with the idea of having a child. Soon though, the frustrated and worried entries began to change course. Jordan was starting to sound optimistic and even showed signs of the fun-loving, carefree guy I fell in love with.

He wasn't a poser like he stated in one entry. He always is hard on himself especially when it comes to his music and how he affects others.

Being seen as an idol to many teenagers, Jordan feels pressure to be a good role model. I'm sure that comes from him not having many people to look up to as a kid.

Jordan doesn't get that he is a real person with his own demons to overcome or that it's okay to not be perfect and it's inevitable that he'll make mistakes. Maybe our baby will play a part in his healing process.

I turned to the last two pages. On the left page of the book was a sketch of shattered pieces that looked as if they had craters on them with a sky backdrop. Written across the page was "Breaking The Moon". On the opposite page were song lyrics.

Where are those grey eyes that stared at those blue skies?

Remember when the moon was ours at night?

And the stars kept our secrets wrapped so tight...

Then life got real and ripped out our hearts

Until they beat no more

Battered us into the darkness

Until we could not see

And you were gone, oh, where did you go?

I am wounded worse than before

You were like CPR to a drowning soul

By day you were my sun

At night you were my dreams

Underneath that moon

That's broken for good, oh how it seems

I love the lyrics. I am touched by them. They made me realize something, though: how little faith Jordan has in love. Though the past couple of months have been hell for us, I am coming out more focused than ever.

I suppose I still have some of the same fears. I had doubted Jordan's commitment to me. I always doubted the strength of his love for me. Though my self-esteem has increased tremendously the past two years, my insecurities still seep in once in a while.

For instance, Bippy Reynolds brings up much insecurity

for me. When she's around, she always takes the spotlight. Growing up, I felt invisible whenever she was in the room.

When she did talk to me, she always put me down in some form. If that wasn't enough, she dated my boyfriend. The fact that he even mentions Bippy in his journal and allowed her to kiss him recently gives me reason enough to question how he feels about me.

However, even when I found out about the kiss, I somehow knew it didn't happen because Jordan was in love with her. I know Bippy is his past. I know she was the first and only girlfriend to break his heart, and that he wanted to believe she cared about him more than to just cheat on him and lie to him.

Unfortunately, Bippy did treat him as if he didn't matter to her. I don't think she is capable of loving anyone more than herself, though, I do believe she loved Jordan. How could anyone not love him?

I knew Jordan would figure everything out; he always did. I can't imagine being with anyone else. It was like he said in one entry: I looked at him like he was my world. Though, the past few weeks taught me something...

I could survive without Jordan.

I could be *me* without him.

I also learned that I don't want to be without him. I know we're good for each other. I want him to have faith in us; faith in himself. It hurts to see he feels this way.

I decided to leave a note in his book in response to everything I've read. I closed the journal and glanced out the window; wishing it was nighttime. I miss the moon. I miss that feeling I have when I think about Jordan. I miss life being as simple as worrying about passing an exam and deciding what to get my parents for Christmas.

I showered and got dressed before heading downstairs. I

worried how Tasha was doing. I feel terrible about having to run out on her like I did. I wonder if she hates me; if she partly blames me for Christian's feelings. I partly blame myself, though I know I have no control over how Christian feels about me.

Breakfast was on the table when I got to the kitchen. Jordan's aunt was on the phone, crying softly. I felt awkward, like I shouldn't be in the room. She hung up the phone a moment later. She noticed me and forced a smile. She resembled Maggie in that moment.

Though Jordan and Aunt Lacey lived together for the past six years, they gave each other their space. Lacey was somewhat of a loner; I guess she had to be since Maggie and Jordan were the only real family she had left. Now, Jordan was her only living relative.

"Morning Haley," she dabbed her eyes.

"Morning."

"Jordan got us breakfast."

I nodded and sat down in front of my pancakes, which were cold now, but I didn't mind. Lacey hadn't touched her food and there was no plate for Jordan.

"Where is he?"

"Um, he told me to tell you he just wanted to be alone for a bit."

I nodded, though I didn't like the idea of him alone. I wanted him in my arms like last night even if we didn't say a word to each other.

"Is there anything I can do?" I asked.

"Sweetie, you being here for my nephew is enough."

It didn't feel like enough. Jordan was all alone and his aunt was about to burst into tears across from me.

The funeral tomorrow would be small considering there was no family left. I wanted Lacey to take some comfort in knowing I truly cared about her sister, and I wasn't just being a supportive girlfriend.

"I really loved Maggie."

Lacey smiled as she cried.

"I know you did, and she loved you. She always feared Jordan would be alone, and when he found you—Maggie was doing better, believe it or not. She just wanted him to be happy."

I smiled. Tasha had told me that once, too—that since I came into Jordan's life, Maggie was happier. She used to have more "not there" moments in the past, which is why this was even more upsetting. I know we all hoped she was getting better, and she was. The development of epilepsy was too much on her mind and body; among whatever other illnesses she accumulated by staying in the nursing home for so long.

Hours passed and Jordan wasn't back. I started to worry. I called him, but his phone was turned off. It was getting dark when I heard the front door open. I lay in his bed the entire afternoon, still feeling discomfort.

Jordan appeared in the doorway. His eyes were red from tears and his skin rosy from the cold. I sat up a little, wincing as I did so.

"Are you okay?"

"Just a little back pain," I waved him off. "I was worried about you."

"Sorry," he said, closing the door before sitting on the edge of the bed. "I'm trying to let you be here for me, but I really…" he took a deep breath. "I don't think I deserve you being here after how I've been acting."

"Jordan, stop beating yourself up," I pulled on his arm. "So you freaked out about the baby… I still love you."

He looked over at me.

"You read my journal… I'm sure you're looking at me

differently."

"Yeah, actually I am. I'm looking at a person who is trying so hard to make everyone happy. You're turning into me," I laughed.

Jordan laughed, too. He always told me I couldn't make everyone happy, and I needed to accept that. He says that's why I was so unhappy in my own life for so long. He was right and I am right about him too.

"That's not such a bad thing, you know—being like you... As long as I don't start eating tofu and freaking out in elevators."

I smacked his arm before wrapping my arms around his neck.

"I'm not upset over anything you said—even the Bippy parts."

"How can that be?" he laughed. "I would be furious."

"Because you're not in love with her."

"I'm not, and I'm sorry that I ever questioned if I even like her. She keeps calling me and leaving me these ridiculously annoying voicemails. She is trying to play me for a fool. I'm sick of buying into her acts."

"Good," I smiled. "So, be completely honest... What do you want? I didn't really find that complete answer in your journal," I said, trying to remain lighthearted in my questioning.

"As far as what?"

"Life," I shrugged.

"You," he said, pushing my hair behind my ear.

For the first time in a long time, I felt my insides flutter. A silly grin came over my face.

"Besides me," I blushed.

"I want to raise this baby with you because I know she'll do amazing things. I want to give her the childhood I didn't have," he said, tears falling from his eyes. "I want to be the husband to you that my dad never was to my mom. I want to prove to her that I learned something from her pain," he now was sobbing.

I hugged him tight, crying with him. He said "husband", and though, I have accepted the possibility of marriage not being in our future—it would be nice to honor our love in an official ceremony someday. I don't care if it's done by a priest or rabbi or guru or some bum on the street—I love Jordan so much and I want to celebrate it.

"You will prove it to her," I whispered. "She's happy when you're happy. Just be happy, Jordan. You know that involves Tortured, right?"

"I know," he said into my hair.

"We'll make it work. You being home with me and the baby and not having your music a part of this world will not make anyone happy."

I said these words into his ear before kissing right underneath it.

"I love you, Haley."

"I love you, too."

He pulled away from our embrace to kiss me softly. I wiped his tears and looked into his sad green eyes. I kissed him deeper and his arms slid down to my waist.

"I've missed you," I whispered, running my fingers up the back of his shirt and kissing his neck.

I pulled away from him and lifted my shirt over my head. He did the same with his shirt before our lips met again in a feverish kiss.

We made love slowly and gently; it was as if we were dancing, better yet, it was like we were having a conversation with our bodies. We were connected mind, body and soul.

Our moon isn't broken. It just lost its way for a while. One thing you can always count on is the moon being there; even when you can't see it. Just feel it. I love you.

♥Haley

Did you see the moon tonight while we made love? It was full and watching us proudly. I love you. Thank you for being everything I need and more. I got this for you as a belated birthday present. I know you're not into fancy jewelry, but I hope you like it. It's not a proposal. I hope that's okay. What this ring represents is my promise to you and our child. I promise to love you unconditionally and undaunted. I promise to be there for our baby with only love and warmth. Please wear this ring as a symbol of my commitment to you.

I love you, Haley.

-J

P.S. – I haven't had a cigarette in five days. I know how much you hate me smoking. And I know you never asked me to quit when we began dating, but I'm doing it for our baby.

Chapter 15

I woke up and it was somewhat cold in Jordan's bedroom. I pulled the blanket up to my shoulders and looked around the room. I expected Jordan to be awake already—either in the shower or getting breakfast; maybe writing by the window, which now I know what he had been writing those nights he couldn't sleep. Instead, Jordan was right next to me; sound asleep. I smiled to myself; happy he might finally be able to get some rest. I know he's been having difficulty. I've been there before.

Thinking about the night before, I turned to look at the alarm clock on the nightstand next to me. Jordan's journal was laid there open with something taped to it. Curiously, I picked up the notebook. I gasped seeing a beautiful white gold Claddagh ring. I pulled the ring off the page and freed it from the remaining Scotch tape. Running my thumb over the heart in the middle of the band, I felt a tear swiftly stream down my cheek.

I wiped the tears out of my eyes in order to read Jordan's note that was written above where the ring was taped to the book. This was his way of telling me how much he loves me. I don't care that it isn't a proposal; in some way, this is better.

The ring is perfect. I'm not into big diamonds or anything overdone. The Claddagh design means more to me than any piece of jewelry could.

Jordan and I are of Irish ancestry, so we are both represented in this ring. The symbolism of the heart in the middle is love, of course. The hands holding the heart represent friendship, and the crown stands for loyalty.

As I admired the ring, I felt Jordan move behind me. His arms wrapped around my stomach while his chin rested in the crook of my neck. I turned my face and kissed him, not caring that we both just woke up.

"I love you so much," I murmured against his lips.

His fingers stroked my jaw as he smiled at me.

"Do you like it?"

"I love it."

"How come you're not wearing it?"

I laughed, "I don't know how..."

"Um, well, you just slide it on your finger."

I laughed harder and lightly slapped his hand that was over my belly.

"I mean—which hand should I wear it on? It means something different if I wear it on my right or left."

"Doesn't the left mean you're taken?"

"Well, if I wear it on my right with the heart facing me, it means I've found love. If I wear it on the left facing out, it means I'm engaged. So, I think I should wear it on my right."

"What does it mean if you wear it with the heart facing you on your left hand?"

"That I'm married," I said, going to put the ring on my right hand.

Jordan pulled the ring out of my hand and took my left hand in his. He put his lips close to my ear as he slid the ring onto my finger.

"In every way that counts, we are married," he whispered.

I looked down at the ring with the heart facing me as I squeezed his hand and placed it back around my stomach. I couldn't form any words. I just lay my head back on his chest.

"Thank you for making today a little bit easier," he said,

and I could hear the change in his voice.

He was crying. Today is the funeral. Today Jordan has to officially say goodbye to his mother. All the pain he's held in for so long will be at the surface. In some way, he might even feel relief. Maggie is no longer suffering. She isn't feeling lonely or confused. She won't look at Jordan as a stranger on some days. She is his angel now. I told him that yesterday, and he didn't say anything, but he did pull me into his arms.

As Jordan and I sat there, holding each other—both mourning his mother, but relishing in our love—the most perfect thing happened. The baby—our baby kicked; right where Jordan's hand was as if it was a bull's-eye the baby was aiming for.

"Oh my God…" he jumped back.

I laughed, "Say hello to your baby."

Jordan rubbed my stomach in awe.

"That's so crazy… Does she move around a lot?"

"Not a whole lot yet, but this week, I'm starting to feel more movement."

"That's insane," he smiled.

We both agreed we should start getting ready—neither of us wanting to leave the safety of each other's arms. As soon as we left this house, pain would rain down on us.

When I sat up in bed to head to the shower, Jordan grabbed my hand and turned my arm toward him. The bruise Christian had left the other day was visible. With everything that happened, I had forgotten all about the engagement party and the disaster it turned out to be.

I didn't even realize Christian had left a bruise until now. I can't believe he grabbed me that hard. How could I explain this to Jordan?

"Did I do that last night?" he asked, concerned.

I shook my head, "No..."

Do I lie to him? Now wasn't the time to tell Jordan about Christian and Bippy.

"I bumped my arm the other day," I said, looking away. "You know how clumsy I am sometimes. Come on, we'll be late..."

I stood up and Jordan called out to me.

"There are fingerprints on your arm," he stood up as well and walked over to me.

He put his hands on either side of my face and forced me to look at him.

"Who hurt you?"

"The person got what he deserves," I told him. "I'm fine, I swear."

"Did Christian do this to you?" he asked.

I could see the anger rising in his face.

"He wasn't too happy with my badmouthing him to Tasha. She slapped him and he grabbed me by the arm after she ran off," I shrugged. "My father stepped in right away and let's just say that Christian's perfect image is ruined."

"I will kick his ass—"

"Jor, I'm fine."

Now, I was the one holding his face in my hands, trying to keep him calm.

"Christian knows better than to come near me ever again."

"You're keeping something from me," Jordan sighed.

"It's over. We really have to go..."

He looked at me and sighed, "Haley..."

"I'm fine. Really, all he did was grab my arm too roughly. I swear."

He reluctantly accepted my explanation for the time, but I hoped he wouldn't ask about it again. I didn't want to tell him just how badly Bippy and Christian screwed him over.

Jordan, Lacey and I rode in the limousine to the funeral home. The car was quiet; the silence heavy with grief. I knew Jordan wasn't expecting many people to show up. Aside from Tasha, the three of us were the only ones who even saw Maggie in the past eight years.

I had left a message for Tasha about Maggie. I wanted to tell her live, but I called her several times and she didn't answer. I knew she deserved to know and get the chance to pay her respects. I hoped she would be there. I just didn't know what kind of state Tasha would be in. Between Christian, the embarrassment of her engagement party gone wrong, and Maggie's death, she must be a mess.

We got out of the limo and walked into the funeral home. Jordan held my hand tensely. He was clean-shaven and in a suit; a contrast from yesterday's scruff and sweats.

We were the first ones to arrive. The smell of flowers was overwhelming. Jordan stared at the coffin as soon as we got into the viewing room. He held my hand tighter while putting a comforting arm around his aunt. I know he feels he needs to be strong for her. The three of us walked up to the casket together.

As hard as it is seeing someone's deceased body, Maggie looked beautiful. She looked like she had in that photo Jordan has of her on his nightstand. His hand trembled around mine. I rubbed my thumb against his skin and I heard an involuntary sob escape his lips.

Lacey was being the strong one. She patted his arm and suggested we say a prayer. She took Jordan's hand and reached for mine. I'm not an organized religion type of person. My family only went to church on holidays, if that. I do pray, though. I have conversations with God all the time. Jordan pretty much feels the same way I do. He believes in God and heaven, which

I'm sure gives him comfort at a time like now. It's a nice thought to think a person you love is in a place full of adoration and looking down on you from above after they die.

After Lacey finished saying the prayer, the old floor of the funeral home creaked from behind us. We turned and Andrew was standing there. I texted him the funeral information, but didn't know if he would be able to make it due to Chuck. I was relieved to see he came alone. Chuck would just make it harder on Jordan today.

Jordan wiped his eyes before letting go of mine and Lacey's hands. He walked over to his brother.

"I wish I got to know your mom better," Andrew said, looking up at Jordan with his big brown eyes. "Dad was telling me about her yesterday."

I wasn't sure how Jordan would react to hearing that.

"Thanks for coming, Drew," he said, before hugging him.

Cami and the band walked in at that moment. For the next ten minutes, hugs and condolences were shared. Sebastian walked over to me and hugged me tightly.

"How are you doing?"

"Okay."

"I never got to congratulate you on the baby," he said.

"Thank you," I smiled. "I'm sure it wasn't exactly good news to you guys when Jordan announced he was quitting," I sighed, rolling my eyes.

"I assumed you wouldn't approve," he shook his head.

"He was just being Jordan," I laughed, watching Jordan and Danny talking. "I'm glad he rethought that decision. I hope you guys don't have any hard feelings toward him."

I looked at Sebastian confidently. He shrugged his shoulders.

"He doesn't tell us much, but I know he has a lot on his

plate. That's why I'm happy he has you. He's a lucky guy," Seb smiled.

"Thank you," I returned his smile.

"Now, if only I can find someone as cool as you," he winked.

"You'll find someone way cooler," I laughed.

Just then, Tasha walked into the room. Jordan immediately went over to her and pulled her into a hug. She was crying on his shoulder. I excused myself and walked over to them.

They were still hugging and Tasha was crying hard.

"Thank you for being there for her," Jordan whispered. "You were a good friend to her."

"I can't believe she's gone," she said. "I'm so sorry, Jordan."

She noticed me then and reached a hand out to me. I took it before wrapping my arms around Jordan from behind. The three of us hugged.

A minute later, Jordan moved out of the way to give Tasha and me a moment.

"Are you okay?" I asked.

She laughed and wiped her tears. I knew it was a stupid question. It's funny that whenever someone cries or goes through something terrible, our natural instinct is to ask if that person is okay. Of course they're not! Logically, we know the answer to the question, but we want to hear the word "yes" escape their lips—to ease our own mind.

Human nature is to hate seeing others in pain. I hated seeing Jordan like this; just like he must have hated to see me sick all the time and upset with him. He was trying to make it okay for me. The thing I realize though is if you're not happy, you can't make someone else happy.

Christian isn't happy. He always wants what he can't have. He wanted Bippy because she was with Jordan and he wanted me because I didn't want him. He could have never made Tasha happy because of that need, even if he tried—which of course he didn't try.

"No," Tasha sighed, answering my question honestly. "But I will be—someday."

"I'm so sorry..."

"Haley, do not apologize for Christian."

"But it's my fault."

"What's your fault?" Tasha asked. "Christian never getting over you? Christian having a history with Bippy and not telling me? Or Christian being a complete asshole and me not noticing?"

I just looked at her.

"You have bad timing—that's the only thing you're guilty of. You could have smacked me upside the head for ever agreeing to marry him. For getting involved with him—"

"You knew I wasn't exactly Team Christian!" I pointed out.

She sighed, "I know, I know. But this is my fault as much as his. I saw all of the warning signs. I just—I ignored them, just like with Ricky. I keep falling for these guys who are over confident and macho, but want to hold me back."

I nodded.

"See, you always thought I was the secure, confident one..." she sighed.

"You are."

"Yes—but I still allow myself to be taken in by jerks. At least you only keep people in your life who aren't out to bring you down. I respect that. You never gave into Christian just because he liked you. You never tried to be like Bippy and those bimbos just to be accepted. You don't pretend to be someone else with

Jordan. You are who you are with everyone—and that's why people are drawn to you."

I stared at my best friend with a blank look on. Here she is going through what probably is the most terrible experience of her life, and she's boosting my ego. She's telling me things about myself that I never thought much of.

I hugged her.

"Thank you for saying all of that. You're not giving yourself enough credit, though," I assured her. "People are drawn to you, too. You don't always have to try so hard, you know? Remember, you can't be tamed—and that's what I love about you. You'll find a guy who respects that rather than sees it as a challenge."

She squeezed me tighter and it felt good to have my best friend back completely. She wasn't in the clutches of some vulture; she didn't think I was trying to steal her happy ending. We pulled apart and Tasha went to say hello to the band.

I saw Drew sitting by himself and I walked over to him and sat beside him.

"Where's your dad?"

"He thought it would be better if he didn't come."

I nodded, "Are you okay?"

"Do you think Jordan resents me?"

"What?" I asked, surprised.

He looked at me, "Dad told me the entire story. I mean, I kind of figured he left Maggie for my mom, but I didn't know I was born while they were still married."

"Jordan doesn't resent you," I sighed. "In his eyes, you're the best thing your father has ever given him."

Andrew smiled at that.

"I told Dad I hate him."

"Why?"

He shrugged, “Because I do. He chased Jordan away. He cheated on Maggie. He’s not a nice person.”

I put my arm around Andrew.

“Your father loves you and Jordan. He just... No one is all good or all bad, Andrew. Sometimes you just have to accept things for the way they are.”

Andrew put his head on my shoulder. I wanted to cry. I didn’t know what to do to make everything better, especially for Andrew. He’s stuck living with a man he hates. I didn’t know how to advise him. Part of me thinks Jordan shouldn’t cut his father out of his life, but then when I see how Chuck acts toward him, a bigger part of me thinks, he’s better off without him.

It’s hard for me to think like that. I love both my parents, and sure, there’s plenty of things I don’t like about them—but generally, I think they’re good people underneath their snobbish and close-minded ways. However, if Chuck was my dad—I think I would have gotten as far away from him as possible, like Jordan did.

Jordan once compared his relationship with Chuck to an abusive spouse. The world would tell you to get out of a relationship where you were physically or verbally abused. Why is it that those same people think differently when it’s a parent and child relationship? It’s so true. A parent is supposed to love their child unconditionally. They’re supposed to create a safe, warm environment for a child to come home to. Chuck didn’t provide that for his children. Growing up, they feared him or felt completely rejected by him.

I think of my child and as much as the pregnancy complicated my life at first—I never doubted how much I would love this baby. I worried about dreams being put on hold. I worried about toys lying around the house and endless diapers. I worried about being overprotective like my parents were, or my kid meeting the wrong types of people in this world, or not making any friends at all. Never once did I worry I would abuse my child in any way. I couldn't even imagine…

"Haley…"

I felt a hand on my shoulder. I was so deep in thought I didn't hear my parents come in. I stood up and felt a sharp pain in my side. I winced before hugging my father, thankful he and Mom came.

"Thank you guys for coming," I said, squeezing him, grateful for my parents suddenly.

I cried softly on his shoulder and when I pulled away, I saw my mother hugging Jordan.

"How's Jordan doing?" Dad whispered.

"Terrible," I sighed.

"He's lucky to have you," he smiled.

I smiled back at him, "I'm lucky to have him."

Jordan and Mom walked over. She was holding his arm in a comforting sort of way. He had a small smile on his face, though his eyes were weary. Showing he is vulnerable to most people is extremely hard for Jordan.

My father looked at Jordan, who offered him his hand.

"I'm so sorry, son," Dad said before hugging him.

Jordan was surprised, I'm sure. I hugged my mother, desperately needing the warmth that comes with a maternal hug.

"How are you feeling?"

"Okay," I said.

"Are you taking care of yourself?" she asked, pulling away looking concerned.

I nodded and smiled reassuringly.

"Thank you both for coming," Jordan said, looking at my parents. "It means a lot."

After the funeral home, we headed to the church. I sat

next to Jordan and my mother sat on the other side of me. I felt her grab my hand. I looked down and realized she was staring at my ring. The look on her face was priceless. I held back a laugh and shook my head to tell her I wasn't engaged. She almost looked disappointed and relieved at the same time.

There were parts during the mass that were difficult for Jordan. He would squeeze my hand tighter and keep his head down. His entire face was bright red. I put my head on his shoulder as a more subtle way of hugging him.

After the mass, we headed to the cemetery. Why were funerals so agonizingly long? There were a bunch of steps of saying goodbye that were the most painful. I couldn't imagine if there was more than one day of viewing at the funeral home like so many people do. To me, for the family involved—it is misery.

On the ride over to the cemetery, Lacey told me about her parents—Jordan's grandparents—being buried there. She went on to list other relatives of theirs also lain to rest long before Jordan was born.

It was upsetting to hear; to know my child wouldn't know many relatives from Jordan's side. Drew would be the only uncle. Chuck and Coryn would be considered grandparents? I don't think Jordan will allow that. Christian would be a cousin to my baby? You can bet he will not be spending any time around my child or me anymore.

As we all walked to the gravesite, I looked around at the other members of Tortured and smiled. They will be part of this kid's family, and so will my parents, and Tasha and Meghan—who will dress him or her up in all of the latest fashions.

For a moment, I imagined how good Luke and Laney would be with a kid. I haven't seen Luke since I humiliatingly kissed him. I didn't know how awkward I will be around him when I do see him again.

We stood around the coffin with roses in our hands. The priest said a prayer before we placed the roses on top of the coffin. Jordan was last to place his rose.

"Always in my heart, Mom," he choked out.

He turned around and hugged me tightly. When we pulled apart, we both noticed Chuck standing a few feet away.

"Jordan, don't fight, okay? Don't do this to yourself today," I told him.

He sighed before heading in his father's direction.

"I just want to pay my respects," Chuck said softly.

Jordan stepped aside without saying a word. He shoved his hands in his pockets and we all stood in silence as Chuck walked over to the coffin.

"Let's get going," Danny said to Cami.

"We're having everyone back at the house," Lacey told them.

"Thank you," Cami smiled.

As everyone walked by me, they rubbed my shoulder or smiled at me. I wasn't used to seeing this particular group of people so somber. My parents walked over to me.

"We're going to head over to Lacey's," Mom said.

"Do you know how to get there?"

"Sebastian said we could follow them," Dad assured me and kissed my forehead.

Lacey walked over to me and I put my arm around her. Drew was next to Jordan almost protectively. Chuck was standing with his hand on top of the coffin in his expensive coat with his head hung down. He was crying and I'm sure we were all in shock.

The great titan Chuck Ashton was showing weakness—or at least what he saw as weakness. For the first time in a long time, his sons were finally able to see some humanity within him.

A few minutes passed and Chuck was still crying. Suddenly, Jordan walked over to Chuck and put his hand on his shoulder. They both stood there for a few more minutes.

Chuck turned toward Jordan and I heard the words "thank you" escape his lips before he walked away from him. We all watched his figure retreating.

Jordan looked over at me and I offered him a smile; I was about to walk toward him when the baby kicked and then a shooting pain ran down my spine. My body physically clenched and I doubled over in pain.

Jordan and Drew ran over to me as Lacey held onto my arm.

"Are you okay?" Lacey asked.

"What's wrong?" Jordan asked worriedly.

I straightened up and took a deep breath.

"The baby is beating me up," I winced, and then the pain passed. "Come on," I said. "Everyone will be waiting for us."

"Haley…" Jordan sighed, with the look he had on earlier when I was trying to elude him away from the Christian topic.

"I'm fine," I assured him.

He looked at me wearily and I rolled my eyes.

"It was just a strong kick."

Once we were back at Lacey's, I felt exhausted. I wanted out of my dress and into pajamas. I sat on the couch with Darren, who was talking about a new Vince Vaughn movie coming out. The band loved any movie the actor made and it was their tradition to go to the movies together any time one was released.

Tasha and Sebastian were in a deep conversation, and I watched on curiously. Jordan had mentioned to me that Sebie hit on Tasha when he first met her. She turned him down since she had a boyfriend at the time. I never asked her if she would have gone out with him had Ricky not been in the picture.

Danny walked over and jumped into mine and Darren's conversation. They began reciting lines from "Wedding Crashers" as I half paid attention. I wanted to take a nap. I felt like I could fall asleep right then and there. I noticed Jordan and my mother talking near the kitchen. They looked tense—we did just come from a funeral, so I shouldn't be surprised, but I was. I wanted to know what they were discussing.

"Haley, are you okay?" Darren asked.

"I'm just tired," I said.

"Go lie down. You look drained," Danny stated.

"I'll be okay—" I said, standing up and wincing.

Danny grabbed my arm to stabilize me.

"Go to bed. Jordan will understand."

"Come get me in a few minutes, okay?"

"Sure," Danny smiled.

I felt like I could barely stand as I made my way upstairs. I didn't even remember getting into bed. Next thing I knew, it was dark. I turned on the light and Jordan was lying in bed next to me, but I don't think he was able to sleep.

"Are you okay?" he asked.

"I'm fine. I'm sorry—I was just really tired."

He sat up and ran a hand through his hair.

"Why didn't you tell me how miraculous you getting pregnant is?"

He looked annoyed and worried.

"What are you talking about?" I asked.

"Your mother told me…about the tumors."

I sighed, "They were benign."

When I was fourteen, I had quite a few problems with my menstrual cycle. It was discovered that I had uterine fibroids. They were noncancerous, but caused me pain and discomfort.

My cycle was still slightly irregular after the fibroids were removed, but the pain was gone. It was a scary time in my life that I tend to block out. My parents were nervous wrecks and I was frightened throughout the whole process. I didn't understand why Mom told Jordan—especially the day of his mother's funeral.

"Haley, don't you think I should know about these things?"

"Jordan, I'm fine. The tumors were removed. Do you tell me about every injury or health problem you've ever had?"

"I broke my nose when I was twelve. Happy?" he sighed.

"How?"

"Haley, stop brushing this off. You didn't tell me you were told you couldn't have kids."

"What?!" I practically yelled. "Just because I had a tumor doesn't mean—"

"Your Mom said..." he sighed. "She said the doctor told her it would be difficult for you to conceive."

I looked at him confused.

"Why would she tell you that?"

"Why didn't *you* tell me that, Haley?" he asked, infuriated.

"Because I didn't know that!"

"What?"

"I was a kid," I shrugged. "They never told me."

I didn't know how to feel about the information. Supposedly, my doctor told my parents to write off being grandparents yet here I am almost five months pregnant.

I was crying when I looked back up at Jordan. He hugged me.

"Our baby proved doctors wrong," I laughed and when I pulled away, Jordan looked incredibly serious still.

"I made an appointment for you tomorrow morning."

“What?” I looked at him strangely.

“Dr. Seodat’s office said she had an opening.”

“But I’m not scheduled to see her until a couple of weeks.”

“Haley, you’ve been in pain.”

“Jor,” I laughed his concern off. “It is normal to feel discomfort when you’re pregnant. I’m fine,” I waved him off.

“You’re not fine, Haley.”

I stared at him, “Why did my mother tell you this? She has you all worried over nothing.”

“It’s not nothing. We’re all worried. Everyone sees it, Hale. They see you’re in pain. You’re always tired. Please, for me, just get checked out.”

Jordan looked insanely worried, and I didn’t know how to feel. I was still reeling that I beat the odds and am pregnant. I felt like I was being kept in the dark about my own health. I had seen Dr. Seodat’s colleague for my last appointment. She did the ultrasound and didn’t see anything wrong with the baby. I held onto that thought.

I was angry with my mother for making Jordan panic like this—it isn’t his nature like it is hers. I was angry at her for keeping things from me. While I fumed over my mother’s inconvenient timing, Jordan’s lips were on mine.

“Please?”

I realized I hadn’t answered him.

“Okay.”

“Thank you. Are you hungry?”

“A little.”

“I’ll get you something,” he said, getting off the bed.

I grabbed his hand.

“How are you doing?”

“I’ll be better once we see the doctor.”

“Jordan, seriously—I’m fine. You need to focus on

yourself."

"So do you," he said before walking out of the room.

I sighed and lay back down in the bed. No wonder why Mom and Dad were so pleasant about the baby news. They thought any chance of me getting pregnant was impossible!

I looked down at my belly and lifted my shirt. Sometimes I felt like my stomach protruded much more than it actually did. It still wasn't obvious I was pregnant, and for some reason, that made me cry.

It made me feel like the baby isn't real; that Jordan and I went through this tough time for nothing.

I then remembered all those nightmares Jordan has been having. The one where Bippy told him I killed our baby came to mind, and now I am more than a bit worried at the thought. What does Bippy know anyway? It was just an anxious dream that doesn't mean anything, right?

February 15th

Haley,

Thank you for being strong for me. Thank you for taking care of me. Please let me take care of you now. I have to travel with the band for the next couple of weeks to promote your song. Here's my real letter to you...

Take care of yourself. I know the stress I put you through couldn't have helped your condition. I know you're in denial that anything is wrong, but I've seen you cover up the pain. I've seen you so weak you can barely move. No matter what, I'm here for you. Say the word and I'll have the band promote the song without me. It would be kinda poetic to take care of the girl behind the song instead of eating up all the media attention like any other sellout. Really, you'd be helping to protect my image. *wink*

Love,

Jordan

Jordan,

Is this a new tradition of ours? Your songbook has become nothing but a book of love letters to each other. Are you okay with THAT image? ☺ You're a true romantic. Shh, I won't tell.

I just wish you wouldn't worry. Dr. Seodat will tell me I'm fine, and the baby is fine. You can go promote MY letter to the world and tell them how much I inspired you. Haha...we all know that's the other way around.

I took pictures of you while you slept last night, even though neither of us slept much. I couldn't help it. I found myself imagining what our baby would look like while watching you.

Will he or she have my blue eyes or your green ones? Will he or she be pale or a little tan like you? Blonde or Brunette? We will be fine. We both love you and now we have Grandma Maggie protecting us.

♥Haley

Chapter 16

Dr. Colette Seodat's office was different than most obstetric clinics, than most doctors' offices period. Instead of white walls lined with advertisements for birth control pills and STD prevention information, there were framed photos of pleasant things. One large painting was of the Boston skyline. A few other frames held various landscape photos while the rest of the frames held images of babies and children with their mothers. I loved Anne Geddes work, and many of the photographs were hers. The walls were warm, pastel colors and various plants were placed around the receptionist's desk and waiting area.

My family physician from Bakersfield recommended Dr. Seodat when I first began school in Boston. My doctor went to medical school with Dr. Seodat's father-in-law. Before I had gotten pregnant, I only had routine exams while I was in school in Boston, which had only been a couple of times. Dr. Seodat had made a lasting impression on me, though. She has a loud, entertaining and take charge personality. She always makes me feel comfortable even though no woman looks forward to seeing her OBGYN.

Jordan bounced his knee as he sat next to me. I watched him for a moment. He was terrified, and that surprised me. I know men don't like to be part of these visits. I know no one likes seeing the doctor, but I had never seen such worry on his face. How badly did my mother scare him? Or maybe he was thinking his dreams were a premonition for something bad to happen. In his journal, he mentioned fears of losing me and a baby all over again. I wonder if the baby in the nightmares was representing Bippy's unborn child or ours.

Just then, Mom walked in. I glared at her.

"What are you doing here?"

I know it came out hatefully, but I was annoyed she would put such worry on Jordan while he was still grieving his mother. I know she didn't mean to hurt anyone, but she needed to stop her neurotic perturbation.

"I'm your mother. I want to be here for you," Mom said, reaching her arms out to me, expecting me to run into them in tears.

I shook my head.

"You have a lot of explaining to do," I said, folding my arms over my chest.

"I'm sorry I never told you that having children was a slim chance for you," she said, as one woman looked up from her magazine intrusively.

"Yeah, well, I guess I'm glad you didn't. Then, I would have worried for nothing," I sighed, looking at her.

"Haley, I am so happy that you were blessed to not have to go through that nightmare of not being able to conceive, but..." Mom said swallowing. "I spoke with Dr. Byrnes and he insisted you see Dr. Seodat immediately."

"I just saw her colleague a couple of weeks ago—I was fine," I shrugged.

Jordan stood up, "But you said you only got a sonogram, right?"

"Yeah, so?"

Mom looked at me worriedly.

"They can't see everything from a sonogram, sweetie."

I looked at both Jordan and my mother's faces. They are scared I am going to lose the baby. They are afraid they are going to lose me. They didn't want to tell me that, but it was hard to hide the look of terror on their faces. I felt myself begin to worry. With every passing day, I imagined my baby—how it will feel to hold it for the first time, what he or she will look like, how its first word sounded, what kind of personality it will have. It never crossed my mind that my baby will not be born.

I glared at both of them for thinking such terrible thoughts. Where is their faith? Where is their positive thinking? What happened to my laid back boyfriend? He should have brushed my mother's worries off, not take them on! I was feeling so much all at once—mostly anger and worry, though. I wanted to get this check-up over with so I could hear Dr. Seodat tell them they are absurd for worrying—that my baby and I are doing wonderfully.

The pain—that is stress related. That will subside now that Jordan and I are okay and the shock of the pregnancy has worn off. Somewhere inside of me, though, wondered if stress alone could cause such terrible pains and weakness, like I am experiencing.

"Haley Foster?" The nurse at the reception desk called.

I turned around to look at her.

"Right here."

"You can come with me," she smiled.

I looked back at Jordan and Mom who were about to walk in with me.

"Can I please do this alone?" I asked with a sigh.

"Haley," Mom cocked her head to the side.

"I promise I will tell you whatever the doctor says. I just—I need some breathing room for this. I can't look at the two of you expecting the worst," I explained.

"Hale, I'm not expecting the worst," Jordan sighed, stepping closer. "I just want you to take every precaution."

I nodded and offered them a smile before following the nurse through a door. We walked down a hallway and into an examining room. Unlike the waiting room, this one made me more uncomfortable with the stirrups attached to the chair reminding me why I was there. The nurse instructed me to change into the paper gown before she stepped out.

The room was cold as I undressed. I quickly put the gown on; not that it offered any warmth. A couple of minutes later, there was a light rapping at the door and Dr. Seodat poked her head inside.

"Are you ready for me?"

She asked me as if she were asking if I were ready to go on a roller coaster. I nodded and she walked in all the way before shutting the door. She always looked so young, but I never asked her age. By looking at her, I would think she is in her early thirties, but considering how renowned she is in her field, I'd say she has a few more years on her.

In some ways, Dr. Seodat reminds me of how Tasha will be in a few years. They both have an outgoing quality about them and a no-nonsense approach to things—yet always make jokes.

"How are you and the little one doing?" Dr. Seodat asked, sitting down in a short stool with wheels.

She rolled over to me with a big smile and I was happy someone was looking at me with confidence today.

"I think we're doing well," I said.

Her face fell.

"Uh-oh, what's up?"

"My mom is making a big deal about a preexisting condition I had as a teenager, but I've been checked out a couple of times and no one has…"

"Wait, what condition?" Dr. Seodat asked, looking down at her chart.

"I had uterine fibroids that were removed eight years ago."

She looked down at my medical history and began thumbing through the pages.

"I see… Your old doctor did not send me that information," she sighed, obviously frustrated she wasn't aware of my full history. "How come you didn't say anything?"

"Honestly, I didn't think about it," I shrugged. "It was so long ago. My mother literally just told me I am lucky I was able to get pregnant. Should I be worried?"

Dr. Seodat kind of shook her head from side to side.

"It's possible you can have a completely healthy pregnancy with no complications. However, considering your problems with your menstrual cycle in the past, you might feel extra discomfort and pain. Have you experienced any pain?"

I nodded, "I have a lot of back pain. I'm also really tired sometimes to the point where I think I'll pass out."

Dr. Seodat nodded and took down notes before tossing her clipboard and pen aside.

"Let's ease your mind and check everything out, okay?" she smiled.

"Okay," I smiled back.

I already felt better. We went through several routine procedures and Dr. Seodat showed no signs of something being wrong aside from my blood pressure being higher than usual. After she finished examining me, I eagerly waited for her to say something.

"Are you still having severe morning sickness?" She asked, holding her clipboard again.

"Um, it's gotten better," I said, trying to remember the last time I vomited, which was a few days ago. "Once in a while it's still pretty bad."

"Headaches?"

"Sometimes," I nodded.

"Dizziness?"

"Yeah, when I'm tired."

"Swelling?"

"In my feet."

This questioning was the most serious Dr. Seodat has been the entire appointment. During the examination, she was singing songs and we were sharing stories about our lives while laughing. She really took my mind off everything.

"I'm going to run these samples to the lab," she said, standing up with two vials of my blood and one of my urine. "I know your next sonogram is next week, but I want to make sure everything's okay now. Maybe you want your boyfriend and mother in here for that?" she asked with a smile.

I smiled in return, "I think they would both be happy to be included in that."

"I'll have the nurse tell them to come in. Be right back—don't go streaking down the halls or anything," she warned.

I laughed, "You know I'm quite the exhibitionist."

She chuckled at my joke considering I held my gown closed as much as I could during the check-up—even while sitting down.

A few minutes later, Jordan and Mom walked in.

"How'd everything go?" he asked, draping an arm over the examining chair while resting the other over my belly.

"So far so good. We have to wait on a couple of tests, but she didn't seem too concerned," I said.

Though now I worried Dr. Seodat just had a brilliant poker face.

"So, the fibroids didn't come back, right?" Mom wondered.

"No—I have some uterine scarring, though. I don't know if that's what's causing the pain or something..." I shrugged.

"Haley, you have to ask more questions," Mom groaned. "This is important."

"Mom, I know it's important, okay?" I looked at her, wanting to cry. "Once the results are in, Dr. Seodat said she will answer all my questions. Since you think I don't take my baby seriously, then why don't you ask for me and keep treating me like *I'm* still a baby?" I asked, getting worked up.

Jordan put a hand on my shoulder.

"Calm down," he said softly.

Mom had her hands on her hips.

"I know you take this baby seriously, but I am concerned about you, too. You will always be my baby, Haley, and I don't want to lose you because you had a slip up with your boyfriend," she said.

I wanted to yell at her. How dare she disregard this baby as if it is a mistake. No, the baby wasn't part of our plan—not now anyway—but obviously he or she is meant to be. Jordan and I are always extremely careful when it came to sex; using more than one form of birth control most of the time.

To be honest, with all the precautions we took, I'm a bit amazed how it happened. I know there's no foolproof form of protection, but what are the odds that my pill and the condom both didn't do the trick? Jordan did wonder if the condom broke one time, but even still, this baby must really want to be born. I especially think so after learning the difficulty level it was for me to get pregnant due to my past health issues.

"Enough!" Jordan yelled at my mother. "Elena, do you think this is helping? Your daughter is crying. She's had a lousy first few months, and maybe that was partly because of me, but I promise I'm here for her. I can take care of her," Jordan said, as if telling her to back off from taking responsibility for me.

"Oh, you can take care of her?" Mom laughed. "By going off on your little tours while my daughter stays home waiting?"

Jordan sighed and I groaned.

"Get out, Mom."

"What?"

"If you can't be supportive, then I don't want you here. I will not tolerate you talking down to me and I definitely won't allow you to talk to my boyfriend like that. When no one else paid attention to my needs, Jordan did. I'm sorry if you see that as a threat, but you can't keep me in this protective bubble forever."

Jordan looked at me surprised. Mom sighed and plopped down in Dr. Seodat's stool. The wheels moved a little as she did—startling her. I almost laughed, and so did Jordan.

"I'm sorry," she said. "I'm just—I love you and I want you to be safe," she looked at me before turning toward Jordan. "I didn't mean... I think you're a great guy who loves her very much."

"I do. I'm not perfect. I don't have the ideal job, but we'll make it work."

Mom smiled and just then Dr. Seodat walked in.

"Well, I hope you all kissed and made up," she said, raising an eyebrow at the three of us.

Mom blushed and Jordan laughed.

"You must be the Dad," she smiled.

"Jordan," he said, shaking her hand.

"Colette Seodat."

She leaned toward me, "You're right—he is gorgeous."

I laughed while Jordan smirked.

"He knows it, too," I rolled my eyes.

Dr. Seodat laughed loudly, startling Jordan and Mom who were not used to her boisterous cackle.

"Let's get a look at this baby of yours," she said before going to wash her hands.

A minute later, my belly was exposed and the cold gel was being applied. Mom peeked over.

"Wow, you're starting to show," she smiled.

I laughed, "I know."

Earlier I felt my baby bump was not enough, but it made me happy that my mother could notice—even if it took me baring my stomach for that to happen.

Dr. Seodat moved the transducer around my abdomen. On the ultrasound screen was my baby, which looked noticeably bigger since my last sonogram. Jordan leaned in closer.

"That's her!" he smiled, amazed.

"Her?" Mom asked. "You didn't tell me you knew!"

I laughed, "We don't know, Mom. Jordan thinks it's a girl."

"Why's that?" Dr. Seodat asked.

"I had a dream a while back about it being a girl," he said, getting quiet immediately following that.

I knew he was thinking about that dream he had where Bippy told him I killed our baby. He thought I was going to lose the baby. I hoped that dream was just a coincidence and not anything more.

I'll admit part of me believes in messages through dreams. Jordan's dream could be some form of clairvoyance or it could just be his own anxiety coming through.

"My mom also thought it will be a girl," Jordan said softly.

I took his hand in mine and squeezed it.

"Well, would you like to know if your mother was right?" Dr. Seodat asked.

I looked over at Jordan and we both answered a simultaneous yes.

"It's a boy," she said.

"Really?" We both asked simultaneously again, almost shocked.

Mom laughed, "What are you two twins now?"

"Oh, and you're having twins," Dr. Seodat said.

"What?" Jordan practically yelled.

"You're lying," I shook my head, catching on.

"Yeah…" she said followed by another one of her enormous laughs. "You are having just one baby girl," she smiled.

"It is a girl?" Jordan asked as I gasped.

"Yup. Grandma was right," Dr. Seodat said as we all stared at the screen.

"A little girl," Mom gushed.

"Congratulations," Dr. Seodat said.

"Is she doing okay?" I asked.

"She seems to be a healthy, feisty little thing… Look at her moving her legs already."

"She takes after you," Jordan said.

"Uh, excuse me? You're pretty feisty yourself," I stuck my tongue at him.

"So, everything is okay then?" Mom asked.

"I'm going to check on the results. Haley, why don't you get dressed and meet me in my office."

Dr. Seodat walked out and Jordan kissed me softly. He ran his fingers through my hair.

"I'm so excited to raise this baby with you. She's our little miracle."

I kissed him a little more passionately than he did me, not caring if my mother was in the room.

"She is our miracle."

About ten minutes later, the three of us sat in Dr. Seodat's office. I was nervous now. Why did she want to see me in her office? What was wrong? How serious was it?

I looked at the photo on the desk. It was of Dr. Seodat with her husband and three children. She has a beautiful family. For some reason, seeing she has children herself made me feel even more confident in her as my doctor. Doctors could have all the knowledge in the world, but still not understand where a patient is coming from—and I need to have that.

Dr. Seodat walked in and sat behind her desk. Jordan was standing by the wall staring at a picture of Dr. Seodat and a red Ferrari.

"Is this your car?"

"Yup," Dr. Seodat answered with a grin.

"Nice," Jordan said before sitting down next to me.

"Okay, Haley...so," she said, folding her hands and looking at me. "It's still on the earlier side to detect this, but you are showing certain signs of preeclampsia."

"Pre-what-a?" Jordan asked.

"Preeclampsia or toxemia."

"I've heard of that before," I said, remembering it wasn't uncommon.

"What caused it?" Mom wondered.

"There's no proven cause, but the scarring on your uterus from the fibroid removal could have played a factor in it."

"Was there something I could have done to prevent it?" I asked, afraid I did something wrong.

"No, sweetie," Dr. Seodat assured me. "Pregnancy messes with your body in a lot of ways. Usually, you can't diagnose preeclampsia until the end of your second trimester, but you fit all of the signs to a tee."

"How dangerous is this?" Jordan asked.

He was more worried than any of us at this point, not having ever heard the term I was being diagnosed with before.

"In most cases, it usually isn't dangerous as long as you can hold the baby to term. However, considering Haley's symptoms are more severe so early on, we need to take some precautions."

"Like?" I wondered.

"Bed rest."

"Bed rest?" I asked. "For how long?"

"Well, as it gets closer to your due date—I want you off your feet more and more," Dr. Seodat explained. "For now, you can follow your normal routine as long as it doesn't involve a lot of physical or stressful activity. Just be mindful of your blood pressure."

I wasn't too happy about this treatment plan. I know everyone will be on high alert and will want to keep me in bed as much as possible. Dr. Seodat also told me to drink lots of water, but what concerned me most was the decision to schedule a cesarean delivery for me. I know they are common procedures, but I also know that something could go wrong. I have been doing my research on pregnancy. I read that there could be breathing complications for babies who are delivered by cesarean.

"Are you sure that will be necessary?" I asked.

"Haley, to be blunt—you're somewhat of a high risk pregnancy. The easier we make the delivery on you, the less chance we have of causing harm to you and the baby."

I nodded. I began to think about school and events. Will I have to drop out of school so close to graduation? According to Dr. Seodat, by my sixth month, I will be limited to bed only. That means no traveling to New York or Vermont or to wherever Jordan may be.

After leaving the doctor's office, Mom hugged me.

"See, it wasn't so bad."

"But it could have been," she sighed.

"Do me a favor and be truthful with me next time it concerns my health—even if you think it will upset me," I groaned.

"I'm sorry," she said. "So, I was thinking..."

"I'm not coming home," I cut her off, knowing exactly what she was planning.

"Then I'll come up here."

"Mom, no. I'll be fine."

"Haley, maybe it's a good idea," Jordan said.

I glared at him.

"I have Tasha and Jordan won't be gone my whole pregnancy."

"I would feel better if—"

"Mom, I can handle myself."

"Haley, can I talk to you?" Jordan asked, pulling me to the side.

"Jordan, I know you're worried, but I don't want to be watched constantly."

"She is your mother, Haley. She loves you and she's the only mother you'll ever have. Let her be here for you, for her peace of mind, for mine...and for yours. There are times in your life when you need to allow people to help you. I've learned that lesson from you. Please," he said.

He was so insistent and I knew it had a lot to do with his own mother. I didn't ever think about how my parents wouldn't be here one day. I shouldn't just cast them aside because they bug me. There is a time to be independent and there is a time when you need to know someone is there to protect you.

If I was busy protecting my child, I suppose I did need

someone watching my back, too. I know Jordan wished he could stay with me every day of my pregnancy, but he had committed to this tour, and was able to finagle several months off to spend with me and the baby.

Walking back over to my mother, I told her she could stay. I didn't know how it was all going to work. Tasha isn't exactly my mother's favorite person and vice versa. At least I have an advantage. I can easily pull the blood pressure card out whenever they argued.

March 17, 2012

Hey Mr. Rock Star! Happy St. Patrick's Day! I'm looking at my Claddagh ring as I write this and missing you. Mom says hi. She thinks it's adorable that we write to each other like this even though we talk every night.

I still have your Late Show appearance on the DVR saved and I've been playing the album for the baby except for some of the angrier songs. We don't want an Emo child now, do we? You're officially big time! Don't worry—you're not a sellout. The only way you could sellout is if you forgot who you were and what this is about—your music; your passion; your fans.

I was talking to our daughter last night and she told me she thinks you're the coolest Dad ever. I have to agree ☺

Anyway, I have to get going. Doctor's appointment today. You won't believe how much I'm showing now! I'll text you a picture of my belly soon. In no time, my stomach is going to be past my boobs. ☹ That's something a girl never wants to happen. It's worth it, though.

Miss you. Can't wait to see what you have to say. I'm mailing the book to Miami today. Love you.

♥Haley

April 3rd

Hey Sexy Girlfriend! I don't care if your belly sticks out more than your boobs—you'll always be hot with those flirty blue eyes and that pretty smile of yours... Am I making you blush yet? Don't let your mom read this, ha-ha! Tell her I say hi.

We're in Philly. Getting closer to you. I'm so happy I get to come home next week. I miss you and that little alien inside of you! Thanks for sending me the new sonogram. I showed the guys and they actually cooed like a bunch of saps at how it looked like she was waving.

I wish I could make this letter longer, but we're about to perform on the Helen Beals Show! I never watch these types of things, but she has the #1 morning show in the country now.

We just met Helen—she asked me about "Haley's Letter" and wanted to know the girl behind it. I told her about you and the baby. She wants to see pictures once she's born, ha-ha! This kid is going to be a star, you know? I'll mail the book out tonight to hold you over until I get back. Miss you.

Love, J

Chapter 17

I sat on the couch watching some rerun of a CW show while Tasha did crunches on our living room floor. Mom had gone to Bakersfield for about a week to see Dad and get some work done. Having her here isn't as bad as I thought it would be. Sure, she jumped over every move I made, but I think this time together has been good for us.

I am now six months pregnant and it is getting harder for me to do my normal routine. Dr. Seodat has been putting more restrictions on me. I won't be returning to school, and that upset me. I want to at least get my degree before the baby is born. Luckily, I did finish my internship so I'll still get the credits for it.

Jordan has been gone for over a month straight, and I am beginning to miss him terribly—not just superficially. It's funny when you hear couples who have just fallen in love gush. On Facebook, Meghan and Mike—who recently got back together—are updating their statuses frequently about how much they love one another. They go on about how much they miss each other when one is at school or work.

In my bitterness of missing Jordan, I feel like saying "try going weeks without seeing your boyfriend and then we'll talk". It's one thing to want to see someone everyday and enjoy it; it's entirely another thing to physically and emotionally need to see someone because you feel something is missing.

Despite this feeling, part of me secretly loves the separation. Not because I want Jordan gone, but because of the excitement of him coming home tomorrow. I love the letters we've been sending each other. I love the late night phone calls with a whispered "I love you" at the end so he doesn't wake the rest of the band on the tour bus. I am thrilled at the fact that Jordan is following through with what he began with Tortured.

He keeps promising me I'll get to follow through with my dreams, too. I told him I already am.

"Haley, a person can't be your dream," he told me.

He is right. To rely on a person for fulfillment is setting yourself up for torment. We both believe in that.

"You're not my dream, Jordan. Dream man, yes," I laughed.

"You are so cheesy," he said, rolling his eyes, I'm sure.

"Being a mother has become my dream. Being loved and happy has always been my dream."

I was crying when I told him this. It's insane to think a few years ago I didn't believe I could be happy. I didn't think I'd fall in love. I always thought I would settle in every aspect of my life—and here I am exceeding all of my expectations of myself and the world.

Still, Jordan wants me to become a professional photographer. He doesn't think it's fair if only he gets to have his career. Once our baby is a few months old, I plan to finish school and I'll see where it goes from there. I don't want to pawn my kid off to some nanny for eight hours a day. I want to raise her. I don't want to be the typical rich chick with a kid who barely sees that kid.

My parents weren't as hands on as I would have liked when I was growing up. Sure, I didn't get stuck with a nanny five days a week, but they were both heavily involved in their careers and their society, that my weekends were spent sitting in a corner at fancy brunches and banquettes while Mom gossiped with friends and Dad made business deals. Elsa did as much babysitting as she did everything else around the house.

Mom actually expressed that regret to me last week while we did something so out of character for us. We watched movies—and not educational and deep movies—I'm talking chick flicks and silly comedies, which I caught Mom laughing at even though she found them "ridiculous".

She even thanked me for rebelling against her and Dad, which shocked me. What parents thanks their kid for that? It's funny how something you do for yourself can influence so many others. I never knew me standing up for myself would ever in a million years bring me closer to my parents. Dad still has some lightening up to do, but he's made great strides himself.

"One-hundred!" Tasha yelled out as she threw herself back down on the floor.

"Finished with your workout?"

She has a big audition for a travelling dance troupe over the summer. She is killing herself to make sure her stamina is up. I have never seen her so lean—she actually has a six-pack! To be honest, it makes me resent her. I was never athletic and was never overly in shape. After gaining fifteen pounds with the pregnancy and not being able to move much, I feel like a sack of potatoes next to Tasha.

"Yup," she breathed. "I'm going to check the mail and then we'll discuss dinner, okay?"

"I'm craving for a salad with croutons and honey mustard dressing!" I said excitedly.

Tasha looked at me funny.

"You're the only pregnant woman in history who craves vegetables all the time."

I shrugged, "My baby is a health nut. She takes after me and not her Daddy, thankfully."

A few minutes later, Tasha came back in with the mail. She tossed me a letter.

"Uh, check out the return address."

I looked to see Charles J. Ashton, Jr. listed on the upper left corner. I was surprised and concerned. I immediately opened the envelope. Two separate letters were inside—one for me and one for Jordan.

In his letter to me, Chuck explained he figured Jordan wouldn't open something from him, which is why he sent mail to me. He also said he wishes well on me and the baby, and hopes he will be allowed to see his grandchild once she is born.

I couldn't resist reading Chuck's letter to Jordan—though I know it was probably wrong of me.

"What did Chuck say?" Tasha asked impatiently.

I sighed, "He basically apologized for exiling Jordan and ever trusting in Christian. He also apologized about Maggie—and for all the bad he's done as a father and husband."

"Wow..." Tasha said. "How do you think Jordan will feel?"

"Honestly, I don't know if it'll change anything for him. And now, this puts me in a really awkward position."

"You're thinking about not giving him the letter?"

I sighed, "I'll give it to him, but the problem is... I never told him about Christian or Bippy."

"What?!?" She yelled. "Haley, how can you keep something like that from him?"

"The timing was so wrong, Tash. His mother had died and he was finally coming to terms with everything that went on with Bippy. I didn't want to stir him up with this. I just—I wish he didn't have to know."

"I know you don't want to hurt him," Tasha sighed. "But he has a right to know the whole truth about his so-called cousin and that slut. This will certainly squash any sympathy he felt toward Bippy's rape claim. How dare she lie to him to try and get him back! I would think you would be infuriated beyond belief, especially with the media rumors going around about Bippy and Jordan dating—I would think you'd want him to know just how deceitful she is."

Tasha was enraged, and I knew some of that fury was over Christian. Whether or not he slept with Bippy before he dated Tasha didn't matter. Tasha was jealous by nature.

"I don't want to hurt Jordan in order to secure my spot as his girlfriend. I don't need to smear Bippy's name for him to want me," I explained.

Tasha looked at me surprised.

"You're too pious sometimes," she laughed. "But I admire that."

"Thanks, but now I'm forced to tell him."

"Or you could not give him the letter?"

"He has the right to make up his own mind about the letter. Besides, I have to tell him the truth—I'm sure it will come out somehow—especially with your temper."

"What does that mean?" Tasha asked with a laugh.

"That you'll probably spout out on some tangent about Christian or Bippy in front of him at some point," I smirked.

A couple of days later, I was getting out of the shower when I heard the doorbell. Tasha was at school and I wasn't expecting anyone. I put my robe on, which was barely fitting now. My hair was dripping wet, and I was going to ignore the doorbell, but when the ringing turned into insistent knocking that wasn't going away—I carefully made my way to the door.

I peered through the peephole and I couldn't see anyone.

"Who is it?"

"Your dream man," the person said as he laughed.

I gasped and swung the door open, not caring that my belly button was poking out of my robe. Jordan stood there in a brown jacket, collared shirt and jeans—with no holes in them.

His hair was trimmed shorter than usual. He looked almost polished—but not stuffy.

I hugged him and he wrapped his arms around me.

"Get inside," he said, pushing me back into the apartment. "Your robe is coming undone."

He kicked the door closed behind him before glancing over my stomach. He pushed my robe back and placed his palms on either side of my bare belly.

"Wow..."

"I'm huge, I know," I frowned, but in fact, I was proud of my bump.

"Wait—I was warned to deny your weight gain..." he smirked. "You're not huge, baby. I can't even tell you're pregnant."

I laughed and wrapped my arms around his neck.

"What are you doing here?"

"You want me to go?"

"You can stay. I just have to kick my other boyfriend out of bed."

He laughed, "You mean Luke?"

I smacked his arm. Jordan loved to tease me about Luke. I confessed about the night before my birthday when I was so angry with Luke for pointing out how much I love Jordan—and how I kissed him. I was worried Jordan would be angry, and at first, he was, but then he laughed about it.

It also helps that Luke has a girlfriend now.

"I wasn't expecting you until later," I pouted. "I wanted to appear more together than this."

Jordan laughed, "My flight got in early. I wanted to surprise you. And I will never," he said kissing my neck. "Ever," he kissed my jaw, "complain about you being half-naked—as long as we're alone," he added with a chuckle.

My body shivered as we kissed, and I looked him over once more focusing on his hair last.

"You hate it?"

"No, I like it. Do you?"

"I guess it's not too bad," he said. "The label gave us a stylist," he shrugged. "I wasn't too happy about the idea, but the girl is pretty cool. She doesn't try to change our style just enhance it."

"Girl, huh?"

"Yup—she's actually a big fan of Meghan's work. And Darren's…" he laughed.

"Uh-oh, Darren's going to break her heart and then you won't have a stylist."

Jordan laughed, "I told him to leave things on good terms."

Darren is the heartbreaker of Tortured surprisingly. He somehow makes friends easily with girls and makes them fall for him. The problem is he screws them over in one way or another and they always end up hating him.

"I'm going to put some clothes on," I said, fixing his collar and snickering at the wet patches on his clothes from my body.

I threw on comfortable clothes and put my hair up before walking out into the living room. Jordan was stretched out on the couch. I waddled over to him before sitting down next to him, curling my legs underneath me and resting my head on his shoulder.

"I'm so happy you're home."

"Me too—I wish I didn't have to leave again in a week," he sighed.

"But then you're home for good for a while," I reminded him.

"How are you feeling?"

“A little bored,” I admitted. “One of my classes, I can still take online, but without school, and you being gone—I’m just killing time. I’ve been shopping online a lot,” I laughed.

“Oh no…” Jordan shook his head.

“For the baby, mostly.”

He laughed.

“What?”

“I actually have baby fever, too. I have about twenty onesies for the kid from all over the country in my suitcase.”

“Really?” I grinned at him.

He looked embarrassed before running a hand through my damp hair.

“I don’t think I can be any happier, Haley.”

I smiled at him and kissed him. My lips began to tremble against his and tears fell from my eyes.

“You cry much easier now,” he laughed.

I wiped my tears. I wasn’t crying out of happiness unfortunately. I was crying at the thought of explaining to Jordan about his father.

“I love you,” I told him. “I know that doesn’t take away all of your pain, but know that I always believe in you. I am connected to you more than anything in this world…”

“You know I feel the same way about you…and I appreciate you telling me that, but where is this coming from?”

“There’s something I haven’t told you,” I swallowed. “Remember how I said there was a big fight between Christian and Tasha at their engagement party?”

“And that’s why she called off the wedding—yeah.”

“I didn’t tell you why they were fighting.”

“I’m not going to like this—Am I?” he asked. “Did he make another pass at you? I knew that bruise on your arm was something more,” he said, his fists clenching. “What did he do to you? I will—"

"Jordan, calm down," I sighed. "Christian always acts inappropriately. You know that. It was never something I couldn't handle. This time, it had nothing to do with me." I shook my head still in disbelief, "Christian told me that he had hooked up with Bippy."

"And you believed him?" Jordan laughed. "He lied about you..."

"Well, I wasn't sure what to believe, but Bippy and your father confirmed it."

"What? You asked them?"

"Of course not. You know I try not to talk to either of them...ever, but your dad had a sudden conscience about the past. And of course Bippy was trying to fish around for information why you weren't with me... I confronted her about what Chuck and Christian said."

"Haley, you actually allowed yourself to be sucked into this petty drama?"

"I was sucked into finding out the truth," I argued.

"I don't think I want to know. I don't know if I can believe any of them."

I reached over to the drawer in the coffee table and pulled out an envelope.

"Jordan, your father wrote you a letter. He's trying to right things."

"He can shove his letter. Nothing will ever be right between us."

I sighed out of frustration.

"Why are you doing this?" he asked.

"Doing what?"

"Ruining things?"

"*I'm* ruining things?"

I looked at him like he was crazy.

"This whole nonsense with my dad and Bippy..." Jordan said with animated gestures. "This is what almost made me lose you. I don't want any part of it."

"I understand that, but you were the one that has always harped on the past."

"What?" he asked as if this news shocked him. "I have moved on from that entire society and made something of myself without them!"

"Yes, you did, but that doesn't mean you're not stuck emotionally."

"Haley, who gave you a psychology degree?" he asked with an attitude.

"Fine. You want to pretend this doesn't all exist on the surface—great. But it's going to keep haunting you, Jordan. It's going to affect us and our baby. So you confront this crap now or..."

"Or what?" Jordan asked, challenging me.

I couldn't say it. Honestly, I didn't know what I was threatening. Would I leave him? Would I keep the baby from him? No.

"Or keep running from who you are," I said.

Jordan looked at me almost hatefully.

"I'm going home to unpack," he said standing up. "I'll call you later."

Now, I was the one to look at him almost hatefully.

"That's real nice. Run away like you always do."

Jordan grunted and punched the wall on his way out. I know I said that last remark purposely to annoy him, but I had to say it. I wanted it to sink into his brain.

He could change his name; disown his family; and pretend his childhood never existed, but it comes out in his songs and in his relationships. I just want him to see that. I don't expect him to call Chuck and tell him he misses him. I just want him to get closure on the past and move on from it.

I picked up Jordan's journal and wrote to him as I cried. When Tasha got back from class, I asked her to drop it off on his doorstep.

April 15, 2012

I hate you for walking out like you did. I haven't seen you in over a month! If you don't want to know the truth—fine. I suppose it really doesn't make a difference. All of the people involved you dislike anyway. I thought keeping it from you would just make you angry with me. Just know Bippy is full of crap when it comes to that whole rape story. Don't you feel any sympathy toward her.

As for your father… I figured you'd want to know why he treated you the way he did. It's not because I think you should welcome him back into your life with open arms. It's because I want you to find answers to underlying questions you may have.

♥Haley

April 16th

I overreacted. I'm sorry. I hate when you're right, you know?

Love,

Jordan

P.S. I'm in your kitchen making you breakfast.

Chapter 18

I woke up and felt like going right back to sleep. Jordan didn't call me last night. I just got a text saying he'd call me "tomorrow". That cell phone I got him for Christmas really was coming back to bite me. I feel like he always uses it inappropriately when it comes to me.

As I glanced at the alarm clock I saw the journal sitting there on the nightstand. Confused, I grabbed it. I read Jordan's brief but pleasant note. I smiled; just when I think he's being a jerk, he surprises me. I think that's what makes our relationship exciting—he keeps me guessing. Though I hate when we fight like we have recently—I love how much stronger we've become through this difficult time.

I could hear Jordan and Tasha in the kitchen, but I also heard another male speaking. I recognized Sebastian's sonorous voice almost instantly. I changed into something more appropriate than the flimsy pajamas I was wearing. I snuck into the bathroom to brush my teeth and tame my hair—it was a wreck.

Someone was making noises by the door and I rolled my eyes knowing it was Sebie. He was big on toilet humor.

"Very funny, Seb!" I called out.

He laughed; probably surprised I knew it was him. I opened the door and his mouth dropped.

"Oh my..."

I smiled, "Say it."

"You look beautiful," he said, not wanting to offend me by

pointing out my belly.

I laughed hard.

"Right—with my big belly and my just woke up look…I'm gorgeous."

"No, seriously… You're a pretty pregnant girl," he said, laughing.

"Thank you. So, what are you doing here in Boston?"

"Well, I…" he said with a sneaky smile on his face. "I promised Tasha last month that I'd be her date for some formal at her school."

"Oh, did you?" I asked, raising an eyebrow.

"I couldn't let her go without a date," he shrugged.

"Uh huh… So what brings you over for my surprise breakfast?" I asked, hearing Jordan and Tasha in the kitchen discussing the new Landry album as something sizzled on the stove.

"I tagged along so I wouldn't be alone in this Red Sox nation," he sneered.

"Ah, I see. Considering most of your attire does consist of Yankee logos, that's probably wise," I nodded.

I pushed the swinging door open in the kitchen and my best friend and boyfriend both smiled at me.

"Morning Mama," Tasha said skipping over to me and kissing my cheek. "This one's a keeper—I didn't know he could cook, too," she nodded toward Jordan.

"I can't really," he laughed. "I only know what my mom taught me."

"Did Maggie cook often?" Tasha asked.

"For me, she did. My dad hired a cook, but I was never into gourmet food—especially as a kid," he laughed.

I remember Jordan telling me how his father tried to force him to eat escargot once when he was seven. Jordan wound up puking all over Chuck soon after.

"So, what did you make?" I asked curiously.

"A tofu scrambler with potatoes," he smirked.

"Seriously? You made tofu?" I gasped, placing a hand over my heart.

"Anything for my babies," he smiled. "Though I still think it's in your head that you get sick from meat," he rolled his eyes.

"Maybe, but after Meghan made me watch that PETA video, I lost my love for meat," I explained.

"Remind me to thank Meghan," Jordan sighed.

A few minutes later, the four of us sat down for breakfast. Jordan may not be happy making tofu, but he makes one heck of a scrambler!

"I think you should quit making music and become a vegetarian chef," I gushed.

"Yeah, okay..." Jordan laughed.

"This is really good," Tasha told him.

Tasha and Sebastian offered to do the dishes. I got the feeling they really just wanted us out of the way.

As I walked toward the living room, I felt pain in my lower back and I winced.

"What's wrong?" Jordan asked, bracing my arm with his hand.

"I'm fine—I just need to sit down."

We got to the couch, and Jordan propped my feet up.

"Comfortable?"

I nodded and he rubbed my belly.

"Thank you for breakfast," I smiled. "Tomorrow I'll make you a peanut butter and Cheerio sandwich, Maggie style."

Jordan smiled a sad smile.

"That was a fun day," he said with a sigh in his voice.

On one of our day trips with Maggie, we brought her to

Aunt Lacey's and I had her show me how to make Jordan's favorite sandwich. I know it will never be the same for him because Maggie isn't making the sandwich for him, but at least it's something. He'll always have the memories.

Jordan took my hand in his.

"Listen, I'm sorry I freaked out last night. And I'm sorry for apologizing for freaking out so much lately," he sighed, annoyed with himself.

The entire time he spoke, he kept his eyes on my belly as he rubbed it. It was soothing. I put my head on his shoulder.

"I won't say another word about it if that's what you want. I didn't want us to have any secrets."

He nodded, "I called Bippy last night."

That was the last thing I expected him to say. Considering he didn't call me, it cut deeply, but there was no need to be jealous. I'm sure cursing Bippy out took a lot out of Jordan.

"I didn't want the burden to be on you, Haley," he said, swallowing. "It was time she told me the truth. Not you."

"Did she actually tell you the truth?"

"About Christian and the baby being his...oh yeah," he sighed. "They deserve each other."

"I'm sure she thinks she's too good for him, though."

"She thinks she's too good for everyone. Do you believe she still had the nerve to want to be friends?"

I laughed, "What did you tell her?"

"To go to hell. And then I told her you were my first love and not her—that any love I felt toward her was under false pretenses."

I looked at him, his eyes still on my belly. I touched his cheek and forced him to look at me.

"I'm fine. It's time for rebirth," he winked.

He kissed my belly before kissing my lips.

I was afraid to ask him about his father. I didn't want to push him. I rested my head in the crook of his neck.

"How do you feel about moving to New York?"

I looked at him confused.

"New York?"

I knew he didn't particularly like Boston—mostly because of the whole Red Sox thing, which was not a good enough reason in my opinion.

"Aunt Lacey is selling her house."

"Why?" I asked, sitting up.

"She wants to get a condo in Florida and travel. She offered me the house, but it's kind of old and... I'd like us to pick out a place."

I looked at him a little taken back.

"Us? As in you and me?"

He laughed, "No, as in me and Tasha. Yes, you and me."

"Oh..."

"Why are you so surprised?"

"We never talked about moving in together."

"Well, I figured now would be as good a time as any. This going from my place to yours is killing me... It's only going to get worse once Little Moonlight is born."

I laughed. Jordan began calling our baby Little Moonlight on the last full moon. We were on the phone, and looking out the window, both exhausted from our day and missing each other. The words just fell from his lips—and though we laughed at the hippy-esque name, I found it fitting.

"So, will you move in with me?"

"Yes," I smiled. "I would love to, but to New York?"

I wasn't sure how I felt about that. I didn't particularly love Boston either, but I didn't mind it. I definitely didn't want to live in Bakersfield. New York does give me comfort in its own way. It is my place to escape from school and family. It is where I met Jordan; it is where I found me.

"I want to be close to the people who are most important to me, Haley. Your parents will come to visit often and we'll go to see them a lot, too, but I know you don't want to live in Vermont anyway. I want to be there for Drew."

I smiled at him. That was enough explanation for me, but he went on anyway. He talked about how his record company is in New York and so were most publicity events—hence he wouldn't have to leave home as much. He discussed the photography opportunities for me in New York and the culture we can expose our child to.

"I'm sold, Jor," I laughed. "What happened to you last night?"

"I didn't sleep," he chuckled. "I thought of all the time I spent being angry, and I got bored with it. Screw all the assholes," he rolled his eyes. "They only did me a favor. I don't need a girl like Bippy—even as a friend, or a cousin like Christian. Or a father..."

His voice lowered.

"Can I have the letter?"

I nodded, and pulled the envelope out of the drawer in the coffee table. I handed it to him.

"I can't snap my fingers and love him, but there has to be some decency in the man for someone like my mother to fall in love with him," he swallowed.

I caught a glimpse of Chuck's decency on the plane trip from Bakersfield to Boston. I hope that side of him will appear more, especially to his sons.

I reached over and hugged Jordan. I am proud of him. We have both changed so much in such a short amount of time.

At first, the baby brought out the child in each of us—the angst, fear and all those insecurities. Now, the baby brought out strength in us that we never thought we had.

The baby kicked me hard as I hugged Jordan and I winced. Pulling away, I rubbed my stomach.

"I think she's jealous," I grimaced.

"My little Daddy's girl," he said, placing a hand on my stomach.

She kicked again and I clenched my teeth.

"Hale, you okay?"

I nodded, "Sometimes I feel like she's the Incredible Hulk ready to bust through my stomach."

"Moonlight, take it easy on Mommy..." Jordan said softly with a smile.

"We need to think of a real name for her."

"You don't like Moonlight?" he feigned shock.

"That could be her Native American name, okay?"

He laughed, "Where's your laptop?"

I tried to get up, but my back was killing me. Jordan insisted on me not moving. He retrieved my laptop from my room before plopping down next to me on the couch. He began searching for names meaning moon, moonlight, moonbeam, and the like. I vetoed the Italian name "Luna" or the Greek goddess "Artemis", which is what Jordan jokingly called out first. He went through dozens of names with "moon" in the meaning. Most of them were odd like "Badr" or "Yue". Since it was part of her heritage, Jordan looked up some Native American baby names with the meaning. I somewhat liked "Jaci", but Jordan wasn't too thrilled about it—saying it reminded him of Jay-Z if said quickly.

As we argued and searched, Sebastian had left and Tasha began to get ready for the formal. I felt like I needed a nap. My head slumped down onto Jordan's shoulder. My eyes fluttered, looking at the computer screen when a name caught my eye.

"Turkish..." I muttered.

"We are *not* naming her Turkish," he said disgusted.

I laughed, "No—that one...the Turkish one."

Pointing at the screen, I focused my eyes and rolled the name off my tongue.

"Aylin."

"It means moon halo," Jordan said.

I looked up at him and smiled.

"I like it. She is our little angel."

"Aylin," he said, thinking about it.

"Aylin Margaret..." I suggested, as a tribute to his mother.

He grinned, "That's a winner."

"Um, what's her last name?"

"I don't know," he furrowed his eyebrows. "Technically, my last name is Ashton."

"But do you want that to be her last name?"

Jordan didn't answer and glanced over at the letter from his father. I felt myself start to drift off to sleep again, and he never answered my question. I liked the ring of Aylin Ashton, I have to admit.

May 23rd

I just finished performing in Chicago. The meet & greet was insane—almost as bad as the NYC fans. We loved it! Seb said no meet & greet will ever compare to the one where you passed out though. He will never let you live that down, you know? The guys say hi.

Chuck called me today. I will probably tell you this on the phone before you read this, but writing to you is therapeutic to me. He told me Drew can move in with us in Boston. He says he just wants us both happy. He said he knows he screwed up. He knows how badly he hurt me. I don't think he does but…

Anyway, I told him I was relieved he would put his son's feelings before his for once, but that we are moving to New York once the baby is born.

He sounded happy… I've never heard him sound happy. Whatever—my relationship with him is what it is. I'm done fighting. I'm done running. But I can't just forgive and forget either.

So… Are you going crazy yet being stuck in the house? At least photography is keeping you busy. I loved the picture of the bird on the ledge and the one of your mother eating tofu made me crack up. You finally wore her down!

My absolute favorite photo though is the one of you with your belly exposed and the heart drawn on it in lipstick.

Miss you. Love you.

Kiss the moon goodnight tonight. I'll feel it.

Tell Aylin Daddy loves her.

Love,

Jordan

Chapter 19

Spring is in full bloom and I want to enjoy it. The winter felt as if it would never end. We even had snow in the first week of April! I am now seven and a half months pregnant and very much ready to be done with the ordeal.

I'm always uncomfortable, always hungry, and always tired. It has been over a month once again since I've seen Jordan, and I wish he was here. He takes my mind off all the discomfort.

Tasha is driving down to New York next week to see Tortured's show and I'm jealous. I only leave the house to go to the doctor. Dr. Seodat is taking strict precaution with me. The preeclampsia has gotten worse, which she predicted it would.

Today I am not feeling well at all. I think it is more emotional than physical, though. Being cooped up without anyone, besides Mom and Tasha, really gets to me. Luke and Laney came to visit me last night, thankfully.

I do everything I can to keep myself entertained. I read just about every book I could find. I watched pretty much every movie that was released this year. Mostly, I take pictures and make scrapbooks—that is when I can get out of bed.

Aside from that, I worry. Though, I am taking every precaution, I am terrified of something going wrong in my pregnancy.

Jordan and I e-mail each other real estate opportunities in New York. I always ask his opinion on baby stuff. I am a little upset I will not have a nursery set up by the time Aylin is born, but Jordan promises me when he gets home we'll get things in order as quickly as possible.

"Sweetie, you should take a shower," Mom said.

I looked at her from my spot on the couch. I didn't want to move.

"I don't have any energy."

"Your father will be here soon. You're just going to make him worry if he sees you all sulky like this."

Pouting, I tried to get up. Mom rushed over to help me.

"Be careful and take your time," she said, walking me to the bathroom.

She was acting strangely. She usually encouraged me not moving, though lately, I haven't been putting up a fight.

The warm water of the shower did feel nice, even if I did rest against the tiles most of the time. I heard some commotion in the apartment as I washed up. I figured Mom had the cleaning lady come over in Dad's honor. I laughed to myself thinking about how Dad would never have watched the silly comedies Mom had with me. He would never have laughed at the story Tasha told us about her getting a straw stuck up her nose on a dare or about Jordan being the one getting me drunk for the first and only time.

I never would have thought Mom would ever be amused by these things either, though. She has been with Dad since she was in college, and sometimes, his thoughts become hers. I hate that about her. I truly believe deep down my mother isn't stuck up—in fact, I bet I'm a lot like the real her. I just wish she didn't always try and hide that side from Dad. He loves me for me. I'm sure he'd love her no matter what, too.

While I was in the shower, Mom came in.

"Wear this, okay?" she said.

I poked my head out of the shower and squinted at the pink maternity dress and leggings.

"Do I really have to get dressed up for Dad?"

"He's here already," she said. "So don't come out naked or anything," she laughed nervously.

I looked at her funny. She didn't answer my question. I was not in the mood to look pretty. I didn't care who was here.

Despite my sluggishness, I blew my hair out straight and wore the outfit. I even put on a little make-up. The entire time I was getting ready I heard music playing somewhat loudly—Billie Holiday—Mom's favorite. I also could make out voices; more than two, I thought. Suddenly, the music stopped. I heard the apartment door close and then silence.

Curiously, I opened the bathroom door. Balloons were practically everywhere. Furniture was moved. Food was set up. This was my baby shower!

Just then, the front door burst open. Mom, Tasha, Laney and a bunch of women charged into my apartment almost scaring me to death. I felt like the baby dropped along with my heart.

Everyone rushed toward me—hugging me, rubbing my belly, and shouting questions. I was overwhelmed. I wasn't used to being the center of attention, especially when I was in such discomfort.

The last time I was thrown a party was for my Sweet 16, and I hated every second of it. No real friends of mine were there. Leslie Tyler came, but Bippy didn't. I'm sure she thought she was too good to come to my party. Not that I wanted her there anyway. My family and the Erikssons were really the only ones there.

Now, I actually like almost everyone at my party besides a couple of my mother's friends I didn't care all that much for, but I knew she considered them important to her. Along with Laney, a couple of girls from school were here; my best friends Meghan and Tasha; my mother's sister and her two daughters showed—though I wasn't that close to them, it was nice to see them. A few other distant relatives and friends of the family were there as well and Jordan's Aunt Lacey came, which made me happy.

"Surprised?" Tasha laughed.

"Yes. I figured a shower was not happening with me being stuck here."

"We figured why not bring the party to you?" Mom smiled.

That she did. There was tons of food and music, which Tasha somehow snuck her iPod into the radio—changing out my mother's old jazz tunes. I actually like some of Mom's music, but I know it isn't for everyone.

I sat down after a few minutes, not being able to stand any longer. Meghan sat next to me with a warm smile.

"How are you?"

"Good."

"I mean…really…" she said.

She didn't know everything, but she knew Jordan and I had hit a rough patch. Who knows what lies Bippy was feeding her on top of everything.

"Really," I sighed. "I miss Jordan. I miss my body," I laughed. "I feel like it's been taken over. Other than that, I'm really happy."

"Really?" she asked smiling.

I laughed, "Really."

Meghan has a habit of overusing words such as "really", "totally" and "like". She isn't an airhead; it is just her personality.

"I have something to tell you…" she began. "I quit working for Bippy."

My mouth dropped.

"Why—why would you do that?"

"Because she's crazy?"

"Meghan, please tell me you didn't do this for me."

"No—though I got sick of her saying how Jordan and her were getting back together. The girl is delusional," she rolled her eyes.

I nodded. Bippy is always confabulating stories of past lovers—usually celebrities. In these stories, she is always the center of everyone's world. I'm sure it came from her parents not giving her enough attention as a child.

"I quit because she referred to me as a 'seamstress' in most of her interviews. She is getting most of the money for a line I created on my own. I'm also quitting because she is rude to me half the time. I don't care if she was getting my foot in the door—I deserve better," Meghan sighed.

"Good for you, Meg," I smiled. "So, what's going to happen to Bippy's line?"

"I'll still get paid a portion of sales. She is pissed and threatened to ruin my name, but I'm not concerned—I have a hook-up with an up & coming celebrity stylist who wants to push my clothing on her clients," Meghan smirked.

"Who's the stylist?"

"Chloe Haas. Sound familiar?"

I thought for a moment.

"Wait, Tortured's new stylist?" I asked.

"Yup," Meghan smiled. "Jordan gave her my number. She's a big fan of mine and wanted to team up with me. So, this will basically lead to me creating my own line," she smirked.

I practically screamed before hugging her. She deserved this opportunity.

Soon I was opening gifts. I didn't know where I was going to keep them all in my apartment. I received practically everything on my registry and then some! Cami sent a child size pink Les Paul guitar that was adorable! Along with the guitar was a onesie with the Tortured logo on it that I loved. Meghan practically made a whole line of clothes for the baby and Tasha got her a little ballerina outfit and the car seat; which I'm sure we would make great use of while traveling along the east coast. And Mom of course bought everything for the nursery without actually buying a nursery!

By the time cake was served, I was ready to fall asleep. I felt like a beached whale sometimes. I just lay on the couch unable to move while people formed a circle around me.

Little by little guests started to leave. Meghan was the last one to go and told me how excited she is for me to move to New York. Tasha isn't as thrilled for my move, but she comes to New York so often, it won't be that big of a deal.

I fell asleep that night with my phone in my hand waiting for Jordan's call. I figured the ringing would wake me up, but it didn't. Instead, a strong tightening in my belly woke me around three am. I sat up and took a deep breath. My belly tightened again, but this time I felt a strong pain. I winced before carefully getting out of bed.

The pain struck me once more, now bringing tears to my eyes. I grabbed my phone as I tried to breathe deeply. I saw the missed call from Jordan and I frowned. He sent me a text saying good night. I dropped the phone feeling the pain even worse than before.

I turned on the lamp by my bed and gasped. My bed sheets had a huge blood stain on them. I panicked now, cupping my hands over my mouth. I felt more pain, and I sobbed. My legs were shaky underneath me.

All I kept thinking is that I am losing the baby. I didn't want to believe that, but I didn't know what else to think. I am a worrier by nature.

I screamed at the thought of my baby dying inside of me. I screamed loud. I didn't know what else to do; that was my only reaction at the moment. I couldn't lose her. Aylin is very much my daughter already. I played her music and read her stories. I told her how her daddy and I met. I fed her. I shopped for her. I love her.

"Baby, don't leave me," I sobbed.

Just then, Mom and Tasha burst into my room panicked.

"Haley," Tasha gasped, seeing the blood on my thighs.

Mom rushed over to me as I hugged her, hoping she could give me an explanation.

"Tasha, call Dr. Seodat. I'm going to get Haley dressed and into the car," I barely heard Mom say. "Sweetie," she said, pulling my face from her shoulder.

My entire body was shaking. I couldn't move other than that.

"Look at me, Haley," she said sternly.

I looked at her.

"You need to put pants and shoes on so we can go to the hospital."

"Mom, it hurts," I said, clutching my stomach, trying to calm down. In all my panicking, I had forgotten about the pain for a moment.

"It's going to be okay."

"The baby…" I said, tears renewing themselves.

"She's still there," Mom said, placing her hand on my belly. "She'll hang in there, but she needs you to hang in there as well."

This was the most calm I had ever seen my mother in a stressful situation. Funny, if she can't find her purse, she's in an uproar, but I'm about to be taken to the emergency room, and she's focused and uplifting.

Mom helped me get dressed and into the car. Tasha got into the driver's seat with the phone attached to her ear.

"Seb, thank God. I know it's late, but I need you to get Jordan," she said, as I slumped across the backseat of her car, trying not to cry out in pain.

"No, Tasha..." I gritted my teeth. "Don't."

"Haley, you have to tell him."

"I don't want him to worry..."

"You know he wants to be here for you..."

It didn't matter what I said. Tasha was already instructing Sebastian to get Jordan to Boston as quickly as possible.

I groaned, and almost felt like passing out. Next thing I knew, I was being placed on a stretcher and brought into the hospital. I heard Mom explaining what had happened to the staff.

I was brought into a room. Mom and Tasha were still with me, thankfully. Dr. Seodat walked in and slight relief washed over me. She would know what to do.

"How ya doin' Haley?" she asked, placing the back of her hand on my forehead.

"Not good. What's wrong?"

"Well, I'm not sure yet. I'm going to find out. You may meet your little girl tonight," she smiled.

I smiled, too. Hearing her say those words confirmed that I didn't lose the baby. I didn't care what pain I went through—I just wanted her safe.

Dr. Seodat gave me a quick examination as well as an ultrasound. She looked at me and sighed.

"The preeclampsia has led to abruption of the placenta from the uterus."

"Is the baby okay?"

"I wish her lungs were developed a little more and her heartbeat is a little slower than I would like... We're going to do an emergency c-section."

"How risky is that for her?"

"She might have some complications, but if we leave her in there—it'll be much worse for both of you," she said, trying to ease my worry about delivering the baby being my best option.

It didn't really work, though. I knew the risks Aylin faced being delivered prematurely, and my instinct was to protect her, but with my own body fighting against her, I felt helpless.

"I am concerned about the amount of blood you lost already," Dr. Seodat told me. "After surgery, you're going to need blood transfusions and be watched closely."

I nodded. I was scared and I hoped Jordan could make it to me in time. I needed him with me, but at the same time, I didn't know if I wanted him to see me like this—frightened and on a hospital bed.

The next hour was brutal. Not only was I in severe pain, but I was being prepared for surgery. Mom told me Dad was on his way. She was trying to keep me positive while Tasha was trying to take my mind off it. That was impossible and honestly, I just wanted them both to be quiet.

I wanted to concentrate on feeling my baby. I wanted to make sure she was still moving inside me, but over the pain—I couldn't feel anything but agony and pressure.

Once Dr. Seodat gave me a spinal tap, I couldn't feel a thing. I was completely numb. She wanted to give me regular anesthesia, but that would mean I would be sedated for the birth. I wanted to be awake to see the baby first thing.

Luckily Jordan wasn't across the country. He was in northern Connecticut. Tortured was touring the east coast. Their last show was in Boston in a week.

Dr. Seodat moved me into the operating room and I wanted to plead with her to wait for Jordan, but I didn't want to put the baby in danger by waiting. I began to cry softly.

"Are you still feeling pain?" Mom asked, holding my hand as they wheeled me into the room.

She and Tasha were both in scrubs now.

"No," I said with shaky breaths. "I want Jordan."

"He's probably almost here," Tasha assured me.

"He needs to be here now."

I realized I sounded like a child, but I suppose I was entitled to feel that way considering the circumstances.

"Can you keep a lookout for him?" I almost begged Tasha.

She nodded and kissed my head before heading out of the room. A curtain was put up so I couldn't see the actual surgery. I felt something, and barely heard Dr. Seodat's words to calm me. I was in a state of shock. I could feel tugging, and I thought about random things.

Everyone's voice around me was muffled. I couldn't focus on what was going on. Maybe it was the lack of blood, but I felt like I was dreaming. I thought about the only other time I was in surgery—to get the fibroids off my uterus. I was a terrified kid. I felt similar to that now.

I thought about the first time Jordan smiled at me. The first time I kissed him. The first time he told me he loved me. The first time I heard "Haley's Letter". The first time we made love. And then I thought about the last time we made love. We had survived a difficult time.

"Haley?"

I faintly heard my name being called.

"Hale?"

The voice was music to my ears. I turned my head, breaking out of my dream world. Jordan was beside me while my mother stood behind him. He was wearing scrubs and a mask. I could see the worry in his eyes.

"Jordan," I said, swallowing.

My mouth was dry.

"Hey," he pulled his mask down, smiled, and kissed my forehead. "You couldn't wait at least another week for me to come home?"

"I'm sorry," I frowned.

I felt guilty for having such a messed up uterus.

"I was kidding," he sighed, putting the mask back on.

Differentiating sarcasm and jokes from the truth was not a strong point for me at the moment. Tasha kept trying to make me laugh earlier and I just wanted to tell her to shut up.

"How ya doin', Haley?" Dr. Seodat called, as I heard a suctioning sound.

"Woozy," I swallowed again. "And thirsty."

Dr. Seodat laughed, "Mom, why don't you get her some ice chips?"

Jordan peeked over the curtain and I could tell he didn't like what he saw.

"Gross, huh?"

"It's just weird," he said.

Mom brought over the ice chips and fed me a couple.

"How was the baby shower?"

"Good," I laughed finally, before feeling more tugging.

Only Jordan can somehow make small talk at a time like this and still keep my interest.

Dr. Seodat and the nurses were moving around faster. Then Mom gasped loudly.

"What?" I asked, concerned.

Jordan peeked over and that's when I heard the crying. Tears filled my eyes and my mouth dropped. It was surreal to think that my baby was here.

"She's..." Jordan said, trying to form words.

"I want to see her," I pleaded, grabbing his arm.

"Hold on," Dr. Seodat said before holding my daughter up so I could see.

"She's so tiny," Jordan said.

And she was tiny, but she was breathing—and screaming, which made me smile. None of her features were distinct to me since she wasn't cleaned and she was scrunching her face up, but she was ours.

"Hi," I cooed to my daughter. "I love you."

"We're just going to clean her up and make sure everything's okay," Dr. Seodat explained before handing the baby to a nurse.

"Sweetie, you did it..." Mom said.

"Dr. Seodat did it," I said, feeling my voice sounding drowsy. "I just lay here."

I heard the room laugh. Jordan looked at me teary-eyed and I smiled. I knew that little girl would have him wrapped around her finger as soon as he saw her.

Suddenly, I couldn't keep my eyes open.

The next time I was conscious, I was in a regular hospital room. I felt nauseous and extremely groggy. I was hooked up to an IV that was sending blood into my body.

"You had me worried."

I turned and Jordan was sitting in a chair by my bed. There were flowers and balloons in the room.

"What time is it?" I asked, squinting, feeling the sun hit my eyes.

"About five."

I had been asleep for over eight hours.

"Why'd I worry you?"

He practically laughed and then turned serious. He glanced down at his hands and then at my face. He looked like he hadn't slept.

"When Sebastian woke me up to say you were being rushed to the hospital, and not because you were going into labor—I was a mess. I took a cab here and made the guy speed..."

"You took a cab from Connecticut?" I asked, surprised.

"Well, I doubt the tour bus would have been quicker," he said.

I laughed, though it hurt. The stitches in my stomach pulled.

"Then I get here and... You were losing so much blood that—you were barely conscious until you were completely unconscious. That scared me," he said, now crying.

"Jordan," I reached out and ran my fingers through his hair.

"It just—What if you didn't wake up like Mom?"

He stood up and cried onto my chest. I hugged him as best as I could. I wish I was able to wrap my arms around him completely. Jordan has been so preoccupied with the tour and the baby that sometimes I forget he's still grieving the loss of his mother. The last time he was at this hospital was when she passed away.

"Jor, I'm fine," I promised him.

At least I think I am. The nausea, drowsiness and pain are what Dr. Seodat prepared me for. I'm sure the blood transfusion isn't anything to be alarmed about. My concern is the baby. Did she need oxygen? How long will she have to stay in the hospital? Who fed her first? I wanted it to be me, but I guess with the whole unconscious thing, I understand.

"Look at me," I whispered.

Jordan lifted his head and looked into my eyes.

"I'm fine," I smiled and took his hand, placing it over my heart. "It's still beating."

He smirked, "It's fast."

"Because you're here," I smirked back.

He pecked my lips and sat back in the chair, sighing.

"How is she?"

I laid my head back against the pillows happy to see Jordan's smile.

"Beautiful," he said, almost disgusted with how simple a word he used to describe her.

"I want to see her."

"The nurse said she'll bring her in as soon as you woke up. I'll go tell her..." he stood up.

"Besides beautiful, is she okay?"

"Sorry—I forgot you've been Rip Van Winkle all day," he laughed.

I rolled my eyes.

"Dr. Seodat said she's amazed at how well Aylin is doing. For a preemie, she's pretty strong. Her lungs are perfect. She's only three pounds."

"Three pounds exactly?" I asked.

He nodded, "The only problem is... She won't eat. They've been feeding her with a tube, but I think she's waiting for you," he winked.

"Did you hold her?" I smiled at him.

He grinned, "I couldn't put her down."

Mom, Dad and Tasha came in a minute after Jordan left. They surrounded me to congratulate me and ask how I was. I was tired, though. I just wanted to hold Aylin and go back to sleep.

The nurse came in with Jordan and Aylin. I tried to sit

up, but winced when I felt another tug on my stitches. Jordan took Aylin in his arms.

"Pretty girl," he cooed to her. "Here's Mommy."

Aylin was placed in my arms and I got my first good look at her. She was completely bald and fair-skinned. Her eyes were closed and her lips pursed. She had Jordan's lips and my nose. She was perfect. I played with her fingers and she gripped my hand. I felt tears roll down my cheeks.

A camera went off. Mom was gushing at "her baby" holding "her grandbaby". Dad was even a mush over his granddaughter.

"Do you think you could feed her?" The nurse asked.

I nodded and looked at everyone.

"Can I get some privacy?"

My parents and Tasha left the room. Jordan walked over to me and rubbed Aylin's head. Her eyes opened and I cooed. She looked at both of us a couple of times and shut her eyes again.

"I'll come back," he said.

"No," I pouted. "I want you to be here."

The nurse loosened my hospital gown for me. I held Aylin up to my breast. The nurse recommended I lay her on top of my chest before trying to feed her and to switch breasts during the feeding. I placed Aylin on my chest carefully. I felt her little hands ball into fists on my skin. She began moving her head around after a couple of minutes. The nurse instructed me to try to feed her now.

I was always shy about getting undressed in front of a doctor or nurse, but after going through pregnancy and labor—you no longer care. It's become routine.

When I held Aylin up to my breast, she instinctively opened her little mouth and began suckling, still with her eyes closed. I smiled down at her as she fed. I looked up at Jordan and he watched intently. I had to laugh. Guys.

"Thatta girl," the nurse smiled. "I'll give you some time with her."

She left the room and I looked over at Jordan.

"That's so weird..."

"Oh no," I sighed. "Now I ruined your image of me?"

"Yes, Haley. You're totally unattractive to me now," he rolled his eyes. "You're so silly sometimes."

"Well, my body's gone through a lot of changes... I'm not the pure virgin you were with."

He laughed and sat on the edge of my bed.

"Now, you're a hot mama," he said leaning over and kissing me.

We sat there talking about plans for our move while Aylin finished eating. I asked Jordan to burp her since I was feeling as if I'd fall back to sleep. I had to guide him through the burping process. He was afraid of hurting her.

I fell back asleep with the vision of the two loves of my life.

December 24th

You're sitting right across from me taking an insane amount of pictures of Aylin. This kid is going to hate you for capturing every bad hair day someday—though her tiny blonde ponytail is "precious" as your mother would say. I'm trying to finish a song, but I can't help to watch you two. Meet me by the fire tonight at midnight. I want to give you one of your presents in private.

-J

Chapter 20

It was hard to believe a year ago I was in this exact cabin clueless to the fact that I was pregnant. The vibe last year was tense. Maybe it was because of Trisha Eriksson's disapproval of Tasha and Christian's wedding plans. Maybe it was just Christian being here period.

All I know is that I remember something missing. Jordan and I were in love, and at the time, the feeling didn't really make sense—I chalked it up to not feeling well. Jordan was also not sleeping well.

After reading his journal, I now realized he was tormented by nightmares of losing me; of losing a baby he had already lost. It's weird to think we had everything then when really—we hadn't even scratched the surface.

It just proves you never know in life. Jordan never knew he was burying his past; he thought putting his feelings down in song was enough. I never knew a baby would change my life this way, either.

Being a mother is different than I thought. It's more difficult; it's nonstop; it's exhausting. At the same time, Aylin's smiling face represents something deeper to me than sleepless nights, dirty diapers and a lifetime of responsibility. She reminds me every day of the love Jordan and I share. She reminds me miracles exist. She showed me a different part of myself; a different side of Jordan, and has given her grandparents a redo on how to treat a child—with warmth and affection.

Since Aylin's birth, the family structure in both mine and

Jordan's lives has shifted drastically. Chuck must have had some wake-up call. After the first letter he wrote to Jordan, more came. Each week, a new letter arrived in my mailbox addressed to Jordan.

At first, nothing changed. Jordan didn't make any attempts. It wasn't until the first time my parents came to visit us after we moved to Manhattan. Aylin was just over two-months old. My father was playing with her allowing a silly side, rarely seen, to come out. I was laughing, and I noticed Jordan staring intently.

I knew he wondered if Chuck could ever be like that with our daughter. He wondered if his father could somehow make it up to him through Aylin.

After that, things started to change; very slowly. Andrew spent most of the time with us—especially once Jordan had to go back on tour. He still lived at home, but he'd come over to our apartment after school to help me out with Aylin. He is great with her and she absolutely adores him.

Chuck came over a couple of times to see her with Jordan's permission. I could tell she got to him. When no one else could, my little baby girl broke the great Chuck Ashton down. The first time he saw Aylin, he was sitting on the floor with her making baby talk and tearing up over how beautiful she is.

Jordan was in no way forgetting his past, but he was trying to move on. Last month, Coryn left Chuck. Apparently, she had been having an affair with her plastic surgeon, who is richer and younger than Chuck. He was so at a loss of what to do that he showed up at our doorstep asking us to take Andrew in for a week until things calmed down.

Jordan tried not to, but he couldn't help feeling bad for his father.

"It's really sad when you realize you're all alone in the world because of the path you chose," Jordan told me one night while we lie in bed. "My dad messed things up so bad."

"But?" I asked, wondering what he was going to say.

"Once the mistakes are made, you can't change them. Now, you're left with nothing and all you can do is try to salvage what may be left. That's what Chuck is trying to do with me. Haley, we're all he has left."

That was true, too. Chuck's sister, Trisha Eriksson, got into a bad fight with him after Christian and Tasha's engagement party. They didn't want to believe the things Christian has done. Apparently, Trisha and John Eriksson also felt the need to vent to my parents about Chuck's opinion of Christian. To the Erikssons' surprise, Mom and Dad decided to confront them on some things they found out about their "dear" son. It's safe to say the Erikssons will no longer spend holidays with us at Foster's Ski Lodge.

In fact, taking their place this year are Chuck and Andrew. It was actually Dad's idea after Jordan mentioned Coryn's bailing on them for the holidays. She decided to go on a Caribbean cruise instead of being with her only son.

I am happy that all of Aylin's grandparents could be part of her first Christmas—I know Maggie's spirit is here somewhere as well. I was sitting with Aylin on the floor while she played a toy piano Sebastian gave her a couple of days ago. I was taking pictures of her from every angle and trying to get her to smile. Her pretty green eyes—the same ones as her Daddy's—looked up at me and there was her million dollar smile to follow.

She was my favorite subject to photograph, and I especially loved to take photos of her with Jordan. The two of them together turn me into mush.

"Getting practice in?" Dad asked, sitting down on the

couch, as he pointed to my camera.

I smiled, "Or I'm just being an obsessed mom."

"Charlie told me you started your own business," Chuck said, sitting down in an arm chair.

Back in September, I was able to make up for my missing credits at a visual arts school in New York. While I went to classes at night, Meghan watched Aylin for me. At the time, Jordan wasn't too keen on Chuck spending that much time with her, so I could never ask him to watch her. Chuck still has a lot of proving to do, and he's still who he is, but it's nice to see there's a heart inside of him.

After I received my degree, I wasn't sure what I wanted to do. While Aylin and I were visiting Jordan on tour, I did some work for the band and even designed some t-shirts. I had learned graphic design skills while in school in New York, and they were coming in handy.

Job wise, I wasn't sure in which direction to go, though. Aylin is still so young and I don't want to leave her with someone else all day. When I showed the band the work I did with the t-shirts, Sebastian thought I should start my own business. I laughed the idea off—never thinking of myself as an entrepreneur or the leader type.

I couldn't get the idea out of my head, though. I imagined what I would call my photography firm, what areas I would focus in, what my logo would look like. I began designing that logo—just for fun—but when Jordan saw it, he told me I'd be a fool if I didn't try my own business out. He will be off for the next few months to do some writing for Tortured's next album, and offered to take care of Aylin for me while I got adjusted to my new business, which I called Moon Halo Photo & Design—in honor of the meaning behind Aylin's name.

My company was officially formed last month, and I

already had several appointments set up in the New Year. With Tortured and Landry already in my portfolio, I was attracting some big name clients. Tasha was referring everyone from her dance school to me for head shots. Meghan asked me to photograph her line which will be debuting at fashion week. The line is "Meggy Lu", a nickname she had since she was a kid.

My career looks promising, and the best part about it is I am able to mostly stay home, which is where my studio is set up. It is comforting only being a room away from Aylin. My job will also allow me to visit Jordan while he is away since I can arrange my schedule the way I want to.

Chuck raised his glass to me.

"Congratulations—the photos you sent of Aylin are beautiful."

I smiled at him and then looked at my daughter.

"That was all her."

Drew sat down on the other side of Aylin and she crawled over to him excitedly. I got up from the floor and stole a picture of Jordan writing. He looked up and rolled his eyes at me.

"After two and a half years, you're still watching me?"

I laughed. He was referring to a picture I took of him while he was sleeping before we began dating. I can't help it—he still fascinates me. I sat down next to him and put my head down on his shoulder.

"How's writing going?"

"I was distracted," he smirked, looking over at Aylin and Drew playing together.

I looked down at Jordan's notebook and smiled.

"You wrote me a letter even though I'm in the same room?"

He shrugged, "Writing to you is the biggest thing I miss about being on the road."

I bit my bottom lip and pulled the book from his hands. I read the brief note, and looked at him curiously.

"Midnight by the fire, huh?"

"Don't ask any questions," he said, pecking my lips and standing up.

My cell phone rang and I walked over to the carpet to get it off the floor. It was Tasha.

"Hey Tash," I answered as Aylin smiled up at me.

Jordan pulled her into his arms and made a face.

"You stink, kid."

I laughed, "That's all you, babe."

He stuck his tongue out at me before taking Aylin upstairs to change her.

"So, how's the Ashton-Foster family Christmas working out?"

I walked into the kitchen so I could talk freely.

"So far so good. Jordan and Chuck haven't argued, though, they don't say much to each other either," I explained. "How are you getting along with Seb's family?"

"Great! They're loud like me!"

I smiled, "Completely opposite of the Erikssons, right?"

"Thankfully—yes. They're fun and warm."

"I'm happy for you."

"Thanks Haley. How's my cute little niece doing?"

"She loves all the attention from everyone. She's happy to have Daddy home, too."

"I miss her. Oh, I forgot to tell you!" Tasha cut herself off. "I ran into Christian."

"When?"

"The other day at this art & music festival Sebie and I went to."

"What did he say?"

"Well, he approached me when I was alone and was trying to apologize. Then, get this; he tried to say you led him on!"

I rolled my eyes and laughed.

"Right, me telling him I am not interested repeatedly and that I love Jordan really kept him hanging on for hope."

"Ugh," Tasha sighed. "Anyway, so then he asks me to get dinner with him, and I laughed in his face."

"Good!"

"Seb came over at that point and pretty much scared Christian away just by looking at him."

"Christian is such an ass."

"I'm so glad to be free of him," Tasha sighed.

"You and me both. I never thought my parents would think of him any less than perfect. Finally, everyone sees the light."

I used to worry about Jordan running into Christian, afraid he would end up in jail for attacking him. However, Jordan told me once: there is no point in fighting Christian—one, it wouldn't be much of a fight and two, Jordan already won. He says me and Aylin are proof of that.

As for Bippy, Chuck had dinner at the Reynolds' home recently. Bippy happened to be home, and of course, the proud grandpa was showing off pictures of my baby girl. Chuck said she walked right out of the room.

I shouldn't take pleasure out of anyone's sadness and I don't entirely. I actually feel sorry for Bippy and Christian—though they definitely got what they deserved. Revenge is sweet, but only to an extent. I can't imagine the load of regret both of them feel for screwing things up so terribly.

After I hung up with Tasha, Andrew walked into the kitchen. Since Coryn left Chuck, things have been a little hard on him. Coryn wasn't exactly the kind of mother to nurture her son. She didn't even try to take Drew with her unlike Maggie did with Jordan. If Maggie had been in a normal frame of mind, Jordan would have been free of Chuck a lot sooner.

"How are you doing?" I asked. "Honestly."

Drew shrugged and sat down on the stool in front of the island in the kitchen.

"Okay. Mom sent me a text a little while ago. A text," he shook his head. "You know, people really should be evaluated before they're allowed to have kids."

I half smiled at him and leaned on the island.

"I agree. You do know that no matter what your parents do, it's not a reflection on you, right?"

Drew nodded.

"You're a great kid. Your mom was just…too young and—"

"But you and Jordan are young," Drew objected. "You're great with Aylin."

"We were just ready."

Drew laughed, "Haley, I'm not stupid. Aylin wasn't planned."

I laughed, "No, but Jordan and I…"

"Are good at it? Mom and Dad are terrible."

I sighed, "Your dad is at least making some sort of effort."

"He's afraid of being alone. He'll get over it."

"You're too young to be so cynical. All you can do is try your best and stand up for yourself when you feel like it's needed. I promise you we'll all love you no matter what…even your parents."

Drew smiled, "Thanks. I never really wanted a sister, but I think of you like one—and I would never want to get rid of you."

I felt tears come to my eyes as I laughed. I walked around the island and hugged Drew.

A little while later, we sat down for the first ever Foster-Ashton family dinner. I have to say my father is being really good about breaking bread with someone he really doesn't like. He didn't have to invite Chuck. Jordan would have been the first one to understand.

My parents were being so welcoming because they thought of Jordan like family now. He has more than proved to them how much he loves me and Aylin.

When she got fussy halfway through dinner, Jordan was the one to put her down for a nap. Not me or Elsa—which is who I'm sure took care of me at parties when I was a baby—but my very cool boyfriend.

It wasn't all for show in front of my parents, either. Jordan always offered to take Aylin off my hands. I know part of it was from guilt when he travelled, but I know a bigger part of it was because he enjoyed every second with our daughter. She filled a void in his life that no one else could fill. My love for Jordan Walsh was taken to an entirely new level when we became parents.

Of course, it wasn't all sunshine and rainbows—we still argued over nonsense like what to watch on TV or how much money we spent—though we were well off, Jordan wanted us to raise Aylin in a modest household. He never wants her to do without, but at the same time, he didn't want her to end up like a rich snob. I think he forgets just who's daughter she is. Sure, I may have an entitlement at times, but if she's anything like me or him—she'll repel people like Bippy and Christian just like we do.

After dinner, I was in the kitchen with my mother. For the first time in years, I convinced Mom to give Elsa the holidays off. Usually, she travelled home late Christmas Eve to be with her family, and I always felt bad. I also convinced Jordan to help me cook dinner tomorrow. I found some recipes and I know Jordan has more of an idea of what he is doing than I do. I've also been practicing by making soups and vegetarian dishes for myself and Aylin. Some things were hit or miss, but I enjoyed cooking—it was another expression of creativity and art.

I was loading the dishwasher as Mom was setting up the coffeemaker. She looked at the machine as if it was foreign and I snickered to myself.

"See, it's not so bad without Elsa."

Mom smiled at me.

"I'm a bit surprised at you, Haley."

I looked over at her confused.

"I mean—we raised you to not have to worry about things like this. And here you are..."

"Are you disappointed?" I wondered in horrid disbelief.

"Of course not," she folded her lips together. "Not in you anyway. I've never been more proud. I'm disappointed in myself," she sighed. "When I was a kid, my family didn't have a lot of money..."

My grandfather was actually considered poor for today's standards. He was a lawyer, too, but had some unwinnable cases early on in his career. His luck changed, though, and by the time my mother was graduating high school, he was able to pay her way through college.

"I was pampered by my father, though. Even when he didn't have the money—he never wanted to disappoint me. I was a brat," Mom laughed.

"I guess that's where I got it from," I smiled.

"Who ever said you were a brat?"

"Jordan. Tasha..."

"Well, I guess you have your moments. I just wish I realized that you weren't like that—you didn't want us to love you with our wallets. You just wanted to be loved, and we didn't know how to just do that. To give you the love you give Aylin..." Mom said, with tears in her eyes.

"Mom, it's okay. I know you love me."

She wiped her tears and I hugged her.

"I'm so happy you found Jordan. He loves you the way you need him to. You were right about him all along."

I squeezed her tightly.

"I hope Daddy feels the same way about him."

"I know he doesn't like to say it," she laughed as I pulled away from her. "But he does. He sees how happy Jordan makes you; how he cares for you and the baby."

Just then, Andrew walked in. We both wiped our tears.

"Mr. Foster sent me in to make sure you girls didn't blow up the place."

I laughed and Mom put her hands on her hips.

"Oh, he thinks he's so funny..." she shook her head.

After dessert, I gave Aylin a bath and Jordan put her to sleep. We all changed into pajamas and each opened one gift. It was a tradition Maggie had, and Jordan wanted to honor that. It was actually Chuck's idea; I know that meant a lot to Jordan.

Chuck wanted Jordan to open his present last. It was an album of photos from Jordan's childhood. Jordan swallowed hard seeing photos of himself with his parents. I had my head pressed against his shoulder as he looked through the photos as if he barely remembered ever seeing them before. Maybe he hadn't.

He stopped at one picture and my eyes widened.

"Is that..." I gasped.

"What the...no way," Jordan laughed. "Where did you find this?"

"It was in a box of photos I put in storage years ago," Chuck shrugged. "These brought back so many memories, and I know they're distant for you, so… I was sure you didn't remember that," he smirked.

"I can't believe it…" I looked over at Jordan. "So you really were my first kiss after all!"

Right in the middle of the page was a photo from when I must have been about four and Jordan around five or six. My blonde hair was in pigtails and I was wearing a red velvet dress. Jordan had a popular hairstyle for that time, which was referred to as the "mushroom cut" and he was wearing a green turtleneck. Our lips were puckered and touching lightly.

"Do you remember this?" I asked looking at my parents.

"Was that the Reynolds' holiday party?" Dad asked Chuck.

"I think so."

"Oh, that was the year we couldn't make it. We were out of town," Mom remembered. "We asked Trisha and John to take Haley for the weekend."

"Look at me, I was still a ladies' man," Jordan joked.

I nudged him and laughed.

"I remember being really awkward, even back then… How did I manage to kiss a boy?" I wondered.

"I'm not just any boy," Jordan winked.

Chuck laughed.

"You were an awkward kid, I must admit," Chuck said to me. "When I found out you and Charlie are dating, I was a little surprised."

"Dad…" Jordan sighed.

"I'm not trying to offend her," Chuck said. "I'm glad to see that you've come out of your shell, Haley."

"Thanks," I smiled.

My parents went to bed after the gift exchange was done. Chuck followed suit not much later. It was a quarter to midnight and Andrew was flipping channels while I checked my phone absently as I yawned.

"Drew, you better get to bed or else Santa won't come."

Andrew looked at him with a scrunched up face as if to say "really, bro?" Jordan made some sort of face back to him that I couldn't see.

"Good night Haley," Drew shot at me before hiking upstairs.

I looked over at Jordan curiously.

"So, what's this gift?"

"It's not midnight yet. And we're not by the fire," Jordan shrugged.

He stood up and stretched; the thermal pajama top rising as he did so. This was his first set of pajamas in eight years. He couldn't exactly stroll around in his boxers like he did at home.

Jordan went upstairs to get my present and I sat down in front of the fire. The faint crackling sound was comforting. This year, the holidays were better than ever.

When you're a child, there's something incredibly magical about Christmas. I would dream of a new doll months before. I loved baking cookies with Elsa. I loved decorating the tree. As a kid, I could even tolerate seeing Christian on the holidays, though back then, we didn't see the Erikssons as often. They usually went to New York to be with their family.

As you grow up, though, the magic of Christmas fades. The stress increases. Families argue. Shopping and decorating become chores. Sometimes you feel alone in a room full of people. I've been there many times.

This year, I haven't felt alone once. The magic has returned. Maybe it had to do with the Erikssons not being here. Maybe it had to do with the evolution of my relationship with my parents. Or maybe it had to do with them fully welcoming Jordan into our family. Ultimately, I know it has plenty to do with Aylin.

She's our Christmas angel this year.

Jordan plopped down next to me, hiding my present off to the side.

"Stop keeping me in suspense," I sighed, getting on my knees and trying to reach for the gift.

He held me back, but I fought him playfully. Jordan pushed me down onto the carpet and I giggled as he tickled me. He kissed my neck softly and then my lips. Our kiss deepened and I wanted him right then and there, but I knew it was too risky.

"Let's go upstairs," I whispered.

He smiled coyly, "Not yet."

"If you got me another tattoo…" I sighed.

I finally did get the dream catcher tattoo on my shoulder blade last month. I was glad I did it; though I whined through the entire procedure.

"It's not a tattoo," Jordan got off me and reached for the small box.

I could tell it was jewelry and I tried to pretend to be happy. I wasn't a fan of expensive jewelry. Jordan knew that.

He took my hand, and I felt his fingers trembling. Curiously, I looked at his face. I couldn't believe it—I knew what his gift was to me.

And I didn't want it. I didn't want him to ask me to marry him.

"No," I spat out.

"I didn't even ask a question, Haley," Jordan sneered.

"Well, the answer is no," I sighed, standing up and sitting in the armchair nearby.

I knew how Jordan felt about marriage and I didn't want him to feel he had to propose to me out of obligation. I am fine with the way things are.

Jordan sat there motionless for a moment before standing up and walking over to me. He stared into my eyes; determined to change my answer.

"Marry me, Haley."

"Why?"

"Because we love each other."

"We don't need marriage to prove that, remember?" I asked, frustrated. "You already promised yourself to me..." I held up my ring finger with the Claddagh ring on it.

"It's not enough."

"It is, Jordan. Who told you it wasn't enough?"

"I did. You deserve to have a wedding and a husband, Hale," he said, getting down on one knee. "I will tie myself to you in every way possible to make you happy."

"That's the problem," I said pointing my finger at him. "To make *me* happy. What would make you happy?"

He cupped my face in his hands.

"You make me happy."

"You don't believe in marriage. I'm not expecting you to disregard that," I said, taking his hands off my face.

"It's time I stopped allowing my past to dictate my life, Haley. I think you were the one to tell me that. Marriage was one of those hang-ups from my past. I've had a lot of time to think on the road about what I want. I have everything I want except you as my wife."

He looked so sincere, and I didn't know what else to do but kiss him. I pressed my forehead to his afterwards.

"Are you sure?"

"Positive. I already asked your parents' permission—"

"You what?" I laughed.

"I want to do things right," he shrugged.

"What did they say?"

"Your mom cried. I think your dad did, too," he laughed.

I laughed, too.

"Mom is probably trying to figure out wedding details already," I rolled my eyes. "I'd like to go a nontraditional route, if you don't mind."

He laughed, "You know I'm up for anything that goes against the status quo." He paused. "Wait, does that mean you're saying yes?"

"Let me see the ring," I sighed.

He smirked and opened the ring box. I laughed hard once I saw my engagement ring with the twenty-dollar price tag attached from Macy's. I loved it. It was fake and cheap with a purple stone—my favorite color. Perfect.

"Is this too much for you?" Jordan teased.

"I love you," I said, going to kiss him,

"Eh, eh—wait," he said, clearing his throat. "Haley Foster, will you marry me?"

"Yes, I will marry you."

Jordan grinned before sliding the ring on; stopping just before the Claddagh ring. They looked hideous together, but I didn't care. I kissed my fiancé. When we pulled apart, Jordan looked out the window beside my chair.

At first, I thought he was admiring our Volvo parked outside. He was the one who decided to sell his Mustang, saying he needed to make sure Aylin would be safe. I was relieved we wouldn't have to worry about breaking down on the side of the road anymore.

"It's a full moon," he said.

"See, we didn't break it after all," I smiled.

Jordan laughed before wrapping his arms around me.

SNEAK PEEK

Expressions
(Dream Catchers Series Book 3)

Letters, Songs & Stories from characters in the "Dream Catchers" Series.

Drew's Envy

From the time I was born, I was a mistake. At least that's what it always felt like. My father was married to another woman when Mom got pregnant with me. I never really thought about that until later. I guess I never realized a lot of things as a child.

Like why my brother didn't want to live with us. Jordan is 11 years older than me, but he is my best friend. It hurt when he left home. It hurt when he blamed Dad for a while, too. I was just a kid when Jordan moved away and when I asked why, he looked at me with that intense expression he rarely looks at me with and said, "Drew, I can't stand your father. I'm sorry, but I need to take care of my Mom."

Your father.

It was clear to me that Jordan didn't want any association with being an Ashton. At the time, I thought that he didn't want me either. After all, I am an Ashton. Jordan called Chuck *my* father and Maggie was *his* mother, not mine. For months, I was bitter; angry with my brother for not wanting my parents, for not wanting to share with me. At seven, that's what it came down to with me—as if he didn't want to share a baseball with me. He wanted his own mother and not mine, not that mine even acted like a mother. I realize that now, though. I realize everything now.

Over the years, I had grown the same hatred toward both my parents. The love for my brother never changed though. The bitterness was always there however. I was jealous Jordan was free to come and go as he pleased. I wanted to be able to make my own decisions. I wanted to move away.

Jordan was always the coolest person I knew. Cooler than my friends who still thought girls had cooties and didn't know anything about Nirvana or Led Zeppelin. Jordan knew everything about music. Even Jordan's friends were awesome. They treated me like I was their age and not some kid they told to shut up and go away. My dad was infamous for that. I was invisible to him.

To Jordan, though, I mattered. He opened up to me about his dreams. He wanted to be a rock star, and not superficially.

He wanted to make a difference. He wanted his music heard. He has so much talent. I was incredibly jealous and amazed by his talent.

"Drew," he'd say. "You'll find your talent. Something that your heart is in. Don't let Dad take it away. He'll try."

Jordan was right. I found my heart in baseball. I found my best friends in my teammates. A couple of them already had their first kiss. Some of them even heard of Led Zeppelin. Baseball was my safe place, and man, I was pretty good at it.

Dad came to my first game where I hit two homeruns. He didn't come to my second game. Or my third. Jordan, however, came to as many as he could. He even made a special trip from Boston for my All-Star game. Dad would make digs about baseball, saying it would not make me smarter or lead me to a professional career. I did well in school just so he wouldn't have a reason to take baseball away from me.

One summer, Jordan gave me a reason to be even more envious of him. He met Haley. I'll admit I was distracted seeing her in the bleachers of one of my games. She is beautiful, and not that beauty that my mom has—where she tries too hard. Haley is and always was just plainly beautiful, even more so after you get to know her.

Jordan fell in love with her and who could blame him? I think I fell in love with her too, and for a couple of years, my crush lasted. Haley always said the right thing to me when I was upset, especially through my parents' divorce. She made my brother incredibly happy, which made me grateful to her.

For a little while, with my pre-teen hormones raging, I worried that my feelings would ruin my relationship with Jordan. It would be the oldest story in the world—a girl coming between brothers. It was right after my niece was born that I realized that Haley is in love with Jordan, not me. I am a brother to her, and after instantly loving my niece as I held her, I realized that Haley is my sister and I love her like one.

Still, I was envious of my brother for the life I could only dream of. By that time, my father was grasping onto a relationship with me. I allowed it out of pity, but to be honest, I don't like my father. I don't like him as a person, plain and simple. I love him in some way—when I remember bits and pieces of my happy childhood memories—I smile, but that's all I can muster for him. He has lost much of himself over the years, even part of his will to fight, which just made things more frustrating. It was hard to not want anything to do with someone who wouldn't scream and threaten you, but instead, sadly brings up the past and is only remorseful for some things and not others. For instance, Dad regrets missing my baseball games, but thinks I deserved getting slapped across the face for leaving my cleats by the door where he tripped over them.

Now, on my college graduation day, I hear the familiar hollering from my brother as I accept my diploma. I smile to myself, remembering how many times I heard those noises from him at my baseball games. I could hear my niece mimicking him; almost as loud as her father and I laughed.

After the ceremony, I made my way over to my family. Mom kissed me quickly, saying she was proud and she'd take me out for lunch tomorrow before leaving. I've come to accept my mother this way, deciding like my father, I didn't like her too much either. Her vapid existence and lack of a nurturing quality was who she always was. I was her ticket to wealth. I suspected for a while that she planned her pregnancy with me in order to tie herself to Chuck permanently, after he didn't divorce Jordan's mother at the beginning of their affair.

Dad hugged me and instead of gushing over my diploma or me getting selected to be in the minor leagues, which is still baffling to me, he went on about my "unbelievable" mother. I practically ignored him as I went to hug my nine-year-old niece, Aylin.

"Congratulations Uncle Drew!"

"Thanks, Ay," I smiled. "Nice hat," I hit the brim of her pink Yankees cap.

I can't believe I will play for the Staten Island Yankees, with the hope that eventually I'd make it to the majors. The Yankees are mine and Jordan's favorite team. Our father is a Mets fan. Maybe we chose the Yankees as a way to say "Screw you" to him, but either way, we love that team.

Haley hugged me next, holding me tight. I could tell she was crying.

"So proud, brother-in-law," she said.

I kissed her cheek, "Thank you."

Before I could make my way to Jordan, a beautiful redhead almost knocked the wind out of me. I've come to expect this from Katie, my girlfriend for the past two years. When she is excited, which is often, she can cause you physical harm. I love that about her, even if I often get smacked in the nose or my foot stomped on.

"We did it!" she said, almost poking me in the nostril with the corner of her graduation cap.

"I know, baby," I laughed. "Congratulations," I murmured before we kissed.

"You too," she said, laying her hand on my cheek.

I looked into her eyes, forgetting momentarily about my family. I am in love with Katie Lawson, who will make an amazing teacher and a wife. I plan to make her my wife someday. For now, we'll be moving into a cozy loft in Tribeca together.

"Hi Katie!" Aylin shouted, breaking mine and Katie's daze.

As Katie hugged Aylin and Haley, I finally stepped over to

my brother.

"I thought you forgot about me, bro," Jordan laughed.

I pulled him into a large hug.

"I will never forget about you," I said. "You're my big brother."

Jordan smiled, "I'm so proud, Drew."

"I owe a lot of this to you," I told him.

I had always wanted to thank Jordan in some way. I just never knew how.

"No, you don't. This is all you," Jordan patted my back. "I admire you so much."

"You do?" I asked, surprised.

"Of course," Jordan laughed. "College, man? Minor leagues? Come on..."

Jordan dropped out of college in his first year. He stopped playing baseball when he was in elementary school because he threw a fit every time he struck out. I'm sure he had a lot of pent up anger as a kid. His music helped with that.

"I love you, Drew," Jordan said, and I couldn't believe it. My big, tough brother had tears in his eyes.

"I love you, too," I said, throwing my arms around him once more.

Somewhere along the way, my envy for my brother turned into pure gratitude. I knew no matter what city he was performing in or what city I was playing ball in, part of us would always be thinking about each other; knowing we overcame Chuck Ashton's wrath and became good people; not just monetarily successful like our father, but human beings worthy of love.

About the Author

Sandy Lo's career began at sixteen when she started writing for her school newspaper in her hometown, Staten Island, New York. Her skills caught the eye of her journalism teacher as well as her Advanced Placement English teacher, who read Lo's first try at writing a novel.

Sandy Lo went onto form StarShine Magazine in 2001 at the young age of eighteen where she honed her journalism skills while also handling the position of Arts & Entertainment Editor at SUNY Albany where she attended for a year before returning to school in New York City.

With StarShine Magazine, Lo gained an international fan base of music lovers, who appreciated her interviews with celebrities like Backstreet Boys, Jonas Brothers, Taylor Swift, 30 Seconds To Mars, Lady Gaga & many more.

In 2008, Sandy Lo's itch to publish a book was eating away at her. She had actively been writing stories since middle school, and finally felt confident in her abilities to achieve this goal.

On January 20, 2009, her birthday, Lo's debut novel **Lost In You** was self-published and received rave reviews from members of the entertainment industry for its accurate portrayal of a popular music group along with its gripping love triangle.

The following year, Lo released **Dream Catchers**, which surpassed her first novel's sales and spawned the sequel **Breaking The Moon**.

In 2010, Sandy Lo was featured in the publication ***50 Writers You Should Be Reading*** released by the producers of The Authors Show.

Aside from writing, Sandy Lo supports Animal Rights and is always looking for ways to make the world through writing.

For more information on Sandy Lo & her projects:

Sandy's Official Website: www.sandylo.com
Official Twitter: www.twitter.com/sandylobooks
Official Facebook: www.facebook.com/sandylobooks

Other Titles by Sandy Lo

DREAM CATCHERS SERIES
Dream Catchers – Book 1
Breaking The Moon – Book 2
Expressions – Book 3
Take Me Home – Book 4
The Reunion – Book 5
Spotlight – Book 6
Book 7 – Coming 2017!

Lost In You
The Watch Dog
Indigo Waters

Made in the USA
Columbia, SC
17 March 2022

57709640R00207